TWO MINDS

She lashed out with a right-armed blow into the underside of his jaw that snapped his head back. As he released his hold on her, she took his feet out from under him and planted a foot to hold him.

Beneath his sobs of pain, she felt confusion and then the expected horror of the alien whisper.

"Pain. Pain," it muttered. *"Clouds. But too well. Soon no need. Soon."*

"Smokey," he said, moving his jaw as if fearing it was broken, "I'm sorry. I don't know what got into me."

She stared, wondering if he was truly ignorant. He slowly picked himself up, surveying the wreck of her gown and his own bruises with shock.

"You don't hate me, do you, Smokey?" he said, his voice small.

"No," she said, thoughtfully, honestly, "not you."

Other AvoNova Books by
Jane Lindskold

BROTHER TO DRAGONS, COMPANION TO OWLS
MARKS OF OUR BROTHERS
THE PIPES OF ORPHEUS

SMOKE
AND
MIRRORS

JANE LINDSKOLD

AVON BOOKS • NEW YORK

SMOKE AND MIRRORS is an original publication of Avon Books. This work has never before appeared in book form. This work is a novel. Any similarity to actual persons or events is purely coincidental.

AVON BOOKS
A division of
The Hearst Corporation
1350 Avenue of the Americas
New York, New York 10019

Copyright © 1996 by Jane Lindskold
Cover art by Dorian Vallejo
Published by arrangement with the author
Library of Congress Catalog Card Number: 95-96054
ISBN: 0-380-78290-1

First AvoNova Printing: June 1996

AVONOVA TRADEMARK REG. U.S. PAT. OFF. AND IN OTHER COUNTRIES, MARCA REGISTRADA, HECHO EN U.S.A.

Printed in the U.S.A.

RA 10 9 8 7 6 5 4 3 2 1

For Kay McCauley—
because she liked this one in particular

1

SMOKEY WAS WITH HER THIRD CLIENT OF THE afternoon when she realized with panic that the man lying on top of her was not human.

He felt human enough moving against and within her. His skin when she tongued his shoulder tasted of salt and man musk. But the mind she touched was not—not unpresent as with the rare human who had a natural shield against her telepathy—but not human.

Her first impulse was to shove him violently away. Her second was to force herself to continue moving against him, to change the rhythm of her response just so, all the while hoping that the body was as human as the mind was alien.

The client's breathing quickened and his pace increased to match hers. Shielding her mind against the random thoughts that beat into her along with the body, she lightly clawed his back, feigning a pleasure she did not feel, doing anything she could to force him to climax and to leave her alone.

After an eternity that the discreetly concealed clock insisted was less than a minute more, he began to peak. Sensing that he was trying to hold something back for later, Smokey threw herself into her job with every trick she had ever learned in her years of turning tricks, determined with a passion close to terror that he would have nothing left, would not come back, would be drained, spent, utterly exhausted.

And although she struggled to be aware of nothing but the movement of body on body, the alien thoughts slipped beneath her hasty shield and fed her fear.

When he had finished, she did not let him rest atop her even a moment as was her usual custom with clients who were paying her highest rates. Taking advantage of his momentary pliability, she pushed him free of her, trying to be gentle when all she wanted was to be out of contact with him and the unnerving sensation of his mind. Not being one of her regular clients, he was not aware of the change in routine, but rolled compliantly onto his back and stared at the ceiling, a dreamy smile just curling the corners of his well-formed mouth.

She'd thought him handsome, when Jules had introduced them, with his slightly weathered fair skin, thick, light blond hair just turning to grey, blue eyes framed with laugh lines. Now she would have welcomed a dozen of the overweight, greasy types that Jules usually brought by.

"That was great, honey," he said, fumbling to pull her back.

She pretended not to see and sat up, swinging her long legs to the floor. The contact of her toes with the fluffy carpet grounded her farther from the alien mind she had touched. Standing, she even managed a smile.

"Would you like a drink, Lee?"

He raised himself on one elbow, running his gaze possessively over her nude form, from the thick mane of black into silvery grey hair that most believed was the source of her street name, over the rounded breasts and down the curves of her slender body.

"I'd prefer if you came back to bed," he said, "and alcohol, in any case, depresses sexual response. I'd be a fool to waste myself with you available."

He gestured arrogantly, and, for the first time in many years, Smokey balked. The client—she could not bring herself to think of him as a man, not after what she had felt—was quite serious, however.

"You've been paid for your time, woman," he said, his smile fading, "and I have no interest in a refund."

Running the tip of her tongue across her teeth, she smiled, resolution taking form.

"Nor have I," she said. "Nor have I."

Crouching alongside him, she teased him with teeth and tongue. The resumed contact was worse, yet infinitely better, for the shock was gone. She ignored his physical contact, keying into his mental touch.

She had two goals—to protect herself from his reading her and to learn something of what he was.

Longer ago than she cared to admit, Smokey had realized that she could read minds. There were limitations—she was not one of the mythical psionics who could read minds that were half a planet away. She needed physical contact with her subject. Probing after specific information was difficult unless the subject was already thinking about the topic.

But Smokey had been using her gift for a long time and could usually direct her client's thoughts where she desired, even when he would have sworn that his entire attention was on his groin. Far more of her income came from her talent for gathering information than from what she was paid for spreading her legs, and this despite the fact that she was one of the most expensive whores on Arizona.

Now she let the client's hands travel freely over her, telegraphing through little sighs and shudders a pleasure she was too frightened to feel. She raised her head from nibbling along the inside of his thigh, noting with abstract approval that his eyes were wide and dilated.

"Don't stop, Smokey," he breathed. "That's too good."

She smiled and bent her head. Stopping just shy of his skin, she looked up again.

"Are you sure you wouldn't like me to take it slower? You must have been working hard—Jules is such a single-minded creature."

He growled and not quite playfully pushed her head back down. "I'll tell you when I've had enough, whore."

But what his mind said in strangely colored images was, *"Work? Not yet. Must feed it or it will waken and fight. Feed it until it sleeps forever. Then can work."*

The thought images flowed with such force and contempt that Smokey could barely refrain from flinching away, as if from a blow. She distracted herself by shifting position and straddling Lee. While she rode him, she could feel the pleasure of his body alongside the mind's detached refrain. As he came there was something else. A sense of betrayal? Sorrow? But the impression vanished too quickly for her to be certain.

Hesitantly immersing herself in the odd rhythms of Lee's thoughts, Smokey asked, "So, are you in the garment trade like Jules?"

She'd learned that direct questions often made clients guarded, but an indirect query made them both verbally and mentally voluble.

Aloud he said, "Yes, imported silks from Old Terra."

His mind said, *"Trade, yes, after a fashion, trade."*

"Genuine Terran silks?" She wiggled against him in a fashion that most men found very distracting. "Are you from Old Terra?"

"Yes," he said, fondling her, "descended from Hong Kong British back a hundred years or so back."

His mind countered, *"Old Terra much more desirable than this world of desert and water valley. Someday."*

"I love silks," she hinted, pulling lightly on his chest hair, "especially Oriental patterns."

Even as his speaking voice was promising her a present from his wares, his inner response was a whispered antiphony, two voices in conflict.

"Mine! You cannot . . ." *"Silk, soft, like the woman's skin."* "Away from me, from mine!" *"Sleep. Be satisfied. Feel. You rise again as a god."*

Bombarded by these impulses, she had little energy to protest when the client smiled, gently shifted her onto her back, and lowered himself onto and then into her.

She had nearly twenty minutes after he left before Jules arrived. Just under six feet tall and superficially muscular with light brown hair and blue eyes, only Smokey knew what lies underlay the man's handsome exterior. His skin as she undressed him was soft and clammy. The amiable expression his face relaxed into concealed an egocentric version of the universe barely more mature than that of a five-year-old child.

Jules chatted about inconsequentialities while she rubbed him down with a light, musky oil he favored. After Lee's disturbing internal dialogue, she found the simple, almost-concentric, rings of Jules's thoughts familiar and even comforting, although normally he slightly repelled her. After she had established sufficient contact to be certain she could read him, she began asking the important questions.

"You're so cheap, Jules," she teased. "All I'm asking you to get me are a couple of flasks of scent. The new guy, Lee, has all but promised me an imported silk robe."

"After Lee already, are you?" he chuckled, (and his mind said, "Good, if Smokey gets him by the balls, I can use her as a bribe").

"Maybe," she purred, nibbling the side of his neck. "He was certainly passionate—almost superhuman."

"Oh? Try me if you think he was so great."

Jules buried his face in her breasts but, as they wrestled, Smokey found nothing in his mind that indicated that he was aware of anything odd about his business associate.

After he had left, replete not only with sexual satisfaction but with an almost atavistic satisfaction that he had "bested" the other men by having the woman last and so obliterating their marks, Smokey touched her call pad.

"Kyu? Smokey here. Hold all my calls unless they're from Gary or Bonny."

She could hear Kyu's smile. "Ridden out after that last lot?"

"Something like that." Smokey rubbed her hands across her face. "Something like that."

2

SMOKEY WAS STILL FEELING DRAINED AND UN-comfortably thoughtful when she arrived home. Bonny met her at the sun-level door and threw her arms around Smokey's waist.

"Mama, guess what happened in physics today?"

"What?" Smokey asked, ignoring the jumble of images that rose from Bonny into her mind.

"Professor Van Druyen was talking about laws of motion and was setting up these balls on the V so that we could see what he meant and Chinue, who lives on Orbital One, made all the balls have terra-cat faces and start mewing!"

"That wasn't very nice," Smokey said mildly, giggling just the same.

Bonny caught her hand and started dragging her. "I put some tea and aspel tarts in the setting room, Mama."

"Sounds wonderful," Smokey replied, following, "but can Wintering get to them?"

Bonny dropped her hand and took off at an all-out run toward the noise of rattling glassware. Chuckling, Smokey paused to hang up her sun hat before following.

Wintering, the chulo who had moved in with them some seasons before, was up in the branches of his favorite perch, a "tree" carved of sandstone by a local artist who was also a grateful client. Bonny was examining the tea tray and setting aside the most damaged pieces for her pet.

As Smokey lowered herself into her favorite chair, Bonny studied her. Tilting her head in an unconscious parody of one of her instructors, she said, "You seem tired, Mama."

Smokey nodded. "I am. Will you pour?"

Lifting the round-bellied teapot with studied elegance, Bonny filled two translucent ivory cups with a pale amber tea.

"Busy day?" she asked, carrying one cup and a selection of pastries to her mother.

"Yes, Jules brought some people in," Smokey said, selecting a fat tart that showed minimal marks of chulo foraging.

While she chewed her first bite, she meditated on how much to say. She had resolved even before Bonny was born that she would lie to her only when absolutely necessary. There was no evidence that her daughter had inherited her talent for reading minds, but Smokey thought that certainly the girl was more empathic than the norm.

Now she studied the nine-year-old. Bonny was perched on the edge of her chair feeding sections of aspel tart to Wintering. Her shoulder-length hair was thick, straight, and the red-gold of sunlit honey; her wide almond-shaped eyes were a thoughtful brown. She was still flat-bodied and slightly chunky, but her features and poise held promise of beauty. In fact, Geisha, one of Kyu's other tenants, had hinted that she would be happy to start Bonny in her mother's profession any time she cared.

Smokey had refused, certainly more coolly than the other woman had expected. Now, feeling her daughter's brown eyes studying her, she realized that she had been avoiding Bonny's question.

"Jules brought in some new clients," she temporized, "and I'm not sure that I like all of them."

Bonny's lips rounded into a defiant pout. "They better have liked *you*," she said, " 'cause my Mama's the best whore on the whole planet—probably in the whole universe."

"Imp!" Smokey blushed at her daughter's praise, but an inner honesty made her admit that Bonny was at least partially right. Her talent made her sensitive to her clients' needs, whether for something as minor as a shift in position to relieve a pinched bit of skin or something as subtle as being aware of a repressed fantasy. That she had turned this talent into a profession even more lucrative and exhilarating than high-priced whoring was a source of pride.

Now, listening with half an ear to Bonny's reports about school, she contemplated telling Gary what she had learned. Reluctantly, she realized that she could not and that her impulse was born of a desire to get rid of responsibility rather than a belief that she actually had information worth selling. If she was to profit from this peculiar encounter, she needed to know more, and that meant further contact with Lee. Shuddering, she tried to convince herself that she didn't want to know more, but curiosity and a tingle of dread told her that while she would not seek him out, neither would she avoid Lee if the opportunity arose.

Outside the setting room, the magnificent sunset that the room was designed to view was just beginning and the fat twin crescents of the moons were paling the scattering of early stars.

"Are you caught up with your studies?" she asked Bonny. "I want to get some exercise."

Bonny nodded eagerly. "Swimming?"

"I was thinking of cycling. The moons will be bright for hours yet, and the day's heat has had a chance to fade."

"Yeah!"

As Bonny ran for the bicycles, Smokey set the tea service on a tray and absently fed Wintering the last of the pastries. With the training of long practice, she put the workday's worries behind her and went to join her daughter.

Sunset was inking the desert orange and pink as they pedaled their bicycles over the packed sand paths that spidered from their residential district up to the ridge-line park. Seen from here, the trees in the valley below were a well-manicured ocean tossed in the evening wind. The ledges along which the residential and business districts were built rose like sand dunes along that ocean's floors.

Winded, they paused at a scenic overlook. A young couple cuddling on a bench gave them a dirty look. Smokey laughed softly.

"Look, Mama." Bonny held out a cupped handful of lavender berries just kissed with a band of darker violet. "Traveler's sharps—ripe ones, too."

"You didn't scratch yourself, did you?" Smokey asked, picking up a berry with pearl-tipped nails.

"No," Bonny replied, slightly indignantly. "My history sim showed how these were some of the first local foods the colonists tried."

"And got scratched to New York and gone harvesting them," Smokey added reminiscently. "Arizona came close to getting named Thornpatch as I remember, but no one but the people who actually lived here thought that was a particularly dignified name for a planet."

"Thornpatch wouldn't be a really good name now, would it, Mama?" Bonny asked, leaning out over the overlook's rail, her gesture encompassing the green valley below.

"Not for the settled areas, Boniface," Smokey agreed, "but there's still much of this planet that's fitter for chulos, gerbils, and native thorn lizards."

Wheels singing against the path, they largely coasted home—a good thing, as Bonny was yawning almost before she had her bicycle in its stall. After the girl was asleep, Smokey puttered around the house, unable to settle down.

Lee had gotten to her more than any man she had laid, at least since she had discovered that love and sex can be mutually exclusive. But it wasn't love or even attraction she felt for him. She knew that the mind she had touched had not been human, but it had not been animal either.

Minds felt as different to her sensing as tastes did to her tongue. Humans might all be chocolate, but some were bittersweet, others milky. This mind did not taste human, yet it had not tasted animal either.

Unfortunately, there was no one with whom she could discuss her unrest. Ever since the experiments with augmenting psi powers went awry a couple of generations before, people with psi tended to keep quiet about it. Telepaths had the most to fear. People tended to deal with clairvoyants as they always had—with a blend of superstition and fascination. Telekinetics were slightly more frightening, but since few could manipulate a significant weight, this power was usually dismissed as a parlor trick.

Telepathy, however, was terrifying. The ability to look into a person's most private thoughts was the last unforgivable invasion of privacy in a coalition of planets that routinely coded and filed everyone at birth. For many years, Smokey had doubted her own ability, but finally had to admit that she wasn't learning everything she knew merely from an unusual sensitivity to body language.

To Gary she excused her ability for finding things out by explaining that she garnered her information through pillow talk. Never one to kill the goose, he let this stay his curiosity.

Frustrated, Smokey went and filled a snifter with a splash of the brandy a starship engineer brought her whenever his ship called in port. The liquor did nothing to dispel her feeling of concern, but she relaxed enough to get to sleep just as the first moon was settling below the ridgeline.

3

MIDMORNING THE FOLLOWING DAY, SMOKEY walked down a quiet, tree-lined street in the Sybarite's District to Kyu's Victorian Mansion. The building was a showpiece, brightly painted in sky blue trimmed with yellow and green. The four-story structure was replete with gingerbread fretwork, balconies, cupolas, and garnished with a full wraparound porch. The porch itself had rounded corners embellished with elaborate latticed gazebos.

The District contained a mixture of gourmet restaurants, opium palaces, and brothels. At this time of day, the types of clients were mixed—star travelers sightseeing or seeking a quick release, business executives entertaining clients, locals out for a lunch more elaborate or exotic than those offered in most Port City eateries.

Seated in a deep white wicker chair, knitting a violet afghan, petite, and Oriental, Madame Kyu surveyed the world outside of her brothel. As always, she was dressed in elegant, severe black. Her fluffy white hair was drawn into an elaborate French braid.

"Good day, Smokey," Kyu greeted her. "There's a package for you behind the bar in the saloon. I can have the girl bring it up with your flowers if you would like."

"Thank you." Smokey admired the efficiency with which Kyu ran her establishment, but she did not precisely like the woman. "I am open for general clients today, unless there are any messages for me."

11

"No messages, yet," Kyu replied.

Smokey knew that Kyu didn't approve of Smokey's selectivity, but as long as the rent was paid, Kyu would not dream of criticizing one the most renowned whores on Arizona.

After a few moments of polite conversation, Smokey went indoors and up the gently spiraling grand stair to the second floor, where her suite was located. Kyu's servant, a middle-aged woman dressed in a black dress with a white apron and a mob-cap, was arranging several bouquets of expensive hothouse flowers—many the scions of alien plants—in vases of cut crystal and delicately etched porcelain.

"Good morning, Smokey."

"Good morning, Eli. Madame Kyu said that there was a package for me."

"Yes, ma'am." Eli gestured with a toss of her head. "It's the large, flattish box. I took the liberty of bringing it up for you."

Smokey nodded her thanks and retrieved the package. The beige card tucked beneath the ribbon was of native card stock, but of a heavy, expensive brand.

Unfolding it, she read, " 'Smokey, I hope this gift gives you the smallest percentage of the pleasure that you gave me. I shall be on Arizona for several more sun cycles and shall certainly hope to have the opportunity to visit you again. Yours, Lee.' "

Pursing her lips thoughtfully, Smokey slipped the gilt cord from the box and took off the lid. Pushing some tissue to the side, she lifted out a floor-length robe in blue-green silk patterned with flowers and twisting Chinese dragons.

"Oh, isn't that lovely!" Eli exclaimed. "Old Terran stuff I'm sure. Nothing Arizonan is that shimmery."

"It is pretty," Smokey said, her heart trembling at the thought of seeing Lee again.

"I'm about finished here, ma'am," Eli said. "Is there anything I can bring for you?"

"Just send some tea, Eli. I should be fine."

When the chime indicating that clients had arrived

jingled discreetly some time later, Smokey was grateful for the distraction. Adorned in a pale blue, lacy peignoir and high-heeled sandals, she wafted down to the Gentlemen's Parlor. Voices told her that there were several available clients and that some of Kyu's other tenants had already arrived. This suited Smokey fine—she preferred the opportunity to make an impression by joining a gathering a few moments late. Rarely had she lost by her delay.

Today she paused in the parlor's arched doorway to survey the group and, incidentally, to let them see her. Three men sat in various attitudes of relaxation on the bountifully upholstered settees and armchairs through which Madame Kyu continued her Mansion's Victorian decor. A fourth man stood near the baby grand piano, apparently ready to turn the pages on the music stand for Ami, a blonde who in her own way was also bountifully upholstered—although not at all Victorian in her attitudes, unless one had garnered those attitudes through research in the "brown manuscripts" of the time.

Four other whores were in attendance already and Smokey knew with a faintly predatory thrill that the competition for who would take the men—and thus their money—had increased in intensity at her appearance.

Moving into the parlor, she seated herself on a pillow-heaped divan and leaned back so that her slender form and graceful curves were both revealed and teasingly shadowed by the fall of her peignoir.

"I'm so pleased that I'm in time for the music," she purred, her tone implying that they had been waiting for her arrival. "Please play, Ami."

Ami could do naught but oblige, though the expression that flickered across her vapidly pretty face betrayed her dislike at being made to seem Smokey's lackey. Hiding a grin, Smokey pretended to attend to Ami's rendition of the "Arizona Waltz" while studying the clients.

The man who sat at ease in the high-backed tapestry

armchair she had seen before. He was the chief purser of the interstellar luxury transport *Roma*. Most of the girls would consider landing him a last option, since he almost certainly was on a fixed expense account, but she wouldn't mind at all. No doubt, he would have some fascinating information—at least some of which he would share voluntarily.

Having identified the purser, she turned her attention to the others. These were most certainly offworlders, probably Old Terran given the *Roma*'s usual route, and most certainly wealthy, or the ship would not have freed a senior staffer to take them to the Sybarite's District. Business travelers, she decided after a moment, and on their first visit to Arizona.

The most interesting of the three was a tall, squarely built fellow with jetty black skin and soft brown eyes. Whereas the others balanced eagerness and anticipation, he was alert, his gaze sweeping the room. He kept glancing over to watch Corrine and Mimosa make practiced conversation with two of the other men, all the while holding his own with pert Geisha. Yet his attitude was not that of a buyer weighing his options, but one of almost clinical fascination. Smokey wondered if he might be an anthropologist.

Patting her hands together as Ami finished her piece, Smokey rose and sauntered over to the dark-skinned man. He looked up, his smile so instantly warm and appreciative that Geisha snorted and stalked off. Smokey couldn't feel too bad—she hadn't quite forgiven Geisha for offering to hold a virgin's auction for Bonny.

"I'm Smokey," she said, holding out her hand.

He took it between thick, dark fingers with calloused tips as if uncertain what to do with it. Then on impulse, he pressed it to his lips. Smiling, Smokey seated herself on the arm of his chair.

"This is your first time on Arizona?" she asked.

"Is it so obvious?" the man laughed. "I'm from Earth—Old Terra, I think you'd call it."

His speech was slow and musical, drawled so that "I'm" sounded more like "Ah-em." His eyes had stopped their restless motion. Their gaze was now fixed on her steel grey eyes with frequent forays down to what the filmy fabric of her robe tantalizingly concealed.

"Yes," Smokey said as if she hadn't noticed his interest. "We call it Old Terra rather than Earth. Earth is just dirt to us."

He laughed, honestly amused, though she had not meant to be funny. The contact with his hand was too slight for her to read his mind, but she didn't need telepathy to tell when she had a man hooked. Kyu would have arranged with the purser to guarantee the minimum acceptable payment for their time—some of these offworlders panicked at the moment of selection and Kyu wasn't about to come up the loser.

Smokey balanced herself so that her thigh brushed the man's upper arm. He slid his arm around her waist.

"I'm Clarence Beauduc of New Orleans, Old Terra," he said, "and I'd certainly like a bit of your time."

"Just my time?" she purred.

His free hand slid under her peignoir. "Not just your time."

"Well, then, come along Clarence Beauduc of New Orleans," she said. "Unless you have your mind set on having me here in the Gentlemen's Parlor."

He paused as if tempted, then got to his feet. She smiled and took his hand. As they strolled up the grand stair, Ami could still be heard playing the piano.

When they were resting, Clarence toyed with her hair. "Smokey isn't your real name, is it? I mean, you picked the name to go with the hair, right?"

"Half-right," she answered. "Smokey's my real name and I designed the hair to go with it."

"Huh," he said admiringly. "I always thought of grey as old lady's hair, but nevermore. Of course, yours is more stylish—jetty black at the top and silvering down to be nearly white at the tips. I like how you matched it below."

Smokey chuckled. "Wouldn't make much sense if I didn't, doing what I do."

Clarence paused and she could hear the questions clamoring to be asked. She stayed quiet, though, and didn't help, knowing that one would finally win to the surface.

"Why do you do what you do, Smokey?" he asked, not even smiling at his tongue twister. "You're a smart lady, I can tell. You could do lots more with your life."

"Flat on my back?" She grinned then sobered, respecting his seriousness. "Would you believe that I like the life, Clarence? I don't streetwalk, no pimp owns my time. I make my own hours and a good living and all for making a few men feel good. It's an honest life."

"What about the lady downstairs, the Oriental with the Queen Victoria fixation? She's not the madam?"

"Oh, sure, Kyu's the madam, but for me that's just like having a landlady. She doesn't get anything on my time unless, like today, I decide to take a walk-in."

"And if I came back?"

"On your own? I'd give her a small cut."

"And if we met somewhere else?"

"And there was money involved? I'd still cut her in." Smokey raised herself on one elbow. "Like I said, it's an honest life, at least for me. Kyu provides a nice, showy house, and I'd be stupid to cross her over a few credits."

Clarence shook his head, "Don't you worry about disease or get lonely for a family?"

"Disease?" Smokey shrugged. "I'm as careful as I can be, see a good doctor, keep up on my shots. I even know something about medicine. I'd actually be pretty safe here anyhow. Most of those clients I don't know are coming in from the spaceport, and most ships scour you out pretty well before they let you take passage. Starshippers are the biggest hypochondriacs I know."

"And a family?" he prompted, stroking the roundness of her breast with the tawny pink pads of his fingers. "Don't you miss having a family?"

Smokey stared levelly at him. "I have a family and, before you ask, yes, they do know what I do. I swear, Clarence, this 'New Orleans' of yours must be the last bastion of prudery on Old Terra. And you must be a rich, rich man to pay my rates to ask such silly questions."

Clarence grinned, his teeth square and white against his lips. "Not 'rich, rich,' Smokey, but I do have a fine research grant. As much as I am shamed to admit it, you've worn me out, and I was enjoying your company too much to 'fess-up. Can I take you to a late lunch?"

Smokey shook her head reluctantly. "I do need to earn my honest living, and I doubt that even your grant would cover paying both for my time and for lunch."

"Maybe not." He cupped her breasts briefly and then swung his feet to the floor. "Dinner?"

She laughed and walked nude to where an apparently antique end table concealed a very modern computer terminal. Checking her schedule, she saw that Bonny had a swim date at the Topaz.

"An early one," she agreed. "If you'd like to try some local food, I can meet you at the Dirty Slate in about five hours. However, I can free up only two hours."

"Another appointment?" he asked, an expression that was quite jealous narrowing his eyes.

"With my daughter," she laughed. "You are nosy!"

"Jus' doing my job, ma'am," Clarence drawled.

"Anthropologist!" she accused with a smile.

"More of a sociologist," he corrected, "and not so much of one to miss that you have a damn cute ass."

"Noticing doesn't cost," she reminded him, "but my time does. Go on and let me earn my keep."

He put on his clothing and turned to leave. "In a few hours then, at the Dirty Slate."

After Clarence had departed, Smokey signaled Kyu that she was again open for business.

"You had a call," Kyu said, with the mixture of aggression and possessiveness with which she regarded Smokey's private affairs, "from that Gary."

"Thanks, Kyu," she answered. "I'll return the call, but I'd appreciate being on the chime."

"Certainly."

Breaking the connection, Smokey activated a signal scrambler (certainly one of the reasons for Kyu's annoyance) and coded Gary. His hawk-nosed, swarthy features immediately built up on her screen.

"Smokey." His smile was tight and thin-lipped, as if it hurt. "Glad to reach you."

"I'm sure," she said. "No doubt that's why you use the VT and don't come on by."

His smile was more relaxed this time. "I can't afford you, Smokey, and I hate taking credit. I've got something here that I'd like you to look into—if you're interested."

"I can't say if I am if you don't say what it is," she sighed, her exasperation only partly play, "and I'll bet you can't talk about it over the VT."

"Wise as well as lovely—Sheba to my Solomon," Gary replied. "Are you free tonight?"

"I have a dinner date, but still a few hours this afternoon."

"And you won't break your date."

"Bad for business," she smiled. "Besides, he's cute."

"Well, I'd better come by this afternoon. Can you schedule me in for about an hour from now?"

"Pretty easily—you can wait if you must?"

"Yes."

Smokey spent most of the next hour with two boys on a birthday jaunt. Neither were virgins, but both believed that they knew a lot more than they did. She rather enjoyed enlightening them and made certain that they left feeling both sated and deliciously scandalized.

She had Gary escorted to her suite about ten minutes later. He arrived looking mildly impatient and more than slightly horny. A wait in Kyu's parlor could do that to a man. She took his briefcase from him and indicated a comfortable seat.

"Tea?" she asked, pouring herself some.

"Yes," he answered. "May I loosen my collar?"

"Take off your shirt if you want." She allowed herself a wicked grin. "I might even forget I'm working if you have something interesting for me."

His peaked brows rose to where his hairline had been the year she first met him, and he opened his briefcase across his knees.

"About a standard ago," he said, "Wickerwork Corporation's liner *Hollyhock IV* was a week late in its run between Old Terra and Icedrake. The official story was drive failure. I had some routine checks made and several members of the engineering crew insist that there was no engine failure. They claim the ship had stopped to investigate a sensor blip. One gal said something—a message capsule perhaps—was picked up."

"Fascinating," Smokey prompted. "Go on."

"Of the three who were—uh—goaded into speaking, one is now dead, accidental, apparently. The other two have been put on a long run and are not expected back in commerce space for two standards."

"The rest of the ship's crew?"

"Let me get back to that," Gary said. "Now, you may wonder why I care about a delay in the *Hollyhock*'s schedule."

"Beyond the fact that it is a premier ship in a rival's fleet?" Smokey said, demurely pouring more tea.

"Yes." Gary coughed. "Beyond that."

"I hadn't, please, go on."

"Since the *Hollyhock* has returned, the company has suddenly undergone a complete change in management strategies. Several new patents have been filed, including one for an improved communications relay, that have led to amazing increases in the value of their holdings. Despite this, they are buying back their own stock at a phenomenal pace—and this includes subsidiary holdings."

"Has the top management changed?"

"No, all the major positions are held by the same people with the exception of one old guy who died of a cerebral hemorrhage half a standard back. His death was almost expected."

Gary called up a file and turned so that Smokey could see the screen. "However, several lesser positions have been changed and in each case the change put someone who was aboard the *Hollyhock* in a post in the management hierarchy. Even odder, I checked into the new patents and again each one is associated with someone from the *Hollyhock*."

"Sounds like you're onto something," Smokey agreed. "What do you have in mind for me?"

"Port City, Arizona, is hosting an Interstellar Conference on R&D for the spacefaring industries. First, I want you to keep your ears open for anything on the *Hollyhock*'s find. Second, I'm going to try and find a way for you to meet up with a Wickerwork representative."

"You want me to pump him," she said.

"There's no one like you for finding things out, Smokey."

She fluttered her eyelashes playfully. "You say the nicest things, Gary. Want to whisper them in my ear?"

He quickly put his briefcase aside and then paused. "Working or not working?"

"Oh, not." She giggled. "How could I charge an old friend? And such a sexy one, too."

"This time you won't," he grumbled happily.

And then she reached for him and as she touched his body and drew him to her, she delved into his mind as he did into her body.

After Gary had left, Smokey reflected on the additional information she had learned. Gary was truly concerned about Wickerwork's increasingly competitive edge, but beneath it she had sensed dread, even fear, as if Wickerwork had obtained something with unbelievable potential. His fears were just that—fears—but despite her inability to find their root, she went off in a thoughtful mood to meet Clarence.

4

THE DIRTY SLATE WAS A SMALL RESTAURANT, literally a hole-in-the-wall of the reddish sandstone ravine in which Port City was built. Smokey greeted the owner.

"I'm meeting a friend for dinner, Fairfield," she said.

"A gentleman?"

"Always," she smiled. "I think I see him."

"If it isn't your date, come back to the bar and I'll buy you a drink."

"Thanks, Fairfield, but that's him."

She snaked her way between the round tables to where Clarence was sitting, his back to her, sipping a glass of chilled wine. Stopping by his chair, she put her hand on his shoulder.

"Smokey . . ." His initial enthusiastic greeting trailed off. "Smokey? What have you done to your hair?"

She spun so that he could see the long, silvery braid that fell between her shoulder blades.

"Didn't recognize me without my hair loose?" She grinned. "Or was it because something else wasn't loose?" Clarence was too dark for his blush to show, but he had the good grace to look embarrassed. "Don't worry, Clarence," Smokey continued. "I'm used to men not remembering my face, but I'm not about to strip so that you can check your memory."

"I . . ." Clarence stood. "Please, sit down, Smokey. Let me signal a drink for you."

When he had seated her and her order was placed he cleared his throat. "Let me start again—Smokey, I'm very glad to see you. You do look quite different with your hair pulled back like that, but very pretty. I rather like being able to concentrate on the delicate beauty of your features."

"Facial?" she teased, then relented. "Very pretty words, Clarence. I tend to pull my hair back when I'm not working. The other style is awfully noticeable."

"And you don't want to be mobbed on the street?"

"Something like that. I guess I don't feel like working when I'm not, and that look is designed to get attention."

"I hadn't realized how much dark hair you had on top. I thought I remembered the silvering effect starting higher."

"It does"—she pushed back her hair at the temple—"but I can brush that underneath."

Fairfield came over with her drink. "Wine for you, Smokey. Can I bring dinner menus?"

"Actually, if Clarence will permit, I can order for us both from memory. I'd like him to try the local cuisine. Clarence, are you allergic to anything?"

"No, but I do watch my salt."

"That shouldn't be a problem. The weather here tends to take it right out of you."

She rattled off a quick order and Fairfield retreated. Then she reached across the table and took Clarence's hand.

"Do you need a refresher on your drink?"

He sipped, mouthing the liquid critically. "This will do, but I've noticed that all the drinks are rather heavy on the ice—even at the expensive places."

Smokey looked puzzled. "Of course the drinks are going to be iced at the expensive places. Ice has always been considered a luxury on Arizona. Even now that the colony is settled, we keep the tradition."

"Must be hard to get drunk." Clarence laughed.

"Not as hard as you'd imagine, since our atmosphere is slightly thinner than Old Terra's. Effectively, even our lowlanders live at what most Old Terran consider 'high altitudes.' People who aren't ready for it tend to get blasted on a few drinks. Natives even things out for them with the ice."

"I like your ice-as-luxury explanation better. From what I've seen, Port City doesn't thrive on altruism. Free market enterprise seems a more accurate description."

"Buy low, sell high," Smokey agreed. "We've few enough people here that it works. There aren't too many shirkers; those who do find that work gets found for them. After a few goes of that, usually people prefer to find their own work."

"Is that what happened to you?" Clarence asked.

Smokey considered. "I don't think so . . ."

There was a discreet rattling of china and silver as Fairfield rolled the cart out of the kitchen. Smokey smiled as she saw Clarence's eyes widen.

"Quite a spread, isn't it?" she said proudly, turning in her seat to help Fairfield set the platters and tureens on the table.

"Are we expected to eat all of that?" Clarence asked.

"No, but I wanted you to have a good sampling. Fairfield will wrap the rest to go."

"Good." Clarence lifted the glass cover off of one dish and sniffed the spicy scent appreciatively. "I recognize the tortillas, but none of the fillings look familiar."

"They probably aren't," Smokey said, spooning an orange paste onto a warm tortilla. "One of the things that shaped local cuisine was that for a long time water wasn't exactly readily available. So—"

"Smokey," Clarence interrupted, rolling up a tortilla of his own, "if you say that the food is good, I'll trust you to stop me before I bite into something too spicy. You're the one I want to know more about. I've decided that you're special."

She chewed slowly, debating how to answer.

"There's not much about me to learn," she said, "and I only said that I'd have dinner with you, not let you interrogate me. I'm just a paid companion, baby, nothing more."

"Yes, but what you know is what I want to know." He popped the end of his tortilla into his mouth and reached for another. "What should I try next?"

"Try the green filling on the bread squares as a chaser," she advised. "The contrast is marvelous."

Each time he tried to redirect the conversation to her life, Smokey fended him away with some delicacy or spicy anecdote. Clarence's interest in the workings of Arizona and specifically of the Sybarite's District was genuine. Beneath it, however, she sensed that his curiosity was becoming more personal and potentially dangerous—dangerous to her hard-won professional detachment.

"If you eat like this all the time," Clarence said, pushing the plate back in token surrender, "keeping your figure must be impossible."

"Not really," Smokey said, her grey eyes twinkling. "Sex if performed with enthusiasm tones the body nicely and burns calories. In any case, I bike or swim almost every day."

"Biking is quite popular here," Clarence noted, toying with a small, yellow fruit. "More than on most planets, I think."

"That fruit is too salty without the sauce next to it," Smokey advised, pushing the plate over. "Try this."

After Clarence nodded his approval, she went on. "I don't know about other planets, but on Arizona the atmosphere is still being fortified. We're encouraged into sports that don't create pollutants. Almost no one owns a personal vehicle larger than a bike, which not only eliminates pollutants, but also cuts down on congestion. Ravines run their own internal transport and planetary government funds an interravine shuttle service."

"Pretty wholesome," Clarence said, "and admirable."

"I never really thought about it," Smokey lied. "Anyhow, you can get fined for doing anything that threatens the ongoing terraforming. Extreme violations can lead to exile. So, we're probably not as admirable as you think."

"Maybe not," Clarence said. "But whatever the reason, the result is admirable. How do you feel about living on a planet that's being terraformed?"

"Well, sweets," she said, licking the dripping end of a jelly roll, "I don't think I'd like to live on an unterraformed planet. And there aren't many planets that welcome humans without some help, right?"

"Just Old Terra, really, though even Mother Earth isn't always very welcoming. Icedrake is supposed to be rather like what Old Terra was back when the glaciers were taking one of their easy strolls. I understand that lots of the critters there are rescued from species endangered by the polluted regions on Old Terra."

"Rescued!" Smokey snorted. "That's altruism—ruin the habitat, then call it 'rescue' to move the creatures. Maybe that's a difference of living on a terraforming world. We think more about how things fit together."

"We think about these things more than our ancestors did!" Clarence protested. "You're being unfair. You can't blame us for the crimes of hundreds of years ago."

"Don't get your heat up, thornbud," she said, raising his hand and nibbling the fingertips. "I don't blame you for anything but thinking too hard about more than simple pleasures. My job is to give you good memories, and you're not cooperating."

"Smokey, just being with you gives me pleasure," he murmured, his eyes liquid brown. "I came to Kyu's 'house' looking for a good informant, and I think I've found something more."

Smokey's eyes widened, becoming silver-rimmed with dark grey as she caught his thoughts. She knew she was more beautiful when she lost her poise, but she couldn't help herself.

"Clarence," she said, deliberately harsh, "I never get involved with tricks."

She pushed back her chair and rose. "Thanks for dinner. I see my time's up. Fairfield will expect you to handle the bill—the men always pay for me."

"Smokey," his voice was low and insistent, "please."

"No." She turned so that he couldn't see her face. "You've paid for my time and now I don't want to see you again. Good-bye, Clarence."

"Smokey." His voice broke.

She hesitated, then put back her shoulders and sauntered out.

Fairfield gave her a wry grin. "Break another heart, Smokey?"

"Yeah," she said. Somehow she didn't feel as cool as she had on similar occasions.

"Good night, Fairfield."

"Good night, Smokey."

She shut the door behind her softly, but the blunt click still sounded dull and final.

5

WHEN SHE GOT HOME, SMOKEY FOUND BONNY in the setting room, still in her damp playsuit, absorbed in a computer program. Wintering was asleep in a companionable heap near the girl's feet, the remnants of a meter-long billipede a crunchy pile along his furry beige-and-tan flank. Outside the long window, the sun was painting the ridgeline rose and gold.

"Bonny," Smokey scolded, "get out of your wet clothes before you ruin that chair."

The girl didn't shift. "In a minute. I've just about got this program clean."

"Bonny!" Smokey drew the round syllables of her daughter's name out into a threat.

This time Bonny looked up. "Mama, please. This isn't just a game—it's important."

Reluctantly, Smokey softened. "You'll clean the chair."

"Promise!"

Seeing that Bonny would be intent for a while yet, Smokey went and changed into a loose white linen shirt that fell past her knees. Belting it with a gauzy grey scarf that Jules had given her, she walked back into the setting room. Bonny had closed the computer and was fingering the chair seat.

"I don't think it's too wet," she offered hopefully. "I was almost dry when I sat down, anyhow."

"Hmm," Smokey said. "Go change in any case. You could get a rash. Have you eaten?"

"A little. Y'mah's mother stopped and got us shuttles, but I could still eat. Did you bring anything home?"

Smokey shook her head. "No, not this time."

"Was it a bad one?" Bonny asked, pausing halfway to her room.

"No," Smokey said, "not really."

"Oh, a nice one. Poor Mama." Bonny shook her head with an almost-adult mannerism. "Since you didn't bring anything, we can have frozfroot instead."

"What a sacrifice!" Smokey laughed. "Go change into your nightclothes, Boniface."

She dished Bonny up a large bowl of the freeze-crystallized fruit and topped it with hot syrup. As an afterthought, she dished up a small portion for herself and carried it with a cup of spice tea out into the setting room. The sunset was gone now and the blue-black sky was not yet washed out by the rising moons. The lesser lights of the space stations were visible and Smokey amused herself by imagining that she could see the starliners and cargo ships purposefully making their way between points.

The faint slap of bare feet on the tiled floor and the rustle of fabric announced Bonny. She was eating as she walked and Wintering was circling her legs hoping for—or perhaps attempting to create—a spill.

"Grandmama Joy in Motion called," Bonny said, slipping the chulo a spoonful of frozfroot. "She said that she'd call back."

Smokey suppressed a groan. Bonny was quite fond of her eccentric grandparents.

"Was she in-system?"

"Uh-huh. She and Grandpapa Bethlehem are just in-jumped on the liner *Ibn Battuta*. They should be in Arizona orbit in two days."

"Two days," Smokey mused. "Why doesn't she ever give me more warning? I've promised Gary I'll do some special work for him. I won't have time to deal with guests."

"I'll do it, Mama." Bonny bounced, not disguising her excitement despite Smokey's evident dismay. "I'm ahead in school, and I'll catch up after they leave."

"Maybe. Let me talk with Grandmama Joy first." Smokey frowned thoughtfully. "We'll see what they're up to."

"Up to." Bonny giggled. "That's good."

"How long ago did the call come through?" Smokey asked, ignoring Bonny's joke.

"I don't know. The house unit told me when I came in." She looked sheepish. "I told it not to bother saving the message because I wanted to go and work on my math problem."

"Don't worry, Bonita," Smokey said. "Joy in Motion is like a bad penny. She keeps turning up."

"What's a penny?"

Smokey was about to answer when a calm, neuter voice announced, "Call incoming. Caller identifies self as one Joy in Motion."

"Bonny, have you been reprogramming the unit's response format again?"

"Uh, aren't you going to answer the call? She's calling from off-planet."

"System, I'll take the call." She grinned at Bonny. "Undo whatever it is you did, capi? I can't handle feeling like I'm in one of those old-time flatties."

The face that built up on screen was slender and oval, with high cheekbones. The unnaturally aqua eyes were wide and fringed with golden lashes several shades darker and more metallic than the pixie cut that flopped into her eyes. Her smile was impish and entirely lovely.

"Hello, Smokey."

"Hello, Mother."

"Must you call me that in that disapproving tone of voice?" The smile didn't fade. "Just call me Joy."

"I'm not disapproving, Joy," Smokey said. "You *are* my mother. How long are you going to be in-system?"

"Well, I'm performing up on the Wheel of Heaven.

Then we wanted to come and visit you and Bonny. In all, I'd guess a few weeks before the *Battuta* will leave. Do you have room?"

Smokey hesitated. "Yes, of course, but I have some work that may give me some odd hours."

"I expect that with the business you're in. We'll just use the time to spoil Bonny."

"Can you get us tickets to your show?" Smokey asked, trusting the impulse fueling her words.

Joy in Motion seemed pleased. "Why, yes. It's been so long since you wanted to come that I didn't even think to offer."

Smokey smiled. "Well then, it's time. Now, Mother, this is costing you. Say hello to Bethlehem and we'll see you after you're in orbit."

"'Joy,' Smokey, 'Joy.' Give our love to Bonny."

The picture faded, but the pixie smile burned in memory. Smokey shook her head thoughtfully, remembering long ago when she was Bonny's age. She wondered how fair her younger self had been to Joy. She wondered . . .

"Mama! Wintering has gotten into the pawpaw jam!"

Over the next two days, Smokey kept alert for mention of Wickerwork's mysterious find, but nothing came her way. She dutifully reported this to Gary when he called.

"Are you free to work tonight?" he asked.

She didn't even bother to consult her calendar. "No, I'm taking in a show."

"Break the date," Gary half ordered. "I'll make it up to you. The R&D conference that I mentioned to you is having a blowout tonight, and I'm fairly certain that I can get you in."

"No," she said, though her curiosity was piqued, and a cowardly part of her was eager for an excuse to avoid Joy. "I can't break this date."

Gary stared questioningly through the screen. "If the money's that good, I'll better it."

Smokey sighed. "It's not, but you can't beat it."

"You aren't getting soft on a client, are you?"

"No," she growled, though unaccountably Clarence's image flashed through her mind. "I'm taking my daughter out and nine-year-olds get hurt if their mothers back out at the last minute—especially if the mother is a whore who has to break dates too often. Leave it, Gary. I've checked. That R&D conference won't end for days yet."

Gary nodded and then smiled in an obvious effort to be conciliatory. "Taking Bonny to a concert?"

"More like a circus," Smokey replied, knowing full well that he could learn if he cared. "We're going to see Joy in Motion."

"The low-gee dancer?" Gary's eyes widened with respect and awe. "Those tickets have been sold out since an hour after the *Ibn Battuta* came in-system. The woman has been declared a Living Art Treasure. You must have fantastic connections to get tickets."

Smokey couldn't resist. "I do—Joy in Motion is my mother."

While Gary was still gaping, she smiled sweetly and reached for the cutoff tab. "I'll talk with you tomorrow."

6

THE SHUTTLE RIDE TO THE WHEEL OF HEAVEN was a routine trip that Bonny's excitement transformed into an adventure. Smokey had made the flight countless times with clients or for work-related events. Bonny made it perhaps twice a standard. The girl tried on the pose of a polished traveler for the first few minutes, but after the streamlined shuttle had been flung into escape, she gave up and smashed her nose to the window, her headphones tuned to the cockpit's chatter.

"There's Port City, Mama," she said, pointing to a wide, green gash in the honey brown terrain. "Which one is that over there?"

Smokey leaned over Bonny's shoulder, smelling the scent of clean little girl mixed with the hint of perfume she'd permitted for the occasion.

"That's Ki'rin Ravine," she answered. "They do research there into what plants and animals can be brought to Arizona. I understand that there are some larger beasts there now—something called a 'chamel.'"

She sensed Bonny's giggle before it reached her ears.

"That's a 'camel,' Mama. Some of my VR school-mates live there and they mentioned it one day when the instructor was late linking in." She turned from the window to face Smokey. "I told Chinue that we were coming to the Wheel. He said that he might come to the dock and meet us."

"He's your friend from your new physics class, right?" Smokey said, feeling Bonny's pleasure that she'd remembered. "That's great. Maybe we can even get him into the show. Joy is having a box saved for us, so there should be room."

By now, Arizona was a tan ball with barely discernible green streaks. Smokey waited patiently but with building excitement as the sphere moved counterspin toward the space station. Beneath her arm, Bonny had also returned her fascinated gaze to the window.

"We're gonna see it, Mama," she whispered, touching her earphones lightly. "The captain says we'll be passing over while it's in daylight."

In response, Smokey hugged her. Below, sharper and brighter than the green streaks, a vaguely oval-shaped blue form was becoming visible beneath them. Bordered by a band of green darker than anything else on the globe, it was like a strange eye placidly gazing up at them.

"That's it, Mama," Bonny said, her tones hushed with respect. "That's the Sea."

Smokey could only nod as Bonny's awe merged with her own very different emotions, flooding her with sensations nearly too powerful to handle, but she held Bonny tighter and stared harder.

"That's right, Bonny, that's Ross Styler's Sea, the largest body of freestanding water on all of Arizona. There's more water there than in all the ravine rivers of Port City, Ki'rin Ravine, Graydon's Gorge, and New Nairobi combined. I remember when it was nothing more than a dream in Ross Styler's mind—odd to see the landscape of a world slowly change."

"How old *are* you, Mama?" Bonny asked. Then her love for a puzzle took over. "Wait, let me remember. Thirty-seven, right?"

Smokey tousled her hair playfully, "Don't say that too loudly, Bonita. A lady who makes her living like I do needs to be timeless."

"I won't tell," Bonny agreed solemnly. "The captain says we should see the Wheel soon. Look! There!"

The space station that had been christened the Wheel of Heaven by commerce-minded individuals was nothing less than a city in orbit. In many ways it was superior to the planet it orbited. A controlled environment kept it ever comfortable; constant traffic from other systems kept it cosmopolitan.

Smokey always enjoyed her visits, but happily returned to the planet. For too many years her home had been purely artificial environments like this one. Her preference was a planet, even a dry, barely habitable one like Arizona.

Still, she had to admit that the snowflake of metal and crystal that glittered against the black velvet starsprinkled void was lovely. It spun slightly, increasingly vast as they closed to dock on the port hub set on one of the outstretched arms. Bonny relayed the cockpit's orders a moment before they came over the speakers and slowly, with the faintest of bumps, they latched onto the space station.

"Slowly, Bonny," Smokey cautioned as they were given permission to debark. "Don't act like a ground bounder. You know how to behave."

Bonny blushed. "Sorry, I got excited."

She was solemnly careful after that, her hands wrapped tightly around the enormous bouquet of pink lilies and pinker roses that she had selected for her grandmother. Smokey restrained herself from taking the girl's hand as they walked through the nearly invisible pressure tube linking the shuttle to the station. The almost-transparent walkways had been routine for the last five years, but they were a change from the pearlescent girder-linked accordions that some part of her still thought of as "normal." Laughing to herself, she realized that she wasn't reassuring Bonny so much as looking for reassurance herself.

A small crowd was milling in the lounge. Near the departure area a young couple was clinging to each other as if they could somehow make unreal the imminent parting. The younger man was crying openly. His older comrade was dressed in a crisp uniform.

Smokey felt a pang, remembering a similar parting when she was sixteen and her first lover had gone into interstellar shipping. He had written a few times before they'd drifted apart. When they had met again about ten years later she had wondered at the pain he had once caused her.

Today she was keyed to the present, not the past, but the pain was there quick and sure. She reached and touched Bonny's arm.

"Do you see your grandmother, Bonny?" She glanced about. "Or Grandpapa Bethlehem?"

"Not yet." Bonny froze. "Yes, there they are!"

Waving her bouquet, she darted across the tiled foyer, shedding rose and lily petals as she ran. Smokey followed with only slightly more decorum.

Wheel of Heaven was probably one of the few places in the commerce worlds where a Treasure like Joy in Motion could expect to come into public and be left untroubled by her legions of admirers. She was kneeling, hugging Bonny, but when Smokey approached she stood and embraced her daughter.

Smokey accepted the embrace, feeling the reserve and fear her mother kept beneath her bubbling exterior. In response, she hugged her more tightly and felt, as with her clients, some of the reserve melt away and be replaced by relief.

Then Smokey turned and embraced Bethlehem, a wiry, fair-haired man who tended to fade into nonentity next to his flamboyant wife. Her father was one of the few men she could not read. When she was younger she had believed that this was because she rarely had extended physical contact with him. Now she suspected that there might be another reason.

"Paging arriving passenger B. Smoke. B. Smoke. Please approach the check-in station for a message."

Bonny looked at her mother, suddenly timid at hearing herself paged in such an adult fashion.

"Should I, Mama?"

"Of course. It's that computer pedestal over by the

doors." Smokey gave her a reassuring pat. "It's probably just your schoolmate looking for you. Go on, and we'll watch from here."

Bonny nodded and scampered off.

"She's growing up nicely," Bethlehem said, his deep slow manner of speaking making his words a pronouncement rather than a comment.

"Bright and social," Joy agreed, "and I think she's pretty now, but going to be lovely later."

"After she survives adolescence," Smokey agreed, remembering her own coltish years.

Only part of her attention had been watching Bonny make her hesitant way across the foyer; she had also been trying to spot the boy that Bonny was to meet. Except for a few traveling with adults, she saw no children. Bonny had arrived at the check-in post. When Smokey looked back again, she saw that Bonny was now in animated conversation with an adult male. Catching her eye, Bonny waved them over.

"Mama, this is Daniel Chinue." She giggled. "Please tell him that I am the only B. Smoke on Arizona."

Smokey offered her hand to Chinue. He was short and stocky, with skin so dark that it had almost-purple undertones. His wooly hair was cropped close and eyes with silver cyber-rims around the irises peered at her over a flat, somewhat pugnacious nose. Despite physically resembling a battering ram, his grip was slight, and the dominant emotion that reached her was surprise.

"Bonny is the only B. Smoke on Arizona as far as I know," Smokey agreed, "and undoubtedly she is the only one in your physics class. By the way, when I'm not 'Mama,' I'm Smokey. These are my parents, Joy and Bethlehem."

Chinue's dark eyes widened slightly in recognition, but he only extended a polite hand in greeting.

"Pardon my surprise, Smokey," he said. "I knew that Bonny was young, but I had not realized how young."

Seeing Smokey's puzzled frown, he halted. "You did not realize the nature of Bonny's class?"

"Nature?"

Chinue sighed. "I see that we have much to discuss. Perhaps I can buy you a drink."

Smokey shook her head, "We are here to see my mother's performance. However, we were planning on inviting Bonny's classmate and his elders to join us. Perhaps you would still be interested."

Chinue smiled as he realized that Smokey and Bonny had shared his error, but in reverse.

"I would be delighted—and honored," he added with a slight bow for Joy in Motion. "I will need to contact my wife. Perhaps we can meet you."

"Ask for Box L4," Bethlehem said. "I will leave word for your party to be expected. How many?"

"Just two," Chinue said. "My son is too young to appreciate the honor."

He gave another of his slight bows. Then with an effort that Smokey hoped Bonny did not perceive, he shook the girl's hand.

"Bonny, you're just like your mother," Joy said to break the awkward silence as Chinue retreated. "Full of surprises."

"We have time for refreshments," Bethlehem added, "before Joy and I need to prepare for the show. What would you like?"

"Easy!" Bonny responded. "Ice cream!"

The theater box that had been reserved for them was as plush as an Elizabethan ball gown, done up in forest green velvet embroidered with pearls and gold bric-a-brac. The theater itself had been configured for viewing in the round and the central stage was a deceptively barren oval that looked all the more elegant for its ornate setting.

Smokey had seen stages like it for as long as she could recall and knew that beneath the gold-dusted blue surface was a concealed matrix of superconductors and circuits far more complex than those used to run many starliners. There was also a tiny cockpit shaped to fit Bethlehem. Its lines were so intolerant of change that

Bethlehem had not gained or lost more than a kilo in all of Smokey's memory.

Bonny was leaning over the balcony's edge, watching the elaborately dressed theatergoers with fascination, when the box's door opened. Chinue entered, dressed in university formals and accompanied by a tiny Oriental woman as delicate as Ming porcelain. She also wore university formals, although her colors were green and gold as opposed to his scarlet and orange. Both, Smokey noticed, wore heavy gold tassels that denoted doctorates.

"Smokey, Bonny," Chinue said, "I would like to present my wife, Mu Tian. Mu Tian is a mathematics professor on Icedrake, but she's on leave of absence to teach in the Arizona VR educational system."

Bonny tilted her head to one side. "I know your name," she said to Mu Tian. "I've been reading your papers on the expanded uses of imaginary numbers."

Mu Tian's eyes narrowed as if she suspected a trick. "You must be mistaken, Bonny. Those papers have never been adapted for children."

"That," Chinue said, placing a blocky hand on her arm, "is one of the reasons that we are here. I suspect we need to get to know Bonny much better."

Smokey had followed this exchange with interest. Now she decided that the time had come for some answers.

"You," she said to Chinue, "are in Bonny's physics class and yet here you are wearing university formals. I'll not claim to be an expert, but that barring and those hood colors usually indicate that the degree taken was in the sciences and from how you've been talking I'll wager that your degree is in either mathematics or physics."

Bonny looked at her mother with undisguised admiration as Chinue muttered, "Physics."

"Now," Smokey continued, "what are you doing in my nine-year-old daughter's physics class?"

Chinue pursed his lips. "How much do you know about the VR school system, Smokey?"

"Not a great deal," she admitted. "My education was mostly shipboard. I do know that the system on Arizona gives Bonny the opportunity to be in special classes that Port City alone could not justify offering. I prefer for her to have contact in the flesh with other children, so the only classes I've enrolled her in have been a few special ones that her local instructors recommended—this one in physics and a couple in mathematics."

"Hmm," Chinue said. "Then let me start at the basics. A VR classroom is just like a normal one in many ways—the lecturers are audible and students are encouraged to take notes and answer questions and interact with each other and the instructor. There is also plenty of hands-on work, which in physics is useful. But the VR classroom has advantages over those I have just noted. For example, students can participate in demonstrations of principles, not just set up models."

Bonny grinned. "The laws of motion were lots of fun. So was atomic structure modeling."

Chinue nodded. "Since everything is a computer-generated reality, there is no difficulty with supplies or space. We can do things even in an isolated solar system like this one that a few generations ago could have only been done at the finest universities."

"Wait," Smokey said, disliking the fanaticism that lit Chinue's features. "I'm not that ignorant. VR techniques like these you're talking about have been used in entertainment forever. I've also heard Bonny talk about her classes. What I want to know is what a doctor of physics is doing in my daughter's class."

"It's VR," he said sheepishly, "and I'm a ringer. In many VR classes, the usual practice is to assign the students personas. Since the actual body is not present, how the person 'looks' in the VR sim can be changed. Education theory has agreed for centuries that random factors like age, gender, and even racial makeup may influence how students and faculty interact. In Bonny's class, all of the students are represented by academic garbed, neuter figures. We use surnames, so even a proper name will not give anything away."

"It's neat, Mama," Bonny assured her.

"So you had no idea that B. Smoke was a nine-year-old girl," Smokey said.

"That's right." Chinue steepled his fingers under his chin. "Now, as I said, I'm a ringer. Since everyone is represented essentially as an equal, I can hide easily."

"Why?"

"Talent scout, you might say," he answered. "Tests have their drawbacks because students often perform outside of what would be usual."

"They freeze," Smokey said.

"Or they study so hard beforehand that they perform better than they would in a more normal situation. The same goes for experiments or reports." Chinue studied Bonny. "Bonny was not in a beginners' physics class, as you seem to think. Her classmates include a geneticist from Ki'rin Ravine, several graduate students, and a professor brushing up on her theory before moving to a post on Guillen."

"I knew that Bonny had been doing well," Smokey temporized, "and that she had outpaced her age group. I simply didn't realize how much. I understand the basics, but Bonny has long surpassed me. Physics and mathematics are not my area."

"What do you do?" Chinue asked.

"I'm a whore," Smokey said. Then, seeing him glance at Mu Tian in shock, she added, "Bonny gets her talent from her father."

"And who is he?" Mu Tian asked.

"He's dead now," Smokey said, feeling a familiar sense of loss. "He was Ross Styler."

The lights dropped to blackness at that moment and Smokey heard the scientists bite back their questions. No matter how essential they viewed what they wanted to know, they would be thrown out of the theater if they interrupted the performance.

Below, a minute violet dust cloud glittered darkly over the center of the raised dais, expanding with just the suggestion of true light to reveal Joy in Motion. She floated over the stage, head and arms thrown back, one leg extended in a point, the other bent at the knee and curling beneath her torso. She drifted there, graceful in her contortion, apparently not even breathing. Then, with a slow rise and fall of her rounded breasts, she came to life.

As her gilded lashes fluttered open, strains of music so faint that they seemed to play in the listener's imagination rather than in the ears came to thread themselves through the audience's breathing. To that music, Joy in Motion began to dance.

Her dance had elements of ballet, if ballet could be freed of the constraints of gravity. She twisted in midair into contortions that would make a supreme yogi descend into jealousy. Gracefully bringing her feet behind her head, she spun, releasing her limbs so slowly that she became a spiral-armed galaxy spinning in violet space.

As she spun and twirled, the music rose and fell, fluctuating with her dance. Critics had long marveled that while Joy in Motion's dance was never the same twice, the music was always perfectly synchronized with her actions.

Smokey was beginning to believe that she understood how this could be so. She wondered that she had taken so long to guess, and with a deep fear she hoped that no one else ever would. The act wouldn't likely be the only thing broken up.

Her revelation intensified her appreciation for the dance and she lost herself in the flips and leaps. Joy became butterfly and star shower, summer breeze and dust storm; Smokey watched entranced but with a pounding heart. When the lights came up for intermission, she struggled to bring herself back to the present concerns.

Chinue and Mu Tian were still jiggling their applause strings when she turned to them. Bonny's eyes were bright and dreamy, but she came to herself when an usher arrived with a tray of liquors and treats "compliments of the house."

"Did you say that Bonny's father was Ross Styler? The Ross Styler?" Chinue asked, his voice still hushed.

"Yes," Smokey nodded. "We met when he came to

help with the Arizona terraforming project. So, Bonny's talents hardly surprise me—she comes from brilliant, creative stock."

Smokey ended her sentence with a toss of her bright mane toward the stage—her reminder that Bonny was the child of art as well as of science. The subject of their discussion, fruit tart in hand, was once again leaning out over the balcony watching the milling people below.

"I didn't think that Ross Styler ever married or had children," Mu Tian commented too casually. "In fact, I am certain that he was homosexual."

Although she had anticipated the line of questioning, Smokey still smoldered.

"I am going to overlook that you have accused me both of being stupid and of being a liar in the space of two sentences," she said, her voice husky, "and I'll answer your questions. Yes, Ross never married—not even another man—and he never fathered children in his lifetime. But we were friends, and when he began to regret his lack, an obvious solution presented itself."

The two scientists were now abashedly silent and Bonny had turned to listen, her expression guarded and critical as Smokey repeated a tale the girl had heard many times.

"We planned that I would bear Bonny and raise her. Ross would make frequent visits and have full parental rights and duties. When he died"—her voice caught despite herself—"I went ahead with our plan with the support of Ross's attorney, who had been helping with our arrangements."

The lights flickered, giving the traditional signal that intermission was nearly ended. Smokey poured herself a splash of smoky Terran whisky, dismayed to see in the ripple of the amber liquid that her hand was shaking. As the lights dimmed, Bonny came and tucked herself onto Smokey's lap. Awash in the trust and fierce protectiveness of her little girl, Smokey didn't even notice when the dance again began.

After the show, Chinue and Mu Tian somewhat stiffly

offered their thanks and hurried off. Bonny looked into the crowd as the retreating robes merged into the sea of color.

"I liked Chinue in class," she said, "but I didn't here—at least after he wouldn't believe anything that we were trying to tell him. And Mu Tian, she's so smart—I know—how can she be so dumb?"

Smokey hugged her. "There's a difference between being smart and being wise, Boniface. Sometimes the more people learn, the more it cuts them off from the way things really are."

The doors to the box opened and Bethlehem joined them. His skin was slightly grey with fatigue, but he looked unreasonably content. He smiled at them, but Smokey was certain that he felt the lingering tension.

"Joy," he said without preamble, "is famished and would like to ask if you two would care to join us for a late dinner on the *Ibn Battuta*."

Smokey was about to accept, but caught Bonny smothering a massive yawn.

"We would," she said, "but I need my beauty sleep and Bonny has had an exciting day. If we hurry we can catch the next shuttle to Port City. Can we come up when Bonny would be able to appreciate it?"

Bethlehem nodded. "You'll be seeing us soon."

"Say good night to Mama," Smokey said, herding Bonny toward the pedslide, "and tell her she was more lovely than I thought possible."

Bonny fell asleep even before the shuttle had undocked from the Wheel of Heaven. Smokey cradled her in her lap and drowsed, her thoughts mingling with the pastel hues of her daughter's dreams until one became the other.

7

FEELING RATHER LIKE A CHILD WHO HAD BEEN cutting classes, Smokey went down to the Victorian Mansion early the next afternoon. Madame Kyu was sitting in her rocker on the porch listening to strains of Dixieland piano coming through the lace-curtained bay window. As Smokey mounted the steps, Kyu smiled her Queen Victoria smile and gestured with one of her knitting needles toward the window.

"How do you like the music?"

"Very nice," Smokey said, though privately she thought that Dixieland jazz in a brothel was somewhat clichéd. "Nice quality recording."

"It's not a recording," Kyu said, her smile broadening into a slightly malicious grin. "I've hired a piano player—I think you are acquainted with him."

"Oh," Smokey replied, at a loss to explain Kyu's grin. "I'll look in and say hello before I collect my messages."

Kyu nodded regally, malice vanished behind the Queen Victoria enigma. Smokey waved and went into the Gentlemen's Parlor. The room was empty except for a man at the piano. He wore pearl grey trousers with a matching vest from which a pocket watch chain trailed. His face was shadowed by a bowler hat slightly darker grey than his suit. He played his way through an elaborate run and then, sensing that someone had entered the parlor, looked up.

"Hello, Smokey," he said.

"Clarence!" Her surprise was genuine, as was the flash of anger that followed. "What are you doing here?"

"Playing the piano, ma'am," he said with a mock-humble duck of his head, "and doing my research."

"I told you that I didn't wish to see you again."

"I remember," he said softly, his fingers rambling into "Melancholy Baby," "but that doesn't mean that I don't want to see you. Madame Kyu was kind enough to give me a job so that I can do my research without contaminating my study sample."

At the mention of Kyu's name, Smokey became sharply aware of the open window. Glaring at Clarence, she stalked off and collected her messages. Jules had sent her a box of sweets and a promise to be in touch. Gary left a short, blunt request for her to call. The others were more routine.

Still seething, she went up to her room, leaving a message to be contacted if any clients came in. Eli had already brought her tea, and she sipped a cup before she returned Gary's call.

"Are you free tonight, Smokey?" he asked. "I really want you to take a go with those Wickerwork engineers."

"I'm free," she said. "You cover all expenses, including the new dress I'm going to need. Information will come at my usual rates, extra if I need to stay out overnight."

"Smokey," he sighed, "whatever else you are, you're not cheap."

"No, I'm not." She smiled. "Mama didn't raise no dumb girlie. Is it a deal?"

"Yes." He looked depressed, but the VT screen flashed that a contract had been recorded.

"Well then, let me go. I need to call Mr'rel's Boutique."

He groaned, but cut off the call.

Smokey tapped Mr'rel's catalogue and assuaged her bad mood by ordering a daring silver silk and lamé evening gown, sandals, and lace silk stockings. As an afterthought, she ordered a baby-doll in emerald green watered satin.

Her temper was almost sweet when the signal chimed. Remembering Clarence, she selected a scarlet teddy trimmed with pale ivory lace and cut high on the sides and low between her breasts. Donning ruby pendant earrings, she tossed on a floor-length confection of creamy spider's silk over the ensemble and stepped into her sandals.

Unlike before, she didn't wait to upstage the other girls. This time she prowled in and didn't even give them a chance. The men were soon bidding for her time. She let it go on until she heard Clarence's playing falter, then she took the two highest rollers up to her suite.

She kept them there for quite a while.

Having made her daily minimum and then some, she called Bonny and arranged to take her to lunch. Over lunch, they decided where Bonny would spend the night, since Smokey would likely be out late. Bonny was less concerned about her mother's work hours than over their meeting with Chinue.

"Am I smart, Mama?" she asked, stopping with a wedge of pepper torte halfway to her mouth.

"You are, especially in certain things like math," Smokey replied, "but that isn't your question, is it?"

"No." Bonny chewed thoughtfully. "Do I have to be an instructor or a researcher just because I'm good at this stuff?"

"No." Smokey shook her head. "No, but I thought that was what you wanted to do."

"I thought so, but now I'm not so sure. Chinue said over the V today that prodigies usually burn out young." She paused. "What's a prodigy?"

"Someone who has a special gift for something, usually a gift that shows up when they are children," Smokey answered. "Chinue called today?"

"Uh-huh, after you left for the Victorian Mansion. He talked for a long time about rare talents and said that I could get a scholarship to anywhere I wanted—even some of the schools on Old Terra."

"What did you say?"

"I told him I couldn't go that far without my mom's permission." Bonny's grin faded. "Mama, I don't want to be a prodigy. I want to be a whore like you and be timeless."

Smokey smiled despite Bonny's seriousness. "Not all whores are timeless, Bonita. In the old days, most 'burned out' before they were twenty. Not all mathematicians have to burn out either. Ross didn't."

A fireball flared in memory, and she squeezed her eyes shut against the pain.

"Not in the usual way."

"Did you love my dad, Mama?" Bonny asked.

Smokey nodded. "In every way but the usual one, Bonny. He was a dear friend, and I wouldn't have had a child with him if I hadn't believed that he was special and that he would be a good father. I wish you had gotten to know him."

"Me, too." Bonny looked guilelessly at her. "Does this restaurant have ice cream?"

Smokey swatted her. "That's for those decadents in orbit, dust devil. Pioneers eat dried lizard livers and like it."

Bonny grimaced. "Yuck!"

"Actually, there is a planet—Icedrake—where a certain type of lizard stores extra sugar in some internal organs. The livers are very sweet and the people there serve them as a dessert. I rather liked them."

"You're teasing me again," Bonny said suspiciously.

"No, really." Smokey inspected the wall menu. "Here the best you'll do is some horrid-looking thing with hot caramel."

Bonny examined the description. "I think I can handle it."

Later, Gary came by to brief Smokey as she was inspecting the delivery from Mr'rcl's.

"You'll be at the function as one of the hostesses," he said, studiously trying not to get distracted by the sight of Smokey deciding just how low she wanted to wear the gown's shoulders. "There's no need to conceal what you do professionally. Several branches of the Entertainer's Guild have been asked to send in people. I have brought you recent holos of the men you need to speak with."

"Speak with?" Smokey pirouetted in her new gown. "Fuck over, you mean!"

Gary dropped her off at the convention hotel, and she easily found directions to the Guild green room. Inside, an assortment of other entertainers were putting the finishing touches on their cosmetics and coiffures. Smokey recognized a butch who did the odd stroll in the Sybarite's District and wandered over.

"Nice tux, Fox," she said, fingering the midnight blue satin approvingly.

"Like it?" The tall, broad-shouldered redhead spun on one black-booted heel and fluffed her white ruffled shirt.

"Love it." Smokey grinned, snapping the other woman's bow tie. "Anyone good here tonight?"

"Well, the music will be live. There are two bands—Sunthorns and Iceweasels—and this place has a really fine sound system"—Fox bared her teeth—"but you know that we won't get much time for dancing, pretty tits."

"Not on our feet, darlings," called a rouged boy as he minced past. "I'm to pass the word that we are to start moseying out anytime. Time to start fishing."

"Yeah." Fox licked her red, red lips. "Let's get out there before the civilians get juiced enough to start screwing each other."

Smokey laughed and, taking Fox's arm, let the butch escort her onto the dance floor. Men, she knew from long experience, often found two women together a powerful aphrodisiac.

As they danced, she scanned the arriving convention-eers for either of the faces she had memorized. Her first turn brought her nothing, but the second time through she saw one—Ettienne Morrel. Morrel was a tall man, well over six feet, but so grotesquely fat that he must have to eat steadily to maintain his weight. She thought he was even heavier than in the recent picture Gary had brought her. Even as Smokey watched, he snagged one of the caterer's trays and loaded his stubby hands with delicacies.

Smokey's initial worry was that his passion might be limited to edibles was quelled when he shoved a couple of sausage patties into his mouth in order to swat the caterer on the rump as she hurried by.

Trailing a few steps behind Morrel came the second man, Adam Chen. Chen was arguing some point with a severe-looking grey-haired woman, much to the amusement of a small throng that clustered around them. With a cheery smile that made her quite pretty, the woman apparently conceded to some point. Amid general laughter, the group broke apart and Smokey got her first clear look at Chen.

Like his picture, he was sandy-haired with brown, almond-shaped eyes. What the picture had not shown was the new worry lines around those eyes or the way he shoved his hands in his pockets and looked over at Morrel, tension in every line of his body. Smokey thought that, even without her expertise, anyone could see that this was an unhappy man.

She let Fox dip her until her grey mane reflected back a silver comet's tail from the polished floor. When she spun up again, Chen's expression had changed. He no longer looked worried. Instead anger flickered across his face, replaced moments later by the bland expression of a novice poker player who draws a royal flush. As he moved to get a drink from a passing tray, Smokey glanced to where he had been looking and froze.

"Scorching sands, Smokey," Fox hissed, her red lips never losing their Cupid's bow pout. "I'll need that arm later if you don't mind."

Smokey felt the other woman's pain and surprise coil back even through the light shield she had been maintaining. Immediately, she loosened her grip.

"Sorry, Fox," she apologized. "I caught my heel on one of the tiles and thought I was going to fall."

Fox softened. "You all right, sweets?"

"Yeah." Smokey kissed her on the mouth. "Thanks to a certain pillar of strength."

Fox chuckled. "Don't kiss me like that, baby, or I'll forget that I'm working. You up to the rest of the dance?"

Smokey nodded and let Fox up the tempo again. Then she glanced back over to where Chen had been looking with such hatred, fighting to restrain her own initial panic. Morrel stood, one hand blocking an automatic caterer in its rounds, the other alternating between gesturing and shoving food into his mouth.

Suitably repulsed, Smokey focused on the man with whom Morrel was so animatedly conversing. She had been right. It was Lee, Jules's client.

Her initial thought was that his presence made her job impossible. Her second was an honest assessment that she wanted it to be impossible; that, if anything, Lee's presence made things easier.

As the dance number ended, she saw Fox giving the eye to a wispy blonde frail who was blushing a very attractive rose in response to the butch's attention.

"Ready, steady?" she purred.

"Smoking," the butch murmured. "Later, 'gater."

Leaving Fox to her vixen, Smokey pretended to notice Lee for the first time. Only as she sauntered over did the question that had been nagging at her take form. What was a garment merchant doing at a high-tech R&D conference?

"Hello, Lee," she said, brushing lightly against the man. "I didn't expect the pleasure of your company."

Lee bared his perfect teeth. "I get around. Smokey, let me introduce you to a couple of my associates, Adam Chen and Ettienne Morrel. Gentlemen, this is Smokey—a woman widely believed to be the best lay on Arizona."

Smokey offered her hand to each of the men, then stole the last of the crumpets from beneath Morrel's questing paw. He hardly noticed, his gaze fixed on the swell of her breasts beneath the silver gown's shifting fabric.

He licked his lips with a crumb-slimed tongue.

"I hope you don't mean to keep her for yourself, Lee," he said. "Not after such a tantalizing introduction."

Smokey managed a smile and a coy dodge as Lee reached to stroke her ass. Driving down revulsion with long training, she fluttered her eyelashes at Morrel.

"I'm a free agent, Ettienne," she said. "I rather prefer the chance to sample all offerings."

Chen chuckled, seemingly enjoying Lee's discomfort. Smokey gave him a languid and provocative once over, pleased to see the promising bulge of an erection even against his loose suit trousers. She gave him her full attention.

"You're very quiet, Mr. Chen," she said, turning so that through a trick of light her dress would become translucent. "Of course, if you're not interested in what I have to offer, I'd be happy to direct you to that best that's here for other tastes. Dirk—the hunk over there with all the muscles and the dark hair down to his ass—is one of the best of the boys."

"Oh, no, Smokey," Chen said, blushing slightly, when his voice caught. "I've never seen anyone like you, and I don't even want to wait for a token dance."

"Hey, don't get hasty," Lee cut in. "She came over to see me first."

"And she's convention entertainment," Morrel added. "Aren't you?"

"That's right." Smokey smiled. "You run your card through the terminal in the room when we enter and leave—you can even tip that way."

"Neat," Lee said, "but that doesn't answer who gets you first and for how long."

"We could all go," Morrel suggested.

"Sorry," Smokey said, "one to a customer—convention rules. Also, it's suggested that we keep visits to under a half hour. Of course, you could always come around for seconds."

Chen drained his drink. "Are we talking or fucking? I could have gotten a good start while you've been nattering on."

"Flip a coin," Lee suggested. "No, that's hard to do with three. How about matching for it?"

They went through some complicated ritual involving credit slip numbers and a chortling Morrel won.

"I'll try and leave you some," he said, grabbing Smokey with surprising force. "Or you can settle for second-best."

Smokey grinned at the two scowling men, certain that they would wait for their chance at her. Then she escorted Morrel to one of the reserved rooms. Morrel opened the door with his convention member's card, and Smokey followed with her thumbprint.

While Morrel fumbled with his pants, she released the clasps on her gown and took off her panties. By the time he had released his girth from the tortured fabric, she was nude except for her earrings. He dropped his trousers with an approving grunt.

"Good," he said, undoing shirt buttons as he sat on the edge of the bed. She sat by him and pretended to caress him.

"I like it best with the woman on top," he said when the shirt was off.

She murmured something as she moved to comply, glad that he had suggested the one position where they could easily make contact without his girth getting too much in the way. As he lay back, she was relieved to see that he already had an erection. Coaxing one from an overweight client could be difficult and she needed for him to be content if she was to have a chance at pumping him for Gary's information.

She straddled him, guiding him into her and talking dirty when she sensed that he liked it. He was more virile than she had expected given his weight and generally unhealthy appearance. Relaxing into the motion, she felt for his mind, and when she found it she nearly lost the rhythm. Beneath the almost-childlike delight of a male getting an unexpected pleasure, she found something she had striven to forget, the calculating fragment of the alien mind.

Fortunately, Morrel misinterpreted her jerking away as the onset of orgasm. Smiling smugly, he grabbed her hips and pulled her more firmly onto him.

"Not so fast, girlie," he panted. "I'm not done yet."

And beneath his words rolled the pulse of an alien refrain, *"Not yet, not yet, but soon, soon. Soon!"*

Smokey tilted back her head and screamed and the shrill cry seemed to black out the noise in her head. Morrel took her howl as indicative of pleasure and pumped his fat hips with something like energy. His building orgasm drowned out the alien voice and she struggled desperately to maintain his peak. When he had finished and the alien voice was again whistling through the ebbing of his pleasure, Smokey pulled herself free from her sweaty perch.

This time Morrel didn't protest, but only smiled at her with a dreamy satisfaction that Smokey found weirdly obscene.

"Let me rest a min, Smokey," he muttered. "I've been working so hard."

"I'm sure you have, Ettienne," she said, battling her own resistance and taking his hand. "What do you do?"

"R&D work, engineering mostly," he said. "I was just an engine jockey until a year or so ago, then I started getting the wildest ideas. I've given up most traveling now."

Smokey felt the beginnings of regret color his thoughts before a memory of his postorgasm contentment flowed over the regret like sweet syrup. The alien voice was silent now, but she suspected its presence in the swift changing of Morrel's thought patterns. As if on cue, he pawed at her, but she playfully drew back.

"I've got to clean up, Etti," she said, print-pressing open a washroom, "but maybe we can get together later tonight or over at my place."

"Hardworking girl, aren't you?" he said, pulling himself into his trousers. "Good pay and easy hours."

"Not like you, Etti," she said, brushing against him, "working so hard."

And the alien thought rippled roughly, *"So. Hard? Near impossible but in physical peace success."*

Once she was freshly dressed and perfumed, Smokey roused the drowsy Morrel and sauntered back into the ballroom. They were barely through the arched doorway when Adam Chen grabbed her by the arm. He smelled strongly of liquor and held a frothing aspel beer in his hand.

"My turn, Morrel," he said, shoving the other man.

Morrel looked at him vacantly, not even a spark of anger in his eyes. When Smokey covertly studied him through her lashes, she was shocked to see that his eyes were completely lacking in intelligence. With a grunt, he ambled off toward one of the caterers, his hands moving like pudgy crab claws.

Smokey didn't have time to do more than file his change in personality. Chen was dragging her by her right arm toward the rooms. She did her best to keep her balance—no mean feat when her sandal heels caught on the carpet.

Reaching the first door with a white "vacant" light, Chen used his free hand to try the door. When it didn't open, he drunkenly slammed his shoulder against it.

"The door will open if you put your convention ID through the lock, Adam," Smokey coaxed, prying his fingers from her arm and guiding them to his card.

"Oh, I forgot." He fumbled for the card. "You're so damn cute, Smokey, and I hadda keep myself distracted from thinking about you screwing that fat slob."

She took his card and opened the door, a pity she rarely felt for her clients making her gentle. Something more than Morrel's having had her first had upset Adam—of that she was certain.

She was also certain of something else—he was far too drunk to perform, and given his current state of mind that would be disastrous. When he was busy fumbling with her gown, she drew a sober/stim patch from the bedside unit and inserted it under the skin between his shoulder blades. She covered the sharp bite of its connecting by raking him with her nails. In his current state of mind, he couldn't separate one pain from the other. In any case, he was far too absorbed with attempting to free her breasts from the trick fastening on the bodice.

Amused, she took his hands.

"It's easier than it looks," she said, with a husky laugh. "You're thinking too hard. Now what do you want?"

"To get at your tits," he growled, "but I thought I'd be a gentleman and not ruin your dress."

"Your wish," she said, pulling at the front of the gown, "is ever my command."

The fabric slid free from her shoulders without resistance. She shrugged slightly and the entire garment crumpled into a silver puddle on the floor.

"The bodice clasp is a fake," she said, stepping out of the gown and then lifting it for his inspection. "It does a good job of distracting attention, doesn't it?"

"Damn! I'll say. You're like that, aren't you—smoke and mirrors." He was sober now, but the truth of the vine was with him yet.

"Oh, no," Smokey said, drawing him to the bed. "I'm no illusion, Adam. Come and see."

He followed eagerly, and as she took him into her arms, she plucked the spent sober tab from his skin. Then she opened her legs and her mind to him. Dreading yet expecting the amoral taint of the alien mind beneath his own, Smokey was genuinely surprised to find that Chen's mind was apparently his alone. His desires were his—simple, male, carnal, with a unique angle that was all his own.

He was accustomed to a smaller woman—his wife, she thought—and found Smokey's height exciting. Obligingly, she stretched her toes to tickle the undersides of his feet, enhancing the difference and his pleasure. As clients went, he was considerate, his concern for her enjoyment not merely a desire to satisfy his own ego.

After Morrel, Chen was a relief, and she entered into her role with an enthusiasm that would have startled those who thought that whores, even in this era, despised the acts for which they were paid. She let him control the motion, keeping her responses subtle and all the more provocative for his ignorance of her skill. When he orgasmed, he was half in love with her, associating the relief from tension, clarity of mind, and intense pleasure with some magic that was hers alone.

Releasing her teeth from his shoulder, she licked the hollow of his throat.

"Happy?" she asked softly.

"Mmm-hmm," he said, relaxing a moment on top of her before taking some of his weight onto his arms. "You're great."

"You're not so bad, Adam," Smokey responded. "In fact, I think you've got a lucky wife."

As she had expected, his response was curiosity, not guilt. "How did you know I was married?"

"This told me." Smokey caressed the traveler's tattoo on his breastbone. "The codes are pretty uniform, but marital status is optional—so I guessed that not only were you married, but that your wife was lucky that you wanted to admit to her existence."

"And here I thought that you were praising my virility." After she giggled appreciatively, he continued, "I forget about that tattoo most of the time, just sometimes when I'm shaving I see it, staring back, and I feel like a piece of meat."

"Nice meat," she said, rubbing her hand along his thigh. "So if you've been shipping so long, why haven't you gotten an invisible mark?"

"Well," he said, distractedly playing with her hair, "I guess I like the idea of an implant even less than getting tattooed. Besides, anyone can read a tattoo—you need a scanner for the implants."

And delving beneath his words, Smokey caught, *"Thought I'd be done with shipping by this point in my career. Would have been, too, but Morrel suddenly becomes a genius, that Lee appears out of nowhere giving orders, and Bayalun starts refusing to speak with me."*

Smokey snuggled him before his thoughts became incoherent emotion. Sitting up so that he could not fail to admire the movement of her breasts, she straddled him and then bent forward to cup the sides of his face in her hands. Faint beard stubble caught under her nails.

"Somehow," she said, "I guessed that a man who still shaved wouldn't like implants."

Most of his attention was centering on the erection building beneath the caress of her buttocks, but she caught a momentary flash of pure, animal terror at the thought of implants. His reaction to the fear was also purely animal and for several minutes she was fully occupied.

As he was panting down from his climax, she glanced at the clock.

"Our time's about up," she said, reluctantly detaching herself. "Feeling strong enough to move?"

He grinned at her. "Smokey, you are something. I'm still as horny as a teenager, but at the same time I feel better than I have in ages."

She playfully slapped his flank, knowing that at least part of his reaction was due to the stimulant in the sober patch she'd given him, but happy to take the credit. In a way, it was deserved. She rarely drugged her clients, but when she did her choice was of the finest quality.

The silver gown in place once more, she thumbed open the door. Chen was babbling cheerful nonsense and promising to look her up again, but as they walked toward the ballroom she could hardly find the wit to reply. Each step that brought her closer to Lee intensified the revulsion building in her. Frantically, she considered making some excuse and leaving with what she had learned, but this would raise suspicions she couldn't afford—not if she planned on working for Gary again in the future.

Resolutely she shook out the silver-grey mane and snagged a drink from the first tray she passed. Lee, as she had expected, was waiting for her. His blue eyes in his handsome face were narrow and feral as he approached.

"Smokey," he said, his teeth white and even in a smile that was anything but friendly, "I'm ready."

She thought about insisting on a break—Guild rules permitted her one—but this would be delaying the inevitable. Instead she took his arm, careful to touch his sleeve rather than his skin.

She smiled a smile as artificial as Lee's own and let him take her from the ballroom. Once in a room, he wasted no time on preliminaries, but immediately began to remove his clothing. Pushing the silver gown once more from her shoulders, Smokey reflected that even the gluttonous Morrel had been more attentive.

Lee turned to her, nude and erect, and gestured toward the bed. "No playing around, Smokey. I saw how you shuttled Morrel and Chen in and out with their half hour and no more. I plan on getting all I can."

Shocked despite herself, Smokey obediently spread her legs and concentrated on guarding her mind from the alien that hid beneath Lee's lust. With her mind closed to him and her body tense with fear and indignation, their coupling was hardly the art for which she was renowned.

Grunting slightly, Lee rolled from her as he finished. Signaling the bedside service unit for water, he studied her as he sipped.

"That was lousy, Smokey," he said bluntly.

"What does it matter to you?" she snapped, her only real emotion relief that she had kept the mind at bay. "You aren't paying for it."

"No, but someone is, and you should give what you're paid for."

"I am—you got your fuck."

"Yeah, but not a Smokey fuck—not like you gave Morrel or even that fool Chen."

"They," she said, sitting up and cloaking herself with her loose hair, "didn't treat me like a dollar streetwalker. You did, and you got what you deserved."

"Oh, I got to treat the paid cunt like a princess," he sneered. "That's rich, Smokey. A whore is a whore."

"No, Lee." She stood and reached for her panties. "A whore is not a whore, as you well know. Go fuck a donut if all you want is to get off. If you want what I have, you treat me like I should be treated. Otherwise, don't bitch."

"Come back here," he growled, "my half hour is barely started and I should demand satisfaction for the time you've wasted insulting me."

"Wasted?" She stepped into her dress. "You're spent, man, you couldn't get it up again if you tried."

He looked down at his limp penis. "It'll be back—meanwhile, you do provide other services."

"No, I've done all I'm going to for you."

She realized that panic was fueling her reaction, but she knew she couldn't risk another contact with the alien mind. Lee's cruel egoism bespoke its presence as clearly as if she had contacted it telepathically. Lee had not been this abrupt, this impersonal their first time. Now he seemed like pure libido without the guiding male.

"Smokey," he warned. "Don't."

"Sorry, Lee," she said, moving to thumb the door. "Maybe when you're human again."

She had scant moments to regret her choice of words, but Lee didn't seem to notice them. Instead he roared and leapt over the bed at her. Horrified, she saw that somehow he had an erection and his intent was clear.

His leap blocked the door and she was forced back into the room. One long arm ripped Mr'rel's creation from her shoulder. She let him pull her inside his reach before finishing the gown's demise with a kick to his side that tore the fabric and planted her foot firmly between his legs.

He howled, and for a terrible moment she thought that he hadn't felt it. She lashed out with a right-armed blow into the underside of his jaw that snapped his head back. As he released his hold on her, she took his feet out from under him and planted a foot to hold him.

Beneath his sobs of pain, she felt confusion and then the expected horror of the alien whisper.

"Pain. Pain," it muttered. *"Clouds. But too well. Soon no need. Soon."*

She drew her foot away, preferring to fight rather than feel more of the insane monologue, but Lee had lost any urge for either sex or battle.

"Smokey," he said, moving his jaw as if fearing it was broken. "I'm sorry. I don't know what got into me."

She stared, wondering if he was truly ignorant. Then she touched the comm tab on the bedside table.

"Maybe someone slipped you something," she evaded.

When convention control answered, she reported the event and put herself on break. Lee slowly picked himself up, surveying the wreck of her gown and his own bruises with shock.

"You don't hate me, do you, Smokey?" he said, his voice small.

"No," she said thoughtfully, honestly, "not you."

8

HER HEAD THE NEXT MORNING FELT LIKE THE end of a three-day champagne binge. After she had pawed a stimpatch from her bed unit and slapped it on her wrist, she rolled from her bed and thumped to the floor. Daylight was streaming around her drawn window shades, and from the outer rooms she could hear Bonny talking to someone.

Hauling on her house robe, she wandered to the kitchen, her head clearing with every step. There was tea waiting in the warmer and she gratefully poured a cup before seeking Bonny.

The girl was hooked unseeing into her VR rig, scribbling equations onto a pressure slate. Wintering lay in a heap on her feet. Leaving her to her class, Smokey went into her office and turned on the privacy field. Gary answered her call with such alacrity that she suspected he had been waiting.

"Smokey, how did things go last night?"

She managed an impish smile, although the sides of her mouth still hurt. "I saw all three of the Wickerwork men."

"Three?"

"Listen, I'll explain, but I don't have any clear answers. I do have some good lines of inquiry for you."

He deflated for a moment. "I suppose that it was too much to hope that you would have any easy solution. I'm ready to take notes."

"First, research an engineer named Ettienne Morrel—he's new to R&D and one of the ones whose picture you supplied."

"Yes, we've looked into him. He's one of their new 'bright boys.'"

"He's not a young man," Smokey said, "certainly not a new kid with the company. I'd like to see if you can find anything about him. I'll even go through the data myself."

"Very well. I'm going to trust your intuition. What else?"

"Check out a fellow named Lee Burshcreek. He was with the Wickerwork people and from what Adam Chen said he's one of the new people on the staff and he's rising fast."

"Lee Burshcreek? I didn't even have him on my listing. He must be off the books completely. I wonder who he's with?"

"Try checking through Jules Boswell," she said.

Gary's brows shot up, but he made a note.

"Anything else, Smokey?"

"Adam Chen is the one on the outside of the Wickerwork team these days."

"Chen?" Gary's eyebrows tried to climb farther and failed. "He was listed on the private and public reports as a major development asset. In fact, if anything the private report was more glowing than the public. He's clean, noble, brilliant, sober . . ."

"Not when I saw him," Smokey said bluntly. "Lee and Morrel have crowded him out."

"There were a couple of female representatives," Gary began.

Smokey smiled, "I wasn't free to see them—and you didn't ask me to. Of course, for a bonus . . ."

Gary laughed, "Maybe. Anything else?"

Smokey hesitated. "No, nothing solid."

When Gary had signed off, Smokey sat reflecting, wondering why she hadn't confided her experiences to Gary, knowing instantly why she had not.

How could she? What she had learned would sound like insanity to anyone who heard it unless she explained how she had learned. And that way of knowing was quite illegal on all the commerce worlds and quite frowned upon on the others.

No, definitely not. Perhaps the discrepancies she had found would be enough to have these men—and their extra minds—locked away. She wished that she believed it.

Bonny linked off the VR as Smokey was refilling her teacup.

"Mama!" She threw her arms around her. "How was the party? Did you bring me anything?"

"Lots of work and lousy tippers," Smokey said, returning the hug, "and there is a box of powder sweets on the front hall table for you."

"Great!" The girl skidded out and rattled off the paper with enthusiasm. There was a solid thump as Wintering came to demand his cut.

Smokey went about routine tasks, her thoughts constantly returning to the night before. Realizing that she was putting herself into a funk, she took Bonny swimming and to lunch before dropping her at her afternoon school. Then she went to the Victorian Mansion.

Relieved not to find Kyu on the porch, Smokey planned on dodging the Gentlemen's Parlor as well, but something about the slow, almost dirgelike notes that shifted out the arched doorway stopped her.

Clarence didn't even look up as she walked in, but continued playing. His pearl grey derby was pushed back on his head and as she stepped closer she caught the sharp, medicinal smell of local whiskey.

"You're drunk!" she said in soft surprise.

He raised his head, pausing in mid-motion as if considering whether the result was worth the effort. His eyes were the color of a fresh bloodstain, the dark brown irises dried blood in the heart of the wound. Wetting his lips with a sip from the water glass of liquor, he studied her.

"Yes," he said, his fingers continuing the dirge as if they were independent creatures. "I am. So's Kyu, and Ami's dead."

Smokey grabbed the piano for support, staring at the sociologist who was looking through her at some horror.

"Dead?" she managed. "Ami? How?"

"Murdered," Clarence replied, focusing on her as if seeing her for the first time, "by some trick. He . . . filleted her. And she must have been alive for most of it to have bled that way."

He emptied his glass and suddenly became clinical. "I'm not a coroner, but I do know that if he had cut her heart out first, not last, she couldn't have bled so much while he was skinning her."

Turning, he calmly vomited into a polished spittoon in the corner behind the piano.

"That's better," he said to no one in particular.

Then he looked at Smokey again. "He asked for you first."

"Me?" her voice squeaked.

"You." His fingers started feeling out the dirge again. "'Course, as you were at such pains to make sure I knew, you're a pretty popular whore. Could just have been your reputation as the best piece of ass on the planet that brought him here. After all, he took Ami fast enough."

Smokey tried letting go of the piano and found that her hands would not loosen. Clarence looked at her, almost with compassion.

"I'd offer you a drink, but it's all gone. I've been drinking since I found her. Kyu sent me up when Ami didn't come down for a parlor call an hour or so after her client had left."

He began to weep, the tears taking color from his eyes, so that Smokey expected blood, not water, to splash onto the piano's ivory keys.

"I liked her, you know," he said. "I love you, Smokey, but I liked her. She'd come and listen to the piano or play something for me. She'd never been to Old Terra, and she liked to hear me tell her about it."

He brought his fist down with a jangling crash.

"I liked her and some deviant could do this and calmly pay his bill and leave and the police are treating her murder like it's an embarrassment 'cause the government wants it kept quiet and she's dead and tortured dead."

Smokey found she could release the piano and hurried to hold Clarence while he sobbed. Involuntarily, she touched his mind and shuddered at what she saw there. Ami dead, not merely skinned, but her flesh peeled from her ribs, legs, arms, revealing the white bone. Her heart neatly placed on the pillow beside her head. The face had been left unmarked, perhaps to better preserve the look of perfect horror and sanity-shattering pain engraved into the china doll features.

Clamping her hands down on Clarence's shoulders, Smokey wept with him. Then her tears dried in shock as the image in his mind changed and her body was the one that lay there in tortured pieces, her face wore the twisted contortions of pain. She absorbed this vision in voyeuristic revulsion, her only relief Clarence's own self-tormenting guilt that better Ami die this way than his Smokey.

Overwhelmed, her tears flowed again. The sound of footsteps and voices forced her to herself.

Detaching herself from Clarence, she scrubbed her eyes dry and tried to compose herself.

"We aren't open, are we?" she asked.

Clarence frowned at her. "I'm not sure. Slip out the side door, honey, and get Madame Kyu. She'll handle them, whatever they want."

Smokey obeyed, hearing the piano play a few bars behind her and then the sound of Clarence speaking to someone. His words were muffled as she pulled the heavy door behind her.

Kyu was sitting in the little kitchen in the back of the house. As Clarence had said, she was drunk. Eli was rubbing her shoulders and cooing at her.

"Smokey!" Kyu said. "You're alive!"

"Yes, I am." Smokey felt all elbows and thumbs, a thing she hadn't since she was fifteen and watching Joy in Motion perform to adoring hordes.

"Kyu, there are some people who have just arrived. Clarence is talking with them."

"We are closed," Kyu said in a drunken parody of her usual manner. "Tell Clarence that we have said so and that our command has been posted on the E-boards and a black wreath has been ordered from the decorators."

Again, Smokey obeyed, though this time she paused to wash her tear-streaked face. When she entered the reception parlor, Clarence had moved away from behind the piano and was in conversation with a man and a woman. The presence of the woman made her almost certain that they were not clients. Still, Kyu's message should be passed on nonetheless.

"Madame Kyu says that we are closed," she said, as they turned to look at her.

"These aren't clients, Smokey," Clarence said. "They're from the law, and they want to speak with you."

"Me?" Smokey felt immediately defensive. "Why? I wasn't even here. I worked late last night and was at home this morning except when I took Bonny to lunch. I don't know anything."

"Easy, Smokey." Clarence crossed to her and surprised her by taking her in his arms. He was completely sober now, though he still reeked of whiskey and vomit. "They're talking to everyone in the Mansion, not just you."

Smokey tried to relax, but something of the tension remained, despite the comfort Clarence was emanating. Spacer brat, entertainer's child, runaway, and later covert psionic and industrial spy, Smokey had no love for the law, but she fought her reaction back and found a shy smile somewhere in her kit.

"I'm sorry," she said, turning within the shelter of Clarence's arms. "This whole thing is still such a shock. I didn't mean to react poorly."

"Madame Kyu let us use one of the smaller parlors for interviews earlier," the woman said. "I think we should adjourn there and continue this more privately."

"Go on, Smokey," Clarence said, releasing her. "I'll send Eli in with some tea for you."

Smokey squeezed his hand as she stepped forward. The male officer smiled at her, which seemed to annoy his female partner. Smokey hid a smile of her own and let herself be directed into the Purple Room.

In this parlor, Kyu had indulged her royal fantasies to the hilt. A handwoven carpet in predominantly purple arabesques sank under her feet. High-backed chairs with flaring, thronclike arms were upholstered in plum velvet embroidered in gold. More gold embossed, carved mirrors over the black marble hearth.

Normally, Smokey found the room overdone, but today she welcomed it as might a wild creature returned to its natural environment. The police paled in the setting, but even in street clothes she blossomed. Almost as reflex, she loosened her hair from the tight chignon she had twisted it into before leaving home. The smoky coils furled out around her shoulders and she tossed her head just enough to encourage them to life.

The frown on the female officer's face deepened, but the male's expression brightened approvingly, an approval echoed by Clarence when he came in with a tray bearing a tea service and a plate of flaky-crusted tarts.

"Eli was busy," he explained, and when Smokey brushed against him to help pour the tea she caught the image of the maid and the madam in a half-dressed embrace. "I'll leave you now."

As he exited, Smokey smiled professionally. "Tea?"

The man nodded, but the woman snapped, "Enough delays! We only want ten minutes of your time."

Smokey couldn't resist a gibe. "That normally costs several hundred credits, but I'll be generous. I firmly believe in cooperating with the law."

She smiled at the man again, pleased to feel her childish panic receding behind familiar rituals.

"How may I help you?"

The woman scowled and the man smothered a laugh in his tea. Smokey took advantage of the pause to examine them. Both wore the trousered khaki-and-russet uniform of the Arizona police, cyber-rims, and carried datapads. Petite with Oriental eyes and sun-bleached hair cut short, the female officer would be cute if she lost her sour expression. The male was tall and broad with a hint of a paunch; his skin, hair, and eyes were all dark.

"Please, Officer Wallon," Smokey said, taking the name from the woman's collar tabs, "ask your questions. I'm still in shock. In fact, I'm still not completely certain what has happened. All I know is that Ami was killed, apparently by a client, and that her murder was brutal."

Her hand shook as she recalled the image she had lifted from Clarence's mind. Wallon heard the cup rattle against the saucer as Smokey set both down, and her expression softened.

"Those are the basics," she said, "and we'll happily brief you further after the interview. For now, we would like to avoid knowledge pollution."

Smokey nodded and the male, Officer Laurie, continued, "We must insist that anything you know not go further than this interview. We especially do not want the Press involved. Your—housemate—was killed by a psychopath and we don't want him dodging us by tracking our progress through the media."

"I understand," Smokey said. "You are certain that the killer was a male?"

"Fairly so," Wallon replied. "Your house does not usually cater to homosexuals, and the last client anyone recalls seeing Ami with was a male. Unfortunately, he wore a domino and was average enough in build and height that we didn't get much of a description from those who were at the Victorian Mansion earlier. He paid in disposable credit slips, so we won't be able to trace him through payment receipts."

What followed was a fairly routine list of questions about Smokey's whereabouts that morning, about Ami, and about the Victorian Mansion's routines and procedures. Only when Smokey refused to present a list of her steady clients did the interview become prickly.

"The man asked for you first," Wallon said in exasperation. "He may come back. Don't you care?"

"I care. I care a scorching lot," Smokey said, "but he clearly wasn't one of my regulars. They make appointments in advance and I had none this morning."

"You don't take walk-ins?" Laurie's expression was not quite a leer, and Wallon looked as if she was going to kick him.

"Not for my regulars," Smokey explained patiently. "I cater to them and I never want them to feel they are lining up for a bit of pussy. I'm not a streetwalker."

"We may get a court order if circumstances seem to show that we will need those names," Wallon threatened.

"Do." Smokey smiled. "I believe in cooperating with the law."

The interview was clearly over and after a bit more verbal fencing, the two officers left. Clarence came from the front parlor as Smokey was returning her hair to its street coil. His piano player's costume had been replaced by more normal slacks and shirt of Old Terran styling.

"Guess you'll be heading home," he said almost wistfully. "Won't be doing work here."

"Let me buy you an early dinner," she offered impulsively. "I'm not expected anywhere for a few hours."

His smile was as brilliant as it was fleeting.

"I'd like that," he said, offering her his arm. "I don't want to go home yet."

"Where are you living?" she asked as they walked to the pedslide.

"I rent a couple of rooms on the Port edge," he said. "Not very native, but I don't know the customs here and a portside hotel is a hotel, no matter the planet. Madame Kyu gives me my meals at the Mansion—part of the pay—and if I don't feel like eating there, the District is great for food."

"You're certainly getting a distorted view of Arizona."

"Maybe, but it's the part that I've come to study, so that's enough."

"Maybe," was her only reply.

They went to a different restaurant this time, but again Clarence let Smokey order. Only when they were picking through the sampler did he comment.

"Arizona food uses lots of dehydrated materials, doesn't it?" He picked up a wedge of dried fruit and bit into it, evident enjoyment eliminating any hint of criticism.

"It does and it should," Smokey replied. "Even though terraforming has been going on for a long time by human standards, the dominant feature of this planet is still lots of dry heat. If we could raise more food here, we'd have a great export business in preserved food. As it is, the more we alter the climate to our needs, the more we alter the dryness."

"Certainly a little moisture in the air won't have that much effect!"

"No, not overall, but older settlers claim they can see the changes in little things like the time needed to dry a load of laundry or sun-dry a meal." She shrugged. "I like being able to take Bonny swimming or to go for a bike ride in one of the ravines without wearing a filter to keep the moisture from being sucked from my throat. Still, some say that humans should have learned from what happened on Old Terra."

"Old Terra's not that bad," Clarence protested. "Culturally, it's amazingly rich, and there is still a variety of climates and cultures that the colony worlds lack."

Their main course came and conversation shifted to how to best prepare the selection of foods. After they had settled back with cups of tea and a choice of sweets, Smokey returned to her earlier topic.

"I've seen Old Terra," she said, "though I haven't visited for more years than someone in my profession should admit. I spent most of my childhood on spaceliners, and whenever we came to a planet I got the educational tour. Monuments, scenic spots, rare and wonderful creatures—the whole blitz."

Clarence shook his head in amusement. "And with all the planets to settle on you chose Arizona?"

"Yeah." She smiled reminiscently. "I wanted a place that hadn't been finished up yet, where I could make a mark—even if just as the best whore. Arizona is also on the wave front of technology. We may suffer from the climate, but we don't miss anything in human advancement. Sands! Lots of the newest developments come from here—especially from the labs at Ki'rin Ravine."

"Easy, Smokey." Clarence chuckled. "I wasn't saying y'all were parochial, just wondering why you chose Arizona. Now I know—I think I've been shorting the place. I'm going to have to take the tours and spend less time in my room."

"Want a guide?"

He looked at her, his dark face serious. "I thought that you didn't associate with tricks."

She ran her card through the pay-all on the edge of the table and slipped it back into her wallet before replying. "You're not, Clarence. I'd like to try you as a friend."

"I haven't changed in how I feel about you, Smokey."

"I know"—she broke the seriousness with a sudden grin—"but you may change your mind when you get to know me."

"I won't," he promised, "but you can have the chance."

They stopped in a shop so that Smokey could replace the dress she had worn into the District with light slacks, a blouse, and a straw hat. She insisted that Clarence wear a hat as well and bought him a wide-brimmed one that matched hers except that the band was purple rather than green.

He offered her his arm, and she guided him down the Port City ravine, explaining the quirks of her adopted world as they descended toward the bright blue stream that cut through the ravine's base.

"Ten years ago," she said as they watched the water run over polished rocks and fall in artistic rills, "this was covered by a clear cap and the only open water was in the geodesic you see down there."

"The flashy topaz thing?"

"That's it," she agreed. "Then a scientist—I guess you could call him an ecological physicist—named Ross Styler came up with a way to create quantities of water from recombined atoms or something like that. I never did quite understand it. The result is Styler's Sea—used to be called Styler's Puddle and some people say that it will become the planet's first ocean. There's even talk of building another installation and starting another puddle. Anyhow, with the increased capacity to create water, the little rivers were opened up. The moisture content of the atmosphere is slowly growing, and we even get mists down in the ravines."

"Impressive." Clarence knelt and cupped the water in his broad, brown palms. "I would like to see Styler's Sea. It must be like a miracle in all this desert dryness."

"I think it is," Smokey said. "Maybe we can make a hadj of it. I've meant to take Bonny now that she's old enough to appreciate it."

"A hadj?" Clarence asked.

"Yes, the word comes from some Old Terran religious practice. It means a holy pilgrimage. Ross said that for Arizonans to really appreciate the Sea and what it meant, they should travel there overland and see the slow changes to the desert as the water has its influence. He thought it would teach people what they were doing with a terraformed planet—lead to respect or something."

"Didn't Styler die before the Sea developed?" Clarence asked. "I seem to recall that from one of the 'About the Planet' tapes I reviewed on the *Roma*. It referred to the Sea as his memorial."

The sharp sense of loss returned, but Smokey managed to talk despite it.

"Ross was a visionary," she said. "He knew that his nixies would work and what the effects would be. The hadj was his dream for a future that he didn't live to see. He wrote about it, though, and even discussed it on interviews that have survived him. As the Sea has grown, so has the custom. Most Arizonans try and make the hadj at least once in their lives. Those who have been here longer try to go every few years so that they can see the changes."

"And you want to take your daughter," Clarence said.

"Yes." Smokey sighed. "She's getting old enough to consider other worlds. I want her to have this one down before she considers moving on, even if that move won't come for years. Moving is easier if there is something called home to return to."

Clarence nodded. "I get homesick for New Orleans, time to time, and I like to think that it's missing me just the same. I know it doesn't, but I pretend."

Smokey looked at him as he played with the water and held back another sigh, this one for herself.

"I need to pick Bonny up from school in a little," she said. "Would you like to meet her?"

Clarence studied her, wiping his already-dry hands on his trousers as he got to his feet.

"I'd like that, Smokey. I'd like that very much."

They took the pedslide to a mid-heights building that burrowed back into the sandstone of the ravine. The double glass doors were tinted emerald and hung with hundreds of tiny brass bells that chimed merrily as they entered. A woman sat on one of the divans in the cool, tiled foyer working on a datapad. She smiled as they entered.

"The children are finishing with dance," she said, glancing up from her work. "They'll be free in a moment."

"Can we go in and watch?" Smokey queried.

"I think so." The woman smiled ruefully. "I'd go in but I need to finish my report before my kids get out."

Leaving the other parent behind, Smokey led Clarence through a smaller door, this one with rose-colored glass. The sound of drum and flute came faintly through, growing more distinct but never loud as they walked in and took seats on the ubiquitous bleachers lining the walls. A few other adults also waited, their attention focused on the group of about twenty boys and girls gathered at the room's center.

The children ranged in age from about seven to twelve standards and most bore the ruddy tan and sun-bleached hair of Arizona natives. Their only clothing was a long, white tunic that hung loose from shoulders to mid-calf and a bright scarf twisted from their foreheads and then knotted to cascade down the back. The colors varied, no two the same, and so a rainbow danced to the delicate strains of flute and the bouncing taps of the small drums each child carried tucked under one arm.

"That's Bonny," Smokey whispered, "the tallish girl in the back—the one with the pink scarf."

Bonny hopped from foot to foot, her face furrowed with a concentration she rarely bothered with for her mathematics, her lips counting her steps under her breath.

"She's very pretty," Clarence said, "but then she would be, with you for a mother."

Smokey grinned. "She's brilliant, too, apparently something of a mathematics and physics prodigy, I've just learned. She'd stay hooked into the VR all day if she didn't need to eat. I don't want her to get an unbalanced view of life, so she has a variety of classes that take her out of the academic realm and make her learn about people."

"You don't bring her to the Victorian Mansion?"

"Not often, especially now that she's getting tall. I want her to develop naturally, at her own pace. I've never seen a case where a sexually precocious child grew up into a happy adult."

"Don't tell me that you believe that age and maturity are the same thing!" Clarence commented with evident surprise.

"Not at all," Smokey replied. "By precocious I mean those kids who start screwing because they're trying to make someone else happy or to prove how mature they are. I guess I don't want Bonny to miss out on puppy love and crushes and all the rest simply because she's learned to be blasé about the mechanics."

The dance circle was dispersing now. Bonny walked

slowly along, giggling with another girl. When she saw Smokey, her face lit up and she came trotting over with a smile for her mother and a curious stare for Clarence.

"Hi!" she said, hugging Smokey to cover a sudden shyness.

Smokey squeezed her briefly, then pushed her back. "Bonny, this is my friend, Clarence. Clarence, my daughter, Bonny."

Clarence extended his hand and Bonny shook it, obviously pleased by this grown-up courtesy.

"I need to wash and change," she said, then, with another quick glance at Clarence, scampered away.

"She likes you," Smokey said. "Good."

"Good?" Clarence replied.

"Yes." Smokey sighed again. "Good."

9

CLARENCE DIDN'T COME BACK TO THE HOUSE that day, saying he had an evening commitment. When chastely kissing him good-bye, Smokey caught enough of his thoughts to confirm that he was pleased by her new friendliness and had resolved not to crowd her into second thoughts.

At home, there was a message from Gary asking her to call, another from Joy in Motion, and a third from Kyu, noting that the Mansion would be closed for about five days while legal matters were resolved and proper mourning was observed.

Smokey discovered that she was relieved at the excuse for a break from clients. Her contact with the force within the Wickerwork men's minds had frightened her enough that, for the first time since puberty, celibacy seemed like an attractive option. Joy and Bethlehem's visit also made the option of a hadj doubly enticing. She coded the number that Joy had left.

"Joy," she said as her mother's face took shape. "Smokey."

"So I see, dolly. We're coming to a break in our shows here and wanted to know your schedule. We would like to come downside and at least kidnap Bonny if you're not free."

Smokey nodded. "I think I can free up—at least for a few days—and I'd like to invite you and Bethlehem to join me and Bonny and possibly another friend on a hadj."

Joy made no effort to conceal her surprise—nor her pleasure. "I'll talk with Bethlehem and work out our timetable. We'll be in touch soon."

"A hadj, Mama?" Bonny asked, wandering up next to her. "Us?"

"And your grandparents and possibly Clarence, if you don't mind."

"That's great!" She paused, serious. "Clarence is one of the good ones, isn't he, Mama?"

"I'm afraid so, Boniface. Let's not tell him, capi? I'd rather give him a chance to get to know us and decide if he really wants to be friends when all the sparkle and shine are off."

Bonny pursed her lips solemnly and nodded. They'd discussed the difference between really loving someone and just thinking that you did enough times that she considered a trial period normal rather than extraordinary.

Before the tone could become too serious, Smokey hugged her. "We'll need to make plans for our hadj, Bonny. I think a tracked crawler would suit us best."

"One with a clear top? And sleeping cubbies?"

"Not clear," Smokey said. "We'll need sun protection. The desert is hot and brighter than the ravines. Sleeping cubbies would be good. I'd like to take at least two days, maybe three. We can take a shuttle back if we need to."

She was clearing her desk to make notes when she saw Gary's message.

"I need to make a business call, Bonny," she said. "Run off to your school station and research hadj routes for me. We want a good one that we can pick up two or three days easy travel from the Sea."

Bonny bounced off and Smokey coded Gary.

"You called earlier," she said.

"Yes, I know you don't like me to call you at home, but I tried Madame Kyu's and got a recording that the Victorian Mansion is closed for the next several days."

Smokey lined up the stray items on her desk, struggling against an urge to start crying. She was proud that when she spoke her voice showed nothing of her inner struggle.

"Ami was murdered by a client—possibly a random psychopath, but we can't be certain."

"A Jack the Ripper?" Gary's voice flatted in disbelief.

"That's the answer that the law is leaning toward," Smokey said, "though I haven't heard any of the official reports."

"I'll check," Gary promised. "Gratis—call it a return for that last lay. Besides, I don't like to think that whoever killed Ami could be stalking you next."

"Thanks." Smokey felt a tightness ease from her facial muscles. "I appreciate that. Now, what did you need?"

Gary's face acquired a lime tinge as he activated his desktop note file. "I followed up on the leads you got for me, and while the Wickerwork mystery is still unsolved, I did find some interesting things. I thought you'd like to be up-to-date if you have a return engagement with one of those guys."

Something quivered in Smokey at the thought of another fuck with Lee or Morrel, but she stilled the response and listened.

"First of all, of the three, Morrel was the only Wickerwork employee on the *Hollyhock* when they found whatever they found. Chen was at a research center on Icedrake, his home base when the company doesn't have him off conferring. Lee wasn't even employed by Wickerwork, but—get this, Smokey—he was on the *Hollyhock* as a passenger and had the cabin next to Morrel."

"What was Lee doing on the *Hollyhock*?"

"He was a commercial traveler for a textiles concern. Actually, he still is, but he's on Wickerwork's payroll, too."

"May I guess?" Smokey stared at her tidy platoon of desk debris with a certain weariness. "He was hired soon after the *Hollyhock* docked—probably at Morrel's recommendation."

Gary nodded. "Morrel himself is nearly as much of a puzzle. Despite his technical background, he was definitely on the support track. His reviews showed him as reliable, but not inspired. Lately, however, he's become one of their hottest debuggers. He apparently has discovered a gift for catching those little lapses that R&D people miss because they're too caught up in the beauty of their own ideas."

He chuckled as if at a memory. "Morrel's apparently no slouch at innovation either. Something my source said put me onto another change. It seems trivial, but I can't be certain. You remember how Morrel looks—fat and sloppy?"

Smokey shivered theatrically. "Vividly."

"Here's a picture taken about a month before he joined the *Hollyhock*."

The holo that filled half her screen was of a man recognizable as Morrel—barely. The man in the picture was solidly built, maybe even a touch overweight, but the obese rolls of flesh that characterized the man Smokey had met were absent. The picture had been taken at a social occasion of some sort and although a tray of pastries and chips rested on the center of the table that Morrel shared with a man and two women, it was nearly full. Smokey noted that Morrel's side of the tray showed only evidence of minor sampling.

"Are you certain that you have the right man and not a relative with the same name?"

"Positive," Gary replied, canceling the holo. "The sandy-haired woman on his right had been seeing him for some time. They broke off soon after the *Hollyhock* returned. She later had a nervous breakdown and was hospitalized. I believe she's been released, though still on a course of neurotransmitters. Morrel was transferred soon after. Complaints filed about his increasing obsession with food have been dismissed as coping with personal stress."

"See who gave the orders to transfer him and to overlook his other problems," Smokey suggested. "Find if there's a connection to the *Hollyhock*."

Gary made a note. "Lee was harder to get information on; he was just an obscure textiles traveler, something of a free agent. We have learned that he had an aptitude for mathematics which he channeled into business ventures with varying degrees of success. Personal detail is harder to find."

"I mentioned that I'd met Lee before. Did you check with Jules Boswell?"

Gary shook his head.

"Jules is nearly as paranoid as you, Gary. He may have something, and he can be bought."

"Since he's your client, do you want to check?" Gary asked.

"No, see what you can do. I may be out of Port City for a few days. With the Victorian Mansion closed this is a good time for me to take Bonny on a trip."

"Going back to the Wheel?"

Smokey laughed. "Nosy! Maybe. Probably Joy and Bethlehem are coming down. We may take Bonny on a hadj."

"Nice idea. Check with me before you leave. I may have something on Ami's death."

"I will."

After signing off, Smokey sat chewing the end of one silvery curl and studying the ruin on her desk as if she could read the future in the scattered junk. No portents shaped themselves, and she shoved herself away, promising silently to tidy up after she had checked out what Bonny had discovered.

By the time they set out on the hadj, Gary had nothing new, but he promised Smokey he would leave a message when he did. After meeting Clarence, Joy in Motion, and Bethlehem, they took a Nonorail to Graydon's Gorge. Stepping from the humming train, hung with the gear that they couldn't leave behind, they were obvious pilgrims. A guide swept smoothly up to them almost before they were fully unloaded.

She was a pretty, freckled girl in her early teens. Her snub nose gave her a saucy look that her blond ponytail only accented. Jumping down from her air scooter, she grinned at their motley group.

"I'm Carmelita," she said. "Welcome to Graydon's Gorge! Can I direct you to an inn or would you prefer to go directly to one of the caravan directors? I can recommend the best."

Bonny, temporarily overwhelmed by Carmelita's brash introduction, interrupted when Smokey started to reply.

"It's early," she said, "and we know what we're doing. So you can just go."

Carmelita cocked an eyebrow. "So, you have it all planned, do you? Tell me where you're going."

Bonny bristled further at the challenge. "I'm not dumb. You can't trick me. If I tell you, you'll either say you knew it all along or try and claim that somewhere else is better. You tell me what you recommend."

"What's to keep you from tricking me?" Carmelita said, resting a foot on her scooter with the amused air of a mastiff challenged by a chihuahua.

"My mama knows our plans," Bonny snapped back, "and I have them written down in my hand memory."

"Well, I'd say Eze has the best caravan service," Carmelita said tartly, "and he gives a ten percent discount to pilgrims that I bring in."

"On top of Entertainer's Guild discounts?" Bonny said. "We don't want to lose those."

"On top," Carmelita assured her. "Are you with me?"

"Sure," Bonny said, tucking away her notes. "We'll go."

When Carmelita was summoning a tabi for their luggage, she grinned. "That was where we were going anyway, weren't we, Mama?"

"You have the soul of a camel trader, Bonita," Smokey said. "Don't forget to tip her. She might make a good native guide."

"Guide?" Clarence said. "Why do we need a guide? Surely Arizona has a satellite network we can use to navigate the crawler by."

"Of course," Smokey replied, mildly piqued. "We may still be terraforming, but we're not primitive."

"Then why do we need a guide?" Joy asked from the shady spot where she had been fanning herself.

"A guide could handle some of the driving and indicate points of interest," Smokey said. "You don't want to miss anything."

"I'm certain that we'll see enough with you to guide us," Bethlehem said, coming forward and placing his hand on her arm. "Joy and I have driven just about every vehicle you can imagine—we'll be fine."

His hand on her arm flowed images of the five of them slowly crossing a swelling dune, pausing to inspect a rock formation or an insect at the heart of a cactus flower. The crawler waited in the background, solitary and somehow majestic. An enormous sense of peace emanated from the scene, broken when Carmelita came swinging around the crawler with a bright, professional smile.

"I surrender!" Smokey said. "You'll just have to put up with me for a guide. I have made the hadj a few times, so I should be able to remember some of the important things."

Carmelita directed them to Eze's Caravans and then retreated, counting her generous tip. Negotiations for a crawler went smoothly, aided not only by Bonny's research but by Eze's delight when he learned that one of his customers was Joy in Motion. He set them up with his best vehicle and then stood waving good-bye to them from the doorway of his establishment, his hand still caressing the spot on his cheek where Joy had kissed him.

Bethlehem drove for the first few hours, through lands that rapidly became dryer and more barren the moment they crept off the rim of Graydon's Gorge. Later, when Bonny had become bored with the apparently changeless panorama of sand and rock and sparse plants, he started teaching her how to work the controls. The nine-year-old couldn't reach the floor panel, but rapidly became competent at the upper control board.

Bethlehem's coaching was gentle, never less than

patient. What fascinated Smokey was not his temperament, but how several times he anticipated Bonny's errors and corrected her before any serious accident could occur.

The route they had chosen would take two days if they hurried, three if they were more leisurely. At first they pushed the crawler until even the night glow of the Gorge had faded. When it seemed as if they were the only people left below the star-flecked firmament, by common consent they stopped the crawler and got out to stretch.

"Night out here is so different," Bonny exclaimed. "There doesn't seem to be anything between us and the stars."

"There isn't much," Clarence said, valiantly trying to conceal his struggle with the thin air. "I'm amazed at the difference between Port City ravine and out here."

On a smooth stretch of sand, Joy was turning slow pirouettes, laughing at herself.

"I'm so clumsy!"

"Clumsy?" Bonny said, attempting to mimic her grandmother's motions and spinning into a heap.

"It's the gravity, Bon," Joy said, joining her on the dune. "I've spent longer than your mother has been alive on ships between the stars, and when I dance I do with only a feather touch of gravity."

"I remember," Bonny sighed, "I remember . . ."

"Said the Chinese nightingale," Smokey finished with a smile. Then, in response to Bonny's puzzled look she added, "It's an Old Terran story that Bethlehem told me when I was smaller than you are now. I'd forgotten, but it was one of my favorites."

Bethlehem smiled.

"Smokey, you said something about that once," Clarence said, "about growing up mostly on ships. It must have been fascinating."

"It was," Smokey said, repressing an urge to glower at her mother. "It was also boring, lonely, and unsettling. We didn't stay on one ship more than a year and even on those we didn't belong anywhere. We weren't passengers, but we certainly weren't crew. Every time I started to make friends with some of the other ship brats, we'd be moving on to another contract. As soon as I could, I left."

Awkward silence followed. Bonny sat frozen next to her grandmother, then with a burst of limbs and sand she ran over to Smokey.

"Don't be sad, Mama. That's over now, and you have me and we're all friends, right?"

Feeling her daughter's distress, Smokey found a smile. "That's right, Bonita. It's all over, and we're all together here, and the desert is lovely."

The girl was comforted, but the adults remained guarded. Clarence was particularly tense and abashed. Sighing within, Smokey caught Bonny by one hand, Joy by the other.

"Night," she said, "is one of the best times in the desert. We're far enough from the Gorge to really start looking at the terrain."

"The moons are bright, too," Clarence offered, "but I'm not sure what we are looking for."

"Nothing," Bethlehem suggested. "We're just seeing."

His words hung koan-like in the dry air, then Bonny released Smokey's hand and skipped forward.

"I know that plant," she said, pointing to a grey-green clump with fat, round leaves. "It's native—a peek-a-boo. When the sun's out, the leaves curl up."

"What's that one?" Joy said, indicating a spiny ball huddled in the shade of a rocky shelf.

"Don't touch!" Bonny said, running over. "That's a dangerous one—an Icedrake land urchin. They carry water inside, but the stickers have poison."

"What I don't understand," Clarence said, hunkering down for a better look at the urchin, "is why the terraformers would import poisonous plants at all."

Smokey nodded. "I remember asking Ross the same thing. He explained that plants or animals chosen for transplanting all had merits that made them valuable—

those urchins store nearly a liter of drinkable water if you know how to get to it. But usually a creature doesn't evolve without learning how to protect itself."

"So why not just gen-eng it to keep the water storage capacity and remove the poison?" Clarence asked.

"Well, how much chance of survival would it have here without its poison?" Smokey grinned. "They'd be split open by every native life-form on this dustball and gobbled by the creatures we've imported as well."

"I see," Clarence said. "What else is there out here?"

They wandered for the next several hours, never ranging far from the crawler that hovered, a fortresslike backdrop to their explorations. When this palled, they picnicked on the sand, watching the moons chase each other toward dawn. If a slight tension of things yet unresolved still shadowed Joy and Smokey, Bethlehem was likely the only one who noticed.

10

CLARENCE WALKED UP BEHIND SMOKEY AND PUT his hands on her shoulders. They'd stopped at twilight, a day deeper across the Arizona desert. Bonny had gone off with her grandparents to sit quietly by a promising heap of wind-scoured boulders and see what came out with the evening's cool.

"Smokey-jo," he murmured, not quite nibbling her right earlobe. "How are you doing, sugar?"

She didn't step away, but she didn't lean into his invited embrace either.

"I'm pretty well," she said, "though this trip is stirring up memories I thought were long settled."

"You mean between you and Joy?" His voice, soft, deep, just barely husky, invited confidences.

"Yes, I hated her for a long time. She was a terrible mother—the great *artiste*. Temperamental. Effusive. Bethlehem was the better parent, but I started hating him, too, because he was so definitely in her camp, so forgiving, so understanding."

"You wanted him to take your side?"

Smokey stepped away, avoiding the pity in his thoughts rather than his touch. She turned and smiled so not as to seem to be rejecting him and motioned for him to sit with her on the spread blanket left from the picnic dinner.

"I thought that was the case for a long time," she sighed. "Now I think that what I wanted him to do was change her—make her into the mama I wanted. He's awfully understanding, Bethlehem is. Too wise to tell me that what I thought I wanted wasn't what I really wanted and that what I wanted no one could give me. He was patient right up to the day I ran away. Then they cut me off for about five years. Probably the best thing for me then, too, but I hated them both even as I learned to stand on my own and be what I wanted to be."

"Lots of hate, Smokey," Clarence offered. "I'm surprised that it hasn't marked you."

"Not all marks show on the surface," she replied.

Uncomfortable silence settled.

"I didn't mean to be rude," Smokey said at last. "It just slipped out. Really that's old history—we've settled this long since. Bonny's questions keep bringing me back."

"Forget it, Smokey," he advised. "Make some new memories."

This time there was nothing tentative about his kiss. He held her then while the two moons danced with the stars in the clear dark sky, kissing the soft sides of her throat and stroking her with fingers that tried to memorize the curves of her body. She relaxed into his arms then, trying not to weep, feeling from his mind only simple single-minded absorption with his exploration.

Eventually, she must have dozed, because her next awareness was of daylight streaming through the crawler's windows. Bonny slept on a bunk above her, one foot poking off the edge of the platform. The rest of the sleep area was empty, so Smokey permitted herself time to meditate and shower. When she emerged into the front compartment she realized that she felt the best she had since the R&D blowout and Ami's death.

Clarence and Joy were playing dominoes at a tiny table to the right and slightly back from the driver's seat. Bethlehem had the crawler on semipilot. He stood watching the game and sipping a mug of tea.

"We stayed up for the dawn," Clarence said, looking up in surprise as she kissed the top of his wool-soft hair. "You slept about twelve hours."

Commandeering Bethlehem's cup, Smokey sipped the leaf green liquid, nodded in approval, and went to pour herself a cup.

"I feel wonderful," she admitted. "I must have been more worn-out than I had realized."

Bethlehem returned from a course adjustment, grinned as Joy drew the worst possible domino, and then cocked a bristly eyebrow at his daughter.

"Popularity wearing you out?"

Smokey considered him, considered her suspicions, and parried.

"Some. And sometimes in my business you learn things about people that you'd rather not know."

Bethlehem narrowed eyes a few shades darker grey than her own. "Knowledge can be useful."

Joy broke the moment by conceding her defeat in a flamboyant heap of crashing dominoes.

"I'm going to rest for a few hours," she said. "Don't let me miss anything important."

"We won't," Smokey promised. "If I read Bethlehem's scanner correctly, we have about two hours until we reach an area where the eco-shift will become more obvious."

"In that case," Clarence said, "I'll sleep, too. Wake me in a couple of hours, okay?"

When they were gone and the bulkhead secured between sections, Smokey asked Bethlehem, "Did you put the idea in their heads?"

His answer would have gotten him life imprisonment on most of the commerce worlds—except for those that would have executed him.

"No, I can only read thoughts and sometimes send them to a receptive party." He smiled gently. "Joy is usually receptive. But I cannot influence those thoughts any more persuasively than if I was merely using my vocal cords."

"Capi," she answered, raising one hand palm out. "I thought so, from little things that you said, did. You must have been capable of this for years. Why didn't I ever figure it out? Did you block me?"

"No, Smokey." He took her hand. "No, nothing so sophisticated. Yes, I've had the ability for a long time. I knew it wasn't just my imagination for certain back when I was about Bonny's age. You know how it is, don't you? Not trusting what you sense, believing despite growing evidence that you are imagining what you feel?"

"Yes," Smokey said, feeling his mind open to her through his touch. "Yes, I remember."

"Said the Chinese nightingale." He squeezed her fingertips. "I never had to block you—not in the way you mean, though for my own sanity I usually avoided your thoughts."

Smokey flushed a deep crimson, half-embarrassed, half-angered that he could read her those years ago and hadn't somehow made things right.

"I never blocked you, though I did maintain my own shields. You didn't have the experience to see the signs; you hadn't yet learned the marks of a telepath. You know them now because you are one and, unlike most, you don't rule out reading minds as a possible solution to a puzzle."

Smokey let her hand stay within her father's with difficulty. "Yes, I understand. But there have been moments this trip when you have all but dared me to guess your secret. Why now? Why after all this time?"

"Partly because it is lonely hiding a talent that isolates when it ideally should unite. Partly"—he took a deep breath—"because from flashes I have caught of your thoughts, I suspect that you have stumbled onto something that will kill you more surely even than being discovered as a psionic."

Smokey felt the throat-choking panic of memory rise as Bethlehem let an image flow to her.

"That," she said with thought. *"That. How did you know?"*

"You have been agitated, daughter," he said, "and you did not always mask the reason for your unhappiness. I wasn't certain until after we joined you for this hadj. You have relaxed some and given some of your worries away."

"Given them away?" Smokey nodded sadly. "And you have taken them up."

"Not from you, Smokey. I have been aware of these creatures for many years." His smile was touched with bitterness. "Did you think you were the only psionic who had detected them?"

"Well . . . I." She faltered. "Yes, I did. I didn't know there were any other psionics who had escaped the Purges. I figured that I was a freak or a throwback."

Bethlehem laughed so hard that tears ran down into the scrub of his two-day beard. Even grasping his hand, Smokey couldn't comprehend the reason for his laughter, only that it was without malice.

"Papa?" She shook him gently. "Papa?"

He gasped himself calm. "I'm sorry, Smokey. A freak or a throwback? Throwback to what?"

She grinned ruefully. "You know, I honestly never thought about that. Even when I considered that Bonny might have inherited my talent, I never considered that I could have inherited it from you and Joy in Motion."

"Me, more than Joy," he said, sharing the last of the tea between their cups. "Joy's ability is latent, rather than developed. Association with me has refined her abilities as far as they can develop—some empathy and a receptiveness to mental contact. I have also taught her to run a surface thought pattern so that her trivial concerns mask her actual thoughts. It's safer than a blank."

He shrugged and grinned. "This does make her appear somewhat flighty to the sensitive, but then—she is."

Smokey winced at his pun. "What is that horror I have been sensing?"

Bethlehem bit back his reply as the door to the sleeping compartment opened and a tousled Bonny walked out, scrubbing her eyes with her fists.

"Have I missed anything, Mama?" she said.

"Not in the desert, Boniface," Smokey said, noting Bethlehem's mouth quirk with a suppressed smile as he turned to adjust the crawler's course.

"Clarence," Bonny announced, "snores. He didn't close his cubby tightly enough. I did so he wouldn't wake Grandmama. How long 'til dark?"

"A bit yet, but we should be seeing changes before then. Hungry?"

"Yes." Bonny hugged Bethlehem and padded to the kitchen unit, busying herself heating breakfast sweets and tea.

"How you can eat yam dumplings for breakfast," Bethlehem commented, "is beyond me."

"I guess it's all what you grow up with," Smokey said. "Remember that one ship where the entire crew were into eating all their food half-rotten and raw?"

"I'll never forget," Bethlehem agreed. "Ever since then Joy and I have spent a bit of our lift allowances for rehydrates. Needed them a few times, too."

"Why?" Bonny asked.

"Well, Bonny," Bethlehem said, patting his chin with two fingers, "most of the time it's just been engine failures, but once the ship we were traveling on was taken by pirates."

"Pirates!" Her eyes shining, Bonny took the copilot's chair. "I can help drive. Tell me about them."

Smokey listened with only half an ear, the rest of her attention on the landscape outside of the window. When she saw the first cluster of flowering cactus, she went and woke Joy and Clarence. When she saw the first cluster of tall, thin grass, she tapped Bonny on one shoulder.

"Look, Bonita. See anything different?"

Bonny searched. "There! Grass! Wild grass, not even in a garden!"

"We've been descending gradually for the last several hours," Smokey explained. "Soon we'll get our first sight of the Sea."

"Is it because the Sea is at the base of a valley that it affects the surrounding area so much?" Joy asked.

"That's right," Smokey said. "Out on one of the plains it would have a lot more struggle to raise the moisture level outside of its immediate environs."

They spread out in the crawler, everyone pressed up near a window, hunting for more evidence of the Sea's effect on the valley basin. Discoveries came with increasing rapidity—a swarm of winged insects, a clump of shrubs with needlelike leaves but extravagant blossoms, a pair of copper and bronze reptiles sunning on a rock.

"What the hell are those—monkeys?" Clarence exclaimed. "There over to the extreme right in the west."

Smokey looked. "Monkeys? I don't think that any nonhuman primates have been introduced . . ."

She caught a glimpse of a retreating tail. "Oh! That looked like a chulo."

"Chulo?" Clarence was puzzled. "Are those native to Arizona? I've never heard of them."

"I think they're from Old Terra," Smokey replied. "They're one of the largest mammals that has been introduced into Arizona's ecosystem—other than humans, of course."

Bethlehem had been calling up information from the crawler's databank. " 'Chulo, also called "coati mundi." An omnivorous mammal, closely related to the raccoon.' Goes on a bit here—probably the most useful bit is that their range of acceptable habitats extends between desert and tropical. They're very adaptable, since after the initial few weeks the young are raised by the tribe rather than by individual parents."

"I never thought much about how terraforming would work," Clarence admitted, three lizards, a peafrond succulent, and a colony of jeweled beetles later. "On Terra most change is viewed with suspicion, even things like returning some polluted zone to a more natural state. When the terraforming worlds are spoken of there's no discussion of the effort taken to change the world on many levels. I used to wonder why it took so long. Now I marvel that it can happen at all."

"I can see why the process doesn't get much coverage," Smokey said. "This isn't very exciting. Arizona has been being terraformed since long before I came here and all we have to show for it is a bit richer atmosphere, a few more plants, and a mess of largely unexciting creatures that are encouraged to meld into the terrain. The greatest success is that the change isn't quick or dramatic and so should continue."

Bethlehem made a startled sound and the crawler lurched slightly.

"I'm fine," he assured the concerned babble. "I was listening and missed avoiding a bit of rock."

"Are you certain?" Joy said. "Maybe I should drive. You may be getting tired."

"No, I'm fine."

Smokey thought that she caught a whiff of something added mind to mind, but it was too faint for her to be certain. She scowled out the window, amazed at how easily those two could make her feel like a kid.

"Hey!" Bonny said. "It's getting purple up high. Let's look for a really good place to stop and see what comes out at dark."

"Shouldn't we leave the crawler and stalk up on foot?" Clarence asked. "We're going to scare everything."

"We haven't so far," Joy commented. "I wonder why?"

"I know! I know!" Bonny bounced in her seat.

"Why?" Clarence asked, snagging her and then dragging her into his lap. "Tell the dumb Terran."

"It's because Arizona doesn't have any really big predators yet," she said. "We learned in school. No one is allowed to hunt anything—even bugs—and the ecosystem is on such a micro . . ."

She hunted for a word.

"Microcosmic?" Smokey suggested.

"Microcosmic scale, a microcosm." Bonny paused, proud of herself for remembering the word. "So humans are not really something that the creatures think of as dangerous. They might avoid us if we were really noisy, but if we're quiet and still, they'll come out and do whatever they would normally."

"I understand," Clarence said. "We're like cows or horses on Terra. They're big, but not really dangerous, so little creatures come out and mix with them."

Later, when the rest were absorbed watching a foraging gerbil stuff his mouth and then dive down one of the many entrances into his burrow, Smokey drew Bethlehem aside.

"The crawler is programmed," she said succinctly, "to automatically chart its way around anything large enough to be damaged by the crawler. We didn't hit a rock. Why did you jump like that?"

Bethlehem studied her. "I don't want to go into it here—now. Let's just say that your lecture on terraforming made me understand something that's been troubling me since before you were born. I could be wrong; let me think it over more."

Smokey touched the side of his face, lightly. "I'll give you time, but don't expect to slip away."

"I don't." He grinned crookedly. "I don't plan on leaving my little girl to the wolves."

11

STYLER'S SEA WAS AT FIRST A PALE BLUE LINE, then a darker oval, and now that they stood on its banks a delightful thing of wet ripples and reflected sunlight.

"What I can't get over," Smokey said, standing ankle deep in the water, "is the smell. The color, the wet, the sparkle—all of that I expect—but not the smell of all this water in one place with things alive in it."

"Smell?" Clarence said. "This water doesn't smell, Smokey-jo. This is the freshest lake I've ever seen. There are reservoirs on Terra that aren't this clean. If you want to smell water, you've got to try an ocean or maybe the Mississippi River."

She shoved him playfully. "I'm not a rube, Clarence. I've seen oceans on several worlds, but this Sea changes the whole place, makes it alive in a different way."

"Mama! Mama!" Bonny came splashing up the shoreline. "Look! It's got eyes and it was looking at me! Really looking!"

Smokey took the freshwater scallop from Bonny's hands.

"Looking?" she teased. "I don't see any eyes. It looks like a greyish, fan-shaped rock to me."

"There are eyes," Bonny insisted. "Blue ones."

Inspiration seized the girl. "I'll set it down, just in the edge of the water. Then you'll see."

Gently, she set the scallop in a clear, shallow pool above the high water mark. She held them all to silence with a finger to her lips, then slowly withdrew it as a glitter of alien blue eyes opened along the shellfish's rim.

"See!" she said triumphantly. "There they are!"

"I see." Smokey hugged her.

"My dad did something good here," Bonny said. "Didn't he?"

"I think so," Smokey said. "I think so."

Clarence, who had been a few steps off talking with Joy in Motion, tilted his head quizzically. When he came over to join her, Smokey knew his question without even touching him.

"Yes, Ross Styler was her father," she said, watching Bonny dart off after a gossamer-winged Guillen dragonfly. "Ross and I were good friends."

Clarence gnawed at the corner of his lower lip. "Didn't you say she was nine? Styler died more than ten years ago—I saw it on the anniversary memorial over there."

Smokey followed his gaze to the sand-scoured malachite pylon standing where the desert was giving way to sparse greenery.

"You *Can* Get Water From a Stone," she recited the inscription from memory. "Yes, Ross died before Bonny was conceived. He was also contentedly homosexual, but there are ways around such things. I wanted a child and so did he. His death didn't end my conviction that he would be a fine sire for my girl. I'm still sorry that he couldn't be alive to be her father as well."

Clarence stood silently for a long while. The sound of Bonny's laughter rang out against the chimes of the insects that darted out over the water and skated between the plants.

"You're an odd one, Smokey," he said at last. "I don't think there's anyone quite like you."

"Probably not," she agreed. "Good thing."

"Maybe," he said. "Maybe not, but I'm still glad we met."

Joy came up to them. "Bethlehem says that he can

radio for someone to collect the crawler and we can finish our hadj on foot. The scanner says that the way around the Sea is only ten or so kilometers. I'd like to make the walk and have a chance to really be outside before we get on a starship again."

"I'll agree," Smokey said, "with a few provisions. First, we wait until the sun is off-force—about an hour from now. Second, someone has to convince Bonny to nap for that time. Third, we pack an oxygen tank for those of you who aren't adapted to the thin air."

"They all sound like good ideas," Bethlehem said. "And I can convince Bonny to nap, easily."

Smokey glanced sharply at him. "You can?"

"Easily," he said, his smile reassuring. "Just like I did when you were her age. I'll tell her stories."

The trek around the Sea was memorable for nothing more than being what it was. A damp wind like nothing else on Arizona caressed them as they walked. Wavelets splashed them with teasing infrequency, like the affectionate tickling fingers of teenage boys. The sun gradually gave up admiring itself in the Sea's blue mirror and spread out a splendor of color before the rising moons.

Bonny dueted with the damselflies, bringing back her treasures to share with the adults. Her shoes filled with sand so often that Joy playfully commented that they were hourglasses rather than footwear. When at last the girl's energy flagged, Clarence carried her on his back while she sang encouraging songs in a voice too shrill for beauty, but lacking nothing in enthusiasm.

When they arrived at the farther shore with the dawn, a bemused passerby with an air of curious respect directed them to an inn. Their rooms were quickly readied, and, without pausing for more than a quick snack, they each tumbled into bed. So it was not until late the next afternoon that Smokey learned of Gary's murder.

She had just finished sharing morning tea and a bowl of fruit pilaf with Joy and was idly scanning the news-strip running through the tabletop when Gary's name and then a small, stiff portrait appeared. Reaching for the reverse, she brought back the story.

"Smokey." Joy leaned across the table and caught her arm. "Smokey, what's wrong? You just went as white as sand."

Smokey looked up with difficulty. "A—business associate of mine has been murdered. Rather violently."

"Like the girl from the brothel," Joy said. "Ami."

Smokey nodded, reading. "Not quite, but the details may have been suppressed."

Chin cradled in hand, she meditated and decided that it could be coincidence, maybe even was. Gary had been in a dangerous business. People didn't take kindly to those who traded in stolen knowledge. But the showy nature of the murder bothered her. Even in the short news-strip there had been a hint of something *outré* about the way Gary had been killed.

Clever murder was never professional. It invited investigation, curiosity. Surely anyone clever enough to track down Gary would be too smart to do something so dangerous. It wasn't like anyone needed warning. Was it?

She realized that Joy was speaking and that she had no idea of how to respond.

"I'm sorry, Joy. I missed what you were saying."

Joy smiled. "I was just apologizing for not being able to stay more than the next couple of days to help. The *Ibn Battuta* won't wait and nasty things happen when entertainers break contracts."

"I understand. Thanks for offering, but there shouldn't be any trouble. My only connections to Gary are so innocuous that I probably won't even be contacted." She tried to smile. "It's just a shock. I'd worked with him for quite a few years. Had him just a few days ago. Now he's dead. Makes everything seem awfully unreal."

"Life," Joy replied, "has a singular talent for taking all

our expectations and revising them without even the courtesy of a 'by-your-leave.' The trick is learning to survive."

Smokey nodded, thinking of a daughter who had run away, a husband who could read minds, of who knows how many other readjustments and reassessments in Joy's life.

"You're right, Mama," she said, "and I am sorry you and Bethlehem can't stay longer. Not because of Gary's death, just because I may finally be old enough to understand."

12

WHEN SMOKEY, CLARENCE, AND BONNY RE-
turned to Port City, a police officer was
waiting at the house. Smokey immediately
recognized her as Wallon, one of the officers assigned to
investigate Ami's death.

"Good afternoon, Officer Wallon," she said, setting
down her travel pack and thumbing the lock. "What
brings you out this way?"

Wallon glared at her. "I've come to speak with you
about the death of Gary Jorgeson. Surely you've heard
that he's been murdered."

Smokey motioned Clarence and Bonny into the house
with a toss of her head.

As they walked by she said, "I've been on hadj these
past several days, but, yes, I saw a news-strip back at the
Sea. Why do you want to see me?"

Wallon sighed, her exasperation tempered by discomfort. She glanced to where Clarence and Bonny were
watching the byplay, the man impassive, the girl plainly
upset.

"I would prefer to speak with you privately," she said.
"Shall I invite you to the station?"

"When you've been so kind as to stop by?" Smokey
stepped back and let her enter. "How could I ever be so
rude? Bonny, go and see if we have any messages,
please."

Bonny nodded and went, not without another suspicious scowl for the officer, who was looking around the entry room with interest.

Clarence cleared his throat. "I can see about getting things put away, Smokey-jo. Don't forget that I promised to take you and Bonny to dinner."

"I haven't." She gave him a quick squeeze, touched by his tacit promise to be there in case Wallon got rude.

"No messages, Mama," Bonny said, running in, Wintering at her heels, "but the chulo ate my orchids."

Clarence started back. "You didn't tell me you kept one of those as a house pet!"

"Oh." Smokey grinned. "That's Wintering. Chulo tribes chase out the males each winter and this one came to live with us. We figured that he was just wintering, but when spring came around he stayed."

"Really cute," Officer Wallon interrupted, clearly piqued at having been ignored, "but if you'll just give me a few minutes of your time, you can get back to your guest."

"Yes." Smokey pulled herself a bottle of juice from the cooler, pointedly did not offer Wallon one, and gestured. "My office is over there."

Once they were settled, Wallon pulled out a pocket memory and pointed it so that both of their images would be recorded.

"This interview is a part of the official record," she stated. "Now, where have you been for the last several days?"

Smokey replied without any indication of her growing irritation, "As I mentioned, I have been on hadj."

"Do you have any other witnesses besides your daughter and Clarence Beauduc?"

"Witnesses? My other companions were Joy in Motion and Bethlehem. They've since returned to the *Ibn Battuta.*"

"Joy in Motion? The dancer?" Wallon clearly regretted showing her surprise as soon as she spoke.

Smokey did not hesitate to capitalize on the officer's discomfort. "Yes, Joy and Bethlehem are my parents—that's a matter of public record."

Something like anger showed for a moment on Wallon's face. Then she was calmly professional again.

"Do you have any witnesses who are not family?"

"Well there was Eze who rented us the crawler, a guide named Carmelita, and the people at the inn by the Sea where we stayed."

Wallon collected names and addresses, then continued, "Once you rented the crawler and left Graydon's Gorge, did you meet anyone?"

"No, no one but insects, plants, and the occasional lizard or chulo." Smokey sipped her juice. "That's part of the purpose for a hadj, you know."

"Yes." Again Wallon scowled. "Why did you choose this time for your hadj? It's rather suspicious that you left town so soon after Ami's murder."

"Not at all," Smokey said, baiting her. "You might even say that poor Ami's death was the reason we left Port City. Clarence and I were very upset by her death, and with the Victorian Mansion closed in mourning we both had time off. My parents had hoped for time with me and Bonny and the trip fell together from there."

Wallon frowned. "I see. That will be all for now."

"Wait," Smokey said. "You haven't explained why you wanted to speak with me."

Wallon's face blanked. "Why, that should be obvious, ma'am. Port City isn't exactly known for murders. Gary Jorgeson left notes addressed to you in his databank. They were well sealed, but apparently you have been doing some rather sensitive work for him. Therefore, you are the only common factor in two of the ugliest murders we've ever seen."

"So I am a suspect?"

Wallon smiled. "You are."

Wallon's meetings with Bonny and Clarence were comparatively brief. Bonny glowered at the officer and refused to answer any questions until Smokey assured her that cooperation was acceptable. Even then, her answers were monosyllabic.

"I don't like her, Mama," she said after the officer had left and they were eating. "There's something wrong about her."

"She's just trying to find a killer, Boniface," Smokey soothed, "and she doesn't like whores."

"She doesn't like you, Mama," Bonny corrected. "I can tell. She wants to get you."

"Maybe." Smokey smiled. "Now, go get some rest, Bonny. You'll have school tomorrow."

"Capi. Good night, Clarence." Bonny hugged Smokey. "Good night, Mama."

She left, Wintering at her heels.

Clarence reserved his comments until Bonny had gone to sleep. "Funny, that officer waiting here for you, like she knew when you'd be coming home."

"Or was just staking the place out," Smokey said. "I don't think she's that bright. I'll never forget her expression when she learned who my folks are."

"How'd she look?" Clarence asked. "Startled?"

"That"—Smokey's smile vanished—"and angry. Maybe I ticked her off. Either way, she's got nothing on me. Arizona's laws uphold innocent until proven guilty.

"Smokey"—Clarence touched her lightly—"I could go back to my place, but I'd rather stay. Guest room, your room. I don't even mind if you charge. I'm just not ready to be alone, not after playing family with you folks."

Smokey looked at him. He was being completely honest with her. With something like horror, she realized that if anyone was being dishonest, it was she. Had years of expecting people to lie, knowing when they did, feeling their manipulations beneath their words, had this made her unable to accept honest love when it was offered?

She didn't mean to take a deep breath, but she did just the same.

"I think I love you, Clarence," she said. "I'd rather have you stay here than just about anything."

She felt his joy, felt the urge to protect her that followed.

"You know that I love you, Smokey-jo," Clarence said, "but don't go scaring yourself. If you want me to stay, I will. Otherwise, I'll see you at the Victorian Mansion come tomorrow."

"Stay," Smokey said, and the words were easier this time. "I want you near. I think I might always want you near, man."

She twinkled wickedly at him, ran her hand down his trousers' front, and squeezed gently.

"I don't think I'm the only one wanting, Clarence," she said. "Come along. My room's soundproofed, which is a good thing, as I recall."

He scooped her up with surprising ease.

"Show me the way," he said, bending his head to kiss her. "I'm no fool."

So she did and they did, and so he was there in the morning when the news brought them word of the murder of Fox.

Bonny had turned on the newsnet to review what she had missed for one of her classes. The commentators were busy discussing the gruesome murder of a member of the Entertainer's Guild on the stroll in the Sybarite's District.

"The woman has been identified as Claudia Raphelian, a butch lesbian commonly known as Fox."

"She's in your Guild. Did you know her, Mama?" Bonny asked.

Smokey nodded sharply and held up a hand for silence.

"Raphelian's body was found," the commentator continued, "in a side street off of the main stroll."

A star glistened on the screen, indicating that visuals of a sensitive nature were available.

"You might not want to look, Bonny," Smokey warned as she triggered them.

The girl turned away, accepting the sharp tone in her

mother's voice without protest. Clarence took Smokey's hand. The commentator's words continued unheard as they viewed the pull-down screen.

Fox hung suspended from an ornate lamppost of decorative iron, her arms and legs behind her. Her throat had been cut so savagely that her head hung to one side, held in place only by a hank of unsevered flesh.

Smokey retched, banishing the pictures with a blind stab of her finger. Clarence blew out his breath in a gusty current that carried his horror and fear.

"Wallon will be here again," Smokey said bluntly. "Soon, I'd guess. If she takes me in, call my parents. I know a good lawyer, so the law won't be able to hold me long. Bonny, if I'm not here, I want you to listen to Clarence, Joy, and Bethlehem."

Bonny nodded, eyes wide and frightened, "Will they put you in jail, Mama?"

"They might try, but I won't stay long. I haven't done anything wrong."

"Why is this happening, Smokey?" Clarence asked. "This can't be coincidence."

"I don't know," Smokey replied, but deep inside she remembered Bethlehem's cryptic comments and knew that it had to do with Lee and with Wickerwork and with what she had learned. Something wanted her not only out of the way but also so discredited that even if she had told anyone anything, her words would mean nothing.

She shivered. "Don't worry, folks, or, if you do, just remember that I'll be back soon."

There was a pounding on the door.

"You would think that they would be polite enough to use the buzzer," Smokey said, trying to be calm for Bonny's sake.

She went and opened the door. "Yes . . ."

Her words trailed off. Bethlehem stood there, a hat shadowing his face as he slipped inside.

"Smokey. Good, Bonny and Clarence are here. We need to get you away."

"Away?" Smokey frowned. "I've been framed, but I can clear it up. I have a good lawyer."

"Contact him later," Bethlehem said. "Grab what you must have. Forget clothes or routine stuff. Hurry!"

She stared at him, aware that Bonny was already moving to obey, towing Clarence behind her.

"Papa, why?"

"Smokey, this is bigger than you know." Bethlehem managed a tight-lipped smile that was anything but reassuring. "Come away and I'll explain later."

There was something in Bethlehem's expression that brooked no argument. Necessary equipment was packed in a few minutes. Clarence stood silently, holding an extra bag of Bonny's mementos. Smokey had far less.

"Grandpapa?" Bonny held her chulo out to him. "Do we have to leave Wintering?"

"He wouldn't be very happy on the *Ibn Battuta*, Bonny," Bethlehem replied gently. "Will one of your neighbors take care of him?"

The girl's eyes were wet with pooling tears, but she managed to nod. "I can leave a note. We will come back, won't we?"

Bethlehem lifted the chulo from her arms and carried him to an open window. Wintering looked back once, then jumped down.

"We will, Bonny, but we must leave now."

Smokey pressed a brief note onto her neighbor's door as they left. Bethlehem led them along an up-ravine trail to where a black hover van was concealed.

"We'll meet with a shuttle from the *Ibn Battuta* and go directly into space," he explained grimly as they rose. "The *Battuta* should be able to leave the Wheel of Heaven without difficulty. She was cleared to depart earlier. Arizona's jurisdiction is limited once off the planet and its satellites. At this point the only warrants for Smokey are planetary."

"How do you know all of this?" Clarence asked, the first words he had spoken other than when assisting Bonny to pack.

"I have connections and I listen," Bethlehem said cryptically. "I'll explain more once we're safely away. I promise."

Clarence narrowed his eyes, then nodded once, sharply as if sealing a contract.

"Clarence is coming with us on the starliner?" Bonny asked.

"That would be wise," Bethlehem said. "The people who are trying to blame your mother for those killings are going to be very angry when they learn that she's gotten away. They might try to use Clarence to get her back."

Clarence's skin was far too dark to pale, but Smokey saw his fists clench involuntarily. She didn't need to read his mind to know that he was remembering Ami's dismembered body, Fox's tortured corpse. He heard the warning underlying Bethlehem's calm explanation.

"I want to come," he said, "and not just to get away. I'd worry too damn much about you—about both of you."

Smokey found a smile. "Good. We want you with us."

The transfer from van to ship's shuttle went so smoothly that Smokey almost forgot how dangerous a maneuver it was. Only when one of her decorative hair combs slipped loose and was lost almost before she could reach for it did sudden vertigo melt her knees.

She stumbled, half-falling, into the shuttle and let Bethlehem drop the acceleration harness over her. Once Bonny and Clarence were secured, he moved into the copilot's seat.

"Ready, Joy," he said. "The van is programmed to land near Ki'rin Ravine after flying an apparently evasive pattern."

The shuttle began to pick up speed even before he finished speaking. Smokey couldn't be certain that she had heard aright until she craned her neck and got a clear look at the pilot.

Joy in Motion was hooked into the pilot's link-ups, a wraparound visor over her eyes, her slim fingers dancing over the control board with same grace her body spun over the grav stage. She seemed to feel Smokey's regard because as soon as the course was locked in, she swiveled her chair and gave her daughter a fond smile.

"You seem surprised, Smokey."

"You know I am, Joy."

"Didn't think that I was good for anything but wiggling like a minnow in zero gee." This time the dancer grinned. "Just goes to show you don't know it all—something that would be good to remember when Beth and I start filling you in."

"I will," Smokey said. "I will. How are you doing, Bonny?"

"Do I have to wear this thing?" Bonny asked, plucking at her harness. "It squashes."

"It should," Joy answered, her eyes tracking readings in her visor. "This isn't a fat tub like those station shuttles you've gone on. This is a ship's boat—and I may as well confess that it doubles as a fighter. If we need to fight, I'd rather have you strapped in."

"Oh." Bonny's eyes rounded respectfully.

"Are we likely to get in a fight?" Clarence asked.

"No, not unless they were smarter—or at least faster—than I think they were," Bethlehem answered. "My guess is that they'll waste time on the van."

"I was asking because I may be a bit rusty, but I did do my bit with the Terra System Patrol." Clarence's expression was wry and Smokey loved him for it. "Old Terra still has this idea that just because we haven't seen any bug-eyed monsters doesn't mean that they're not out there, and so we had better be ready for 'em. I was a pretty fair shot and kept up with it for fun afterward."

"Good," Joy said. "And interesting."

"The captain of the *Ibn Battuta* has agreed to rendezvous with us along her assigned flight trajectory," Bethlehem explained, Smokey suspected more to soothe their nerves than because they needed to know. "According to my checks, they started departure protocols from the Wheel on schedule. We should meet in a couple of minutes. When we dock, the hangar should be empty. If it isn't, don't speak to anyone. The crew has orders not to notice you, but we won't push their tolerance."

"You're cozy with the captain," Clarence commented. "That's good."

"Yes, we are, and, yes, that is good," Bethlehem responded. "However, we need to refrain from openly playing on this. We don't want the crew to resent us, especially since in this case we are using our connection to abscond with a fugitive suspected of a series of rather grisly murders."

"We're coming in now," Joy said. "Lean back and watch."

Joy matched courses with the moving liner and the *Ibn Battuta* swallowed her ship's boat without protest. As Joy ran through the power down, Bethlehem assisted them with their harnesses and then parceled out the baggage among them.

No one waited in the cavernous hangar, but neither Bethlehem nor Joy wasted motion or word until they had shepherded them out of the working decks and into the passenger section where their quarters were.

Inside, Bethlehem didn't even set down Bonny's spare carryall before he tabbed the intercom.

"Captain nu-Aten," a contralto female voice answered.

"Bethlehem, Captain. We're aboard."

"Acknowledged. Stay in quarters until jump clear is signaled. I will expect you and your party for dinner. Private and informal, but we have business to discuss."

"Capi," Bethlehem replied. "We'll be there."

Once the connection was broken, he set down Bonny's bag and then sagged into a chair. Joy rubbed his shoulders until he sighed and summoned a smile.

"Welcome aboard the *Ibn Battuta*," he said. "We were hoping to have a longer time to explain things to you, but Captain nu-Aten's 'invitation' speeds up the timetable. We'll show you where to stow your gear and give you a chance to reorient. Then, I'm afraid we are going to need to tell you about a war."

"War?" Smokey said, instinctively reaching for Bonny. "You said war?"

"That's right." Joy's expression revealed lines of weariness and fear that Smokey had not noticed before. "War."

13

"PERHAPS WHEN YOU HEAR WHAT WE HAVE TO tell you," Bethlehem began, "you will think us overdramatic. But before we begin—Clarence, we've shanghaied you. There is time for you to cut your losses and take this trip as a free cruise. The *Battuta's* next stop is Guillen and there is regular travel between there and Old Terra or even back to Arizona if that is where you want to go."

Clarence stared levelly at him. "Cut my losses? What do you mean?"

"He means," Joy said, "that you don't know enough to be in any real danger, especially if you sever your connections with Smokey. We can help you come up with a plausible reason for your departure and for the rest you can have a free cruise on a fine luxury liner."

"I know what you've said about a war," Clarence said firmly. "I know someone wants to make Smokey out to be a killer—no, not even a killer, a psychopath. I can't forget that."

"Actually," Bethlehem looked uncomfortable, "you could. I'm skilled in hypnotism and you're probably receptive. I could help you—in fact, I'd insist, but it would need to be done soon. The more you know, the harder resculpting your memories would be."

Clarence shook his head, his voice rising. "No, and not for the reasons you think. You think I just don't want you messing with my head. There's more. I'm sure you can't make me forget what I know without altering how I feel about Smokey, and I don't want to lose that. I'll take your war, whatever it is, rather than give her up."

He stopped suddenly, looking embarrassed at his outburst, but Bethlehem only grimaced at Joy.

"He means it," he said.

"I know"—she smiled—"even without you telling me."

She turned her attention to the others. "I realize that this is very strange. It's so strange that I hardly know where to begin."

"Why did you give Clarence a chance to retreat and not Bonny?" Smokey said. "She's only a child."

"Mama!"

Joy interrupted Bonny's protest with a raised hand. "There is no 'out' for Bonny, not short of giving her a completely new identity. She's your daughter, Bethlehem's granddaughter. She may have some of your talent. Beyond this, once the identity of her father is learned, she will become doubly valuable."

Smokey tore a hand back through her hair. "I don't understand."

"No," Bethlehem said, "as Joy said, the problem is complicated. The best way to explain would be to tell you how we became involved. That's what we planned on, but the captain has made this impossible. There are things that you need to know before tonight's meeting."

"So"—Joy drew a ragged breath—"we're going to be blunt and tactless and hope to give you the 'whys' later."

"Go on!" Bonny said. "Tell us!"

"Easy, Bon-ton," Bethlehem said. "This is a lot harder than telling your mom when you've done something wrong—like when you broke that vase Ross had given her. Or what happened at your friend Esther's sleep-over."

Bonny's mouth dropped open in a soundless shout. "How did you know? I never told anyone."

"Because I'm a telepath," he said, "a psionic. I read minds."

Smokey could feel the jolt of Clarence's shock beneath his impassive exterior. Bonny's only reaction was curiosity and confusion.

"I don't understand," she said. "In school we learned about psionics in history class. About the Purges and how there aren't any more."

"That's not true, not completely," Bethlehem said. "My parents escaped the Purges and the extermination campaigns that continued afterward. They raised me with the secret, and when I started showing the talent they showed me how to hide it."

"Is that one of the stories we don't have time for?" Bonny asked.

"I'm afraid so," Joy said, "at least not now, but there is an important thing here. Psionic talent can be passed on, you see, just like grey eyes or a talent for math."

"I'm a telepath," Smokey admitted softly, not daring to look at Clarence, "though not as strong as Bethlehem. My talent seems to work best when I'm touching someone."

Clarence had been sitting next to her, his knee brushing against hers. He jerked as if to pull away. Then, deliberately, he wrapped his arm around her.

"Good," he said. "Then you know I truly love you."

She leaned against his arm. "I know."

Bonny tilted her head quizzically. "Am I a psionic?"

"I don't know, but probably so," Bethlehem said honestly. "Talent varies in how long it takes to show, but given your mother and what I know of your father, I'd guess that you are. How does that make you feel?"

"Weird," she said. "Special, but scared too."

"We'll talk more about this," Bethlehem promised, "but I need to go on. Humans are largely latent psionics. The theory that I prefer is that it is an old hunter-gatherer trait that went from being an asset when humans lived wild, nomadic lives to being a disadvantage when they settled down into fixed communities."

"Whoa!" Clarence interrupted. "I can guess it would

be a disadvantage, sort of like living in a small town where everybody knows—really knows—everybody else's business."

"Not every race gave up psionics," Bethlehem continued. "In fact, in some races the talent grew stronger rather than weaker."

Smokey felt her heart begin to pound, fearing, knowing, what Bethlehem was leading up to.

"You don't mean human subgroups, do you?" she said. "You mean races—aliens—separate from what evolved on Terra."

"That's right," he said. "Alien symbiotes, useless, as far as I know, on their own, but quite potent with a host. I don't know where they came from first, whether they evolved or were created. From what I can tell, they don't keep histories like we do or, I should say, they didn't. Long association with humans has changed them just as long association with them has shaped our race."

"Wait! Slow down!" Clarence almost shouted. "Do I understand you correctly? Are you really saying that there are psionic aliens out there? Like in the old thrillers?"

"Or even older myths and legends," Joy replied. "Yes, that's what he—we—are saying. They have been around since the early days of human civilization. One of the wilder theories even argues that they have had something to do with how human civilization has evolved."

"This is too much," Clarence said. "I . . . ."

"No," Smokey said anticipating his words, feeling his confusion. "Joy and Bethlehem are not crazy. I've felt—sensed—these things. Twice."

"What do they look like then?" Clarence asked. "Why haven't scientists found them?"

"They don't 'look' like much. They are tiny—microscopic," Bethlehem said, "and they break down very quickly after death—you might as well look for a soul. However, the signs of their occupancy are often apparent, especially if you know what to look for."

"Science, especially social science," Joy continued

with a dry smile, "has often credited the disproportion-
ately large number of extraordinary achievements—
good and ill—by physically abnormal people as a result
of learning to accommodate those abnormalities. The
reverse is more likely true. The symbiote is largely a
mental presence, but reaction to it can lead to physical
disfunction. Sometimes the result is illness, other times
a less apparent warping."

Smokey remember Ettienne Morrel and nodded.

Clarence growled. "I feel at a disadvantage. I don't
read minds, never have sensed one of these bogies."

"But you've seen their work," Bethlehem said. "The
murdered whore, Ami, was surely killed by a man who
had a mental symbiote."

Clarence shuddered. "Still sounds like a campfire
tale."

"With good reason," Joy said. "What better way to
trivialize inquiry than to encourage such folklore? No,
the symbiotes don't 'rule' us. I'm not even certain that
they were fully aware for millennia, but association with
humans has changed them."

"Someone started calling the mental symbiotes
'doppels'—a shortened form of the German word *dop-
pelgänger,* since they are like an invisible double within
their host," Bethlehem continued. "The doppels are not
a single, united group. From what I have learned, they
vary in personality and preferences nearly as much as
humans do. However, there are essentially three general
groupings."

He ticked them off on his fingers. "Those who are
largely not self-aware, who simply prefer to survive as
they can. We call these Riders. Then there are those who
are self-aware, but who usually limit active interference
to their own Host. We call these Guests.

"The last group is where our adversaries come from.
They're also the most comparatively recent group and
the only one that tries to coordinate a coherent effort.
Their goal is gaining control of the human race in order
to shape it into a more beneficial host group. They not

only dominate their Hosts to do this, but have found ways to manipulate through the essentially passive Riders."

"Let me guess"—Clarence laughed nervously—"you call these Drivers."

Bethlehem's grin was wry. "Among other things. They're real devils, and for the last couple of generations they have been taking the fight to those humans who know of their existence."

"We're losing," Joy said bluntly. "If we don't find a way to defeat them, within Bonny's lifetime there won't be a human without a Rider or a Driver. The human race can forget free will or anything else."

The silence that followed her words was broken by a soft, triple chime.

"That's dinner," Bethlehem said. "I wish we had time for more, but one does not keep the captain waiting."

"Is she fighting on your side?" Bonny asked as they rode the lift to the Officers' Deck.

"Yes," Bethlehem said. "In her way."

The door to the officers' mess slid open almost before Joy's hand left the call tab. The room they entered was furnished simply, with an oval table and chairs. A sideboard stood along one wall bearing glasses, bottles, a tray of delicacies.

The woman sitting at the head of the oval table was slim and fine-boned almost to the point of emaciation. Her skin was a dark, rich olive brown and her nose pronounced. Eyes and hair were both midnight black, though her hair was streaked with rust.

She was also, Smokey noted when she rose to greet them, barely four feet tall. Suspicion dawning, Smokey turned to her father, but he was already making introductions.

"Captain nu-Atcn, this is my daughter Smokey, my granddaughter, Bonny, and their friend, Clarence Beauduc." He turned to them. "This is Captain Ha'riel nu-Aten of Guillen. In her you also address a Guest, one who has been with her family for three generations."

"She's . . ." Smokey fumbled for the words to ask.

Captain nu-Aten found them for her. "That's right, Smokey. I'm possessed."

14

"IT'S REALLY NOT SO TERRIBLE," THE CAPTAIN explained when the uproar her announcement triggered had been stilled. "If 'my' Guest had not chosen to make itself known to my father, I doubt we would have ever known it was there."

Smokey forced herself to chew a mouthful of the excellent curried rice and chicken that she had been served, calming herself so she would not sound hysterical when she spoke.

"I don't mean to sound rude, but how do you talk with it? I mean, if it's part of your brain—isn't that like schizophrenia?"

"Probably many cases of mental illness are people who have doppels they cannot deal with," nu-Aten replied. "However, Guillen has a strong mystical tradition running alongside the scientific. My father had the mental map to deal with the concept and his Guest was very careful in how it made itself known. When we say that we've had our Guest in the family since my grandparents' day, that's accurate with some qualification. The doppels can reproduce and what I have is a copy of my father's Guest. One of my grandparents' Guests transferred to one of my siblings. The other died with my grandmother in the vehicle accident that killed her."

"Why did the Guest contact your father if it had been there all along?" Clarence asked.

"To get help with the War, of course." The captain poured herself wine.

"The doppels fight each other?" Bonny asked, her spoonful of pineapple poised in midair.

"Yes," nu-Aten explained patiently. "I think that Bethlehem told you, the doppels differ as often as humans in their opinions on issues. My Guest belongs to a faction that wants the symbiotic relationship to continue without overt coercion of the Host. With that belief, it hardly could have tried to control my father like some sort of organic robot."

"No, I guess not," Smokey said. "But don't you feel strange, knowing that there is a creature in your head?"

"Don't you feel strange knowing that you can read other people's thoughts?"

"Yes." Smokey dared her to answer as honestly.

"Well then, yes, I do," nu-Aten shrugged, "but it's been a part of me since I was small and has helped me far more than it has harmed me. I live with it."

Smokey swallowed a horde of other questions, most of which she suspected were impolite. Watching Clarence chase a grain of rice around his plate, she suspected that he was doing the same.

"The Psionics Project may have been the turning point in our relationship with the symbiotes." Bethlehem addressed the tension by lecturing. "When humans began to accept and cultivate those dormant talents, suddenly the doppels' presence was no longer concealed. Perhaps because humans were ill equipped to deal with those abilities in any case—my parents both had stories of colleagues who went mad when they were Awakened—learning of the presence of alien minds coexisting with human minds caused not just a reaction, but a revulsion."

Captain nu-Aten pressed a button by her seat and a covered tray rose from the recessed center of the table.

"I have dispensed with the steward, so dessert is simple. I did learn, however, that Bonny liked ice cream."

"This revulsion," Clarence asked as they served themselves, "and the doppels' desire to defend themselves from it, could this be the source of the Psionic Purges? There are many theories, but no one has ever developed a conclusive explanation as to why public reaction to psionics switched so quickly from acceptance, curiosity, and even eagerness to a jihad against those with the Talent."

"Your training in human cultures shows," Captain nu-Aten said with an approving nod. "I believe that is precisely the source of the Purges. For perhaps the first time in all of their coexistence with humans, the majority of the doppels acted in concert. Hosts were encouraged in certain ways of thought. The more susceptible—those who were already apprehensive about the wisdom of awakening the Talents—became agents of the Purges."

"And afterward," Smokey guessed, "there were those doppels who wanted to continue manipulating human affairs on the grand scale. These became the Drivers."

Bethlehem nodded. "There had always been doppels who wanted a larger range of control, but they had never had any reason to unite. Now, not only had they united, but they had even found a class of humans who made better than average tools, those who, in a sense, already had largely marked human culture."

"The media?" Clarence guessed.

"No," nu-Aten said. "You are too close to see the answer. The best tools were scientists, especially those with a bent for the social sciences. Not only did they regularly make new discoveries that reshaped how basic facts and elements were perceived, but they had the talent for revealing the implications of those discoveries to other humans."

"But," Smokey said, "I don't understand why all of a sudden I am being framed as a slasher."

"You detected the presence of a Driver," Joy said, "and then most certainly gave yourself away. Only one kind of human can threaten the Drivers' plans, and that is a psionic—especially a telepath or empath. When you were revealed—or at least suspected—as such, they had to discredit you. That would mean creating a situation so horrid that even if you had said anything or left any records, your words would be discredited."

"Left?" Smokey said.

"After you had been sufficiently discredited," Bethlehem answered steadily, "you would have died, probably a 'suicide.' "

"I didn't think that I gave myself away," Smokey protested. "I was shocked the first time, but I was almost ready for it with Morrel, especially when I saw him in Lee's company. I was rather abrupt with Lee, but he was a brute. No decent whore would have tolerated his behavior."

"You forget," Bethlehem said. "The doppels have much more experience than humans at detecting Talents. You caught all the little signals that I let 'slip' when we were on our hadj. You don't know enough about how to hide the signals. I imagine that this 'Lee' was fairly certain why he revolted you."

"And if he learned who your parents are," Joy said, "ironically that would have sealed the case against you."

"You've been fighting these doppels for how long?" Smokey asked.

"Since a few years after you ran away, long before Bonny was born," Joy replied. "Bethlehem had held suspicions, but he didn't act on them until they started after him."

"I am a psionic," he said with a shrug. "When they learned of me, they set out to exterminate me. I am a public person because of my association with your mother. As with you, the need to discredit me meant that any murder needed to be prepared for in stages. I got wind of their plans and took out insurance against them."

Catching the expression of concern that flickered across Joy's face, Smokey decided that she didn't want to know what that insurance entailed.

Captain nu-Aten rapped her glass with her ice-cream

spoon. "We need to redirect our discussion. No matter how fascinating the past is, we need to prepare for the present."

Bethlehem nodded, a deferential gesture.

"As Captain nu-Aten noted before, scientists fascinate the Drivers. Lately, they have instigated a campaign to inhabit potentially useful humans. They'll often entrap them," he sighed. "The doppels don't take a human host easily. It's especially hard for the Drivers, who are very active in their possession. Usually, the humans need to welcome them, consciously or not."

"Three times?" Clarence said, trying to chuckle.

"Something like that," Bethlehem said. "In fact, that may be the source of those legends, as you are beginning to suspect. Now, one of the favorite ways for this entrapment to occur is to leave some puzzle and then 'assist' those who are solving it. This helps the doppel get a hold, but often its position is not yet secure."

"Wait," Clarence said. "A puzzle?"

"That's not a very clear explanation," Joy admitted. "It's our shorthand. Usually there's some artifact, mechanical or electronic, often with an apparently alien mark."

"They'd all want to be the first to figure it out," Bonny said, "and get all the prizes. I've seen this in class. People don't like to share ideas because you might steal them—Lobachevsky's Lesson."

"Puzzles!" Smokey drummed a triumphant tattoo on the tabletop. "That explains the Wickerwork situation."

Briefly she summarized what she had learned in doing her research for Gary. Her parents and Captain nu-Aten showed no surprise, only recognition of the pattern.

"Yes, that is the way it happens," Captain nu-Aten said. "Tell me, did you hear anything about recent mental breakdowns from anyone in that group?"

"No . . . Wait, yes, there was a woman, I think. She wasn't one of the *Hollyhock*'s crew, but she had a steady relationship with Morrel. After they stopped keeping company, she had a severe breakdown."

Again, nu-Aten nodded. "That also fits the pattern.

Not everyone can adapt as a Host to a doppel. As best as we can tell, the failure rate for Driver Hosts is the highest."

"No wonder," Clarence said. "They're not just living in your brain, begging your pardon, Captain, but they're messing with how you think. If they want you to do something you think is wrong, it could make you crazy."

"Many Drivers," Joy added, "rescue their Hosts from a breakdown through misdirection—representing themselves as angels or such. Others, the crudest operators, manage by distracting the Host through amplifying some basic animal urge."

"Like for sex," Smokey said, "or food."

"That's right," Joy said. "Bethlehem tends to avoid physical contact—a throwback to the years of his Awakening. In your line of work perhaps it was inevitable that not only would you encounter a doppel, but that you would know one when you met."

Smokey shuddered, remembering Lee's hard, crude fucking. Fleetingly, she wondered what he had been like before the Driver dominated him. She let the thought go for Bonny was asking the question she herself had been reluctant to ask.

"Grandpapa, you said that this is a war, but"—the girl wrinkled up her nose and spoke very quickly—"but we're not winning, are we? How can we win if they're in our heads?"

The last words were almost whispered. Bethlehem traded a solemn glance with Joy and then reached across the table and took Bonny's hands.

"No, Bon-ton, we're not winning, not in the sense that we're stopping the Drivers. We're not losing though, not as long as we can do things like save Smokey or warn others."

"As to how we can win," Captain nu-Aten continued, "just because the doppels are in the minds of their Hosts does not mean that they are invulnerable."

She rubbed her temples as if meditating on the wisdom of explaining this complex problem to a nine-year-old. Then she went on.

"Killing the Host will often kill the doppel. I say 'often' because the rare doppel can flee to another Host if one is available. However, that is such a drastic course of action that we use it only when we must. Even the Drivers don't resort to mass homicide."

"I see," Bonny said with charming gravity. "What can we do?"

"From my family's experience as Hosts," Captain nu-Aten replied, "we know that the doppels can voluntarily transfer Hosts. One of our projects is trying to learn how this process can be triggered involuntarily. Then we can trap the Drivers ourselves after forcing them from their Hosts."

"That sounds promising," Smokey said.

"It is more promising than practical at this point," Bethlehem admitted. "Our prototypes have either failed to oust the Driver or they have ousted the Driver but left the Host somewhat insane."

"Somewhat?" Clarence queried, disbelief framed in the arch of his eyebrows. "What do you mean by 'somewhat'?"

"Some are left with a depression-like apathy that, as best as we can tell, comes from the loss of the Driver as a motivator," Captain nu-Aten replied. "Others persist in a variety of socially objectionable habits. The best we have been able to achieve has been a complete rejection of the experience. Memory regresses to the point when the Driver took control and nothing of the time under direction remains at all."

"This amnesia response," Joy added, "is the most common reaction when a Rider is removed."

"Are these reactions typical of what happens when a Guest transfers Hosts?" Clarence asked.

"No." Captain nu-Aten's lips curved in an odd smile. "Not to the best of either of our knowledge."

"At our next port of call," Bethlehem said, "there is a base of operations for our action—our war. It is an outgrowth of the Psionic Underground that developed in response to the Purges. However, this branch is restricted to those who have had some experience with the doppels. We're taking you there. You'll be both safe and in a position to be helpful."

Smokey studied her lover and her daughter. Clarence held the lower portion of his face in one broad, black hand. His warm brown eyes were steady. As clearly as if she was reading his mind, Smokey could tell that he was unshaken in his determination to remain with her.

Bonny chewed on the edge of her ice-cream spoon, her eyes unfocused yet strangely thoughtful. Smokey touched her hand and sensed no confusion or fear, just a trust in her grown-ups and an eagerness to help. Beneath this ran the abstract impressions she often found when Bonny was at work on her mathematics.

Bethlehem's lips curved in a stiff smile and she blushed hotly as she realized that he could possibly read her thoughts. She resolved immediately both to learn the low-level babble that Joy had perfected and to be more careful about her body language.

"How do you feel about our plan, Smokey?" Joy asked. "Will you do as we ask?"

"The only alternative," Smokey replied, "would be to return to Arizona where the police force is looking to lock me up for murders that I didn't commit. And I can't ignore what you've told us."

"We'll be working on clearing your record," Captain nu-Aten interjected. "This is not a permanent exile."

Smokey hid her relief. She had been striving to conceal images of spending the rest of her life within this elaborate Psionic Underground. Quietly, she resented the sense that she was no longer her own woman, that Mama and Papa were back in control and she the child again.

"Good," was all of her thoughts that she verbalized, "but I insist on helping, not just hiding out. I don't think I could ever do my job again knowing that I might touch a Driven mind."

"Then we are settled"—the captain pushed her chair back from the table—"and my duties call. You are free to roam the passenger sections of the ship. You will find that a suite has been reserved for you. Enjoy the *Ibn Battuta*'s hospitality. I am certain that we will meet again."

When she had departed, Bethlehem gave each of them a key card. "This will allow you into the suite which has been reserved for you and into all first-class accommodations. Despite her friendliness this evening, Captain nu-Aten runs a very tight ship. I suggest you review all the rules posted in the suite."

"Grandpapa," Bonny said, "will I be able to use a computer? I don't want to get too behind in school."

Bethlehem grinned. "Yes, there is usually computer time available. I'll even see if I can get you into the shipboard V-net classes, if you want."

"That would be great," Bonny replied.

Standing beside her daughter, hand just brushing her arm, Smokey caught a fleeting glimpse of something that was gone before she could trace it. Looking at Bethlehem, still beaming like any proud grandfather, she quickly hid her suspicions. Living near another telepath was going to be tougher than she had thought. She could do it; she just wondered if Bethlehem's belief in free will extended to his own daughter.

15

THE STARLINER'S SCHEDULE COULD HAVE RUN twenty-four hours without division, and for the crew Smokey knew that it did. For the passengers, however, there was artificial day and night designated less by light or its absence than by elaborate meals, culminating in an evening banquet, and entertainments scheduled to give the illusion of daytime play and nighttime formality.

Mornings were often spent on lessons. From her father, Smokey learned a variety of ways to shield and conceal her thoughts, ways much more elaborate than the light shield that she had taught herself. Bethlehem also drilled her on a variety of subtle signals that psionics used with each other and in a bit of telepathic etiquette.

During one of these lessons, growing frustrated with the constant drill, Smokey stomped her foot and kicked the sandal she had been dangling from her toes across the room—acting for all the world as if she was Bonny's age rather than a mature professional.

"Smokey!" Bethlehem sounded more weary than upset, but Smokey caught a chiding note nonetheless.

"'Smokey!'" she repeated mockingly. "'Smokey!' I'm so damned tired of this shit. Over and over the same sun-scorched stuff! 'Clear your mind, Smokey. Focus on something neutral, something that won't draw attention to the flow of thought going on underneath.' It's so gritty! So . . ."

Her outburst trailed off when she looked at Bethlehem. The expression on his rugged features was amused, rather than angry. She had seen the same patient expression on her own face when Bonny grew cranky. And that was precisely what she was being—a cranky child.

With a burst of insight, she realized that she never would have behaved so rudely toward any other person. Had another instructor kept her too long, she would have found a reason to excuse herself—an appointment, a headache, anything. Only because Bethlehem was her father had she permitted herself a temper tantrum.

A hot flash flooded her cheeks, and she didn't need to touch Bethlehem to know that he had followed her train of thought perfectly. Yet the smile he gave her was rueful rather than smug.

"Have I been pushing you too hard, Smokey?" he asked softly. "Have I forgotten that you have limits, too? If so, I apologize . . . It's simply that . . . well, you're my daughter. I have so much more incentive for teaching you than I have ever had with another student. I'm sorry."

"Me, too," she said. "Really."

"Let's take a break then," he said. "There's some white wine in the cooling unit."

"Sounds good," she agreed.

The wine wasn't bad, the break even better. Leaning back in comfortable chairs, the stars glimmering through the viewport in front of them, they shared silence.

"It was a little like the emperor's deathbed for me," Bethlehem said after a time.

"From the story of the Chinese nightingale?" Smokey asked. "What was it like?"

"My awakening as a telepath," Bethlehem said. "Do you remember how in the story the emperor woke up and found Death sitting on his chest and all his good and bad deeds whispering at him from all around him?"

" 'Remember! Remember!' " Smokey recited, doing just that. "Is that what you mean?"

"That—yes—and, now that I think about it, the poem I read you years ago by Vachel Lindsay called 'The Chinese Nightingale.' Really, it doesn't have anything in common with the fairy tale except for a coincidence of title, but the two stories are linked in my mind because both of them deal with memory—memory and nightingales."

Smokey thought for a moment. "The Lindsay poem, that's the one about the Chinese launderer who listens to a magical recitation of events that may have happened to him in another incarnation, right?"

"That's it," Bethlehem agreed. "The beautiful princess, the wizard, and the dragon that flies out of the flag to carry them to a hidden palace. I'm pleased that you remember it."

Smokey beamed.

"From the time I was in my early teens," Bethlehem continued, "I knew that I could read minds. I'm not boasting, but even then, untrained and uncertain, I was a far stronger telepath than you are now. I had a natural gift for shielding myself, too, which is probably all that saved my life."

"Uh, huh," Smokey said, pouring herself a touch more wine. "What does this have to do with Chinese nightingales?"

Bethlehem smiled. "You won't forgive me my flight of fancy, will you? Very well. Like Chang the launderer or the emperor on his deathbed, I started by hearing whispers, whispers that seemed to me at first to be telling me things about my own life. After I had been hearing them for a while, I began to realize that what I was hearing was not magical voices, but the thoughts of other people—I realized that I was a psionic."

Remembering her own experience with her awakening Talent, Smokey nodded.

"You knew you were a psionic?" she asked. "I mean, you didn't think you were crazy or something?"

"No, I knew," Bethlehem said. "On Old Terra, where

I was born, urban lore was filled with tales of pre-Purge psionics who exploited the honest folk around them. Like lots of kids, I went from fearing them (along with creatures under the bed), to admiring them, to even wanting to emulate them."

Smokey smiled. "I'm always amazed by the love-hate relationship children have with goblins, gangsters, and other terrors."

"The terrors have power," Bethlehem said, "and a child does not, so, of course, the terrors are something to be admired even as they are feared."

"And what happened to you?" Smokey asked. "After you learned you were a telepath? What did you do with the gift?"

"Nearly got myself killed," Bethlehem said. "I was young, arrogant, and far, far too confident that the prejudice against psionics that I knew existed would apply to everyone except me."

"Wait a moment," Smokey said. "When you were briefing us before, you said that your parents were psionics, that they had trained you and taught you how to conceal the talent."

Bethlehem grinned sheepishly. "That . . . Well, Smokey, I bent the truth a little. I didn't want my behavior to be a bad example to Bonny. You see, everything happened just as I said with one omission. I left out the word 'tried.' My parents *tried* to teach me, but at first I was a recalcitrant student.

"I started using the Talent to get by without working," Bethlehem admitted frankly. "Studying seemed to be a waste of time when I could pick answers out of an instructor's head. I feigned dyslexia so that I was safe from computerized or written exams. Classroom questions were even easier.

"But I was too clever—and too lazy—for my own good. Rather than taking the time to rephrase what I saw in an instructor's mind, I would give it back in nearly identical form. Smug and sassy, sometimes I would hint at secrets they wouldn't like revealed. Nothing serious, but it was amazing how uncomfortable an instructor would get if I hinted at how pretty a particular girl looked—especially a girl the instructor had been indulging in a few innocent fantasies about. Or if I touched on a bit of institutional politics that, realistically, I should have known nothing about."

"They caught on," Smokey said. "Didn't they?"

Bethlehem twirled his wineglass between his palms. "That's right. There was a female instructor I had a thing for—she was older than I realized, and quite pretty in a suave, sophisticated fashion that my adolescent self found incredibly attractive. To make a long story short, I started making her gifts of bits of gossip. When I gave her a rumor that I had plucked from another instructor's mind, she added it to some private suppositions of her own and . . ."

"Why didn't you read her suspicions?" Smokey interrupted. "Why didn't you catch that you were putting yourself into danger?"

"I did and I didn't," Bethlehem said. "I could tell she was interested in me, but in my naive machismo, it never occurred to me that her interest could be anything but a reflection of my own simple, carnal obsession."

Smokey nodded, recalling the scattered shapes of thoughts when the thinker was not actively putting them into words.

"She also may have had some basic idea of how to create a shield," Bethlehem continued. "In fact, I suspect that she did. Such knowledge was more widely available in those days when the Purge was fresher in the memory. She may have even received some basic training in her youth."

He sighed. "In any case, naive fool that I was, I continued scribbling my own death warrant on every test I took, on every oral examination that I was presented. The enforcement officers came calling for me one day after school. I had just done triumphantly well on a test—a test that unknown to me had been created to provide definitive proof that I was reading the answers from my examiner's mind rather than drawing on my own knowledge. They took me to a very private, very secluded prison complex, and there I heard the whispering of minds within minds for the first time."

Smokey shivered.

"My interrogator was possessed of a Guest, a Guest who had become convinced that non-Guest–directed psionics were a threat to the continued existence of the doppels."

Smokey grinned. "Probably correctly, huh?"

"Probably," Bethlehem said. "I was reluctant to accept one—I fought it like the devil, which, to me, it was in a way. When I was worn-out, shaken to tears that shattered my self-possession to the core, then I would hear the whispers, whispers that reminded me of all, good and ill, that I had done with my Talent."

He paused, finished his wine. "Mostly, to be honest, it was ill rather than good."

"I, uh, I understand that the agents of the Purge usually killed the psionics," Smokey said hesitantly. "Not that I'm complaining or anything, but how did you survive?"

"Unintentionally, the same instructor who had turned me in also helped to keep me alive," Bethlehem said. "She would come to visit me, to check on the progress of my 'reeducation' and 'resocialization.' The Purge, remember, was official; the slaughter of the psionics was not. I was young—the word given to the public was that research was being done on how to shut down the psionic centers within the brain."

"How did they explain the hundreds of psionics who were killed?" Smokey asked. "Even my history books mentioned those."

"The deaths were usually explained as the result of the psionic resisting incarceration," Bethlehem said. "Sometimes videos would be shown of the psionic using 'dangerous psychic powers.' It fed the fear and kept to a minimum the suspicion that genocide was the goal of the Purges."

"So the Guest you mentioned wanted you to take on a Guest of your own," Smokey said, still puzzled. "Why? Didn't you say that psionics are a threat to the doppels?"

"Uncontrolled psionics are. Controlled or—shall I say—directed, a psionic is a valuable ally. However, the chances of one accepting and adapting to a Guest are very slim."

Remembering her own experiences, Smokey nodded. "I can see why this would be the case. To have something whispering within your mind and to know that it was not really a part of you . . ."

Bethlehem filled his goblet, then with a shrug drained the rest of the bottle directly into his mouth. With a faint shiver, he continued speaking.

"I listened to the whispers night after night, day after day, and like the Chinese emperor in the fairy tale the weight of Death grew heavier and heavier on my chest. At last, my nightingale came to sing for me."

Smokey stared at him, uncertain if he had gone quite mad. "Your nightingale, Papa?"

"You remember the fairy tale, Smokey," he said. "When the emperor was on his deathbed, the nightingale he had banished in his pride and arrogance returned to sing for him. One by one, the nightingale convinced Death to relinquish the things it had taken from the emperor."

"His sword, his flag, his . . . something," Smokey said. "I remember. Who was your nightingale?"

"My parents," Bethlehem said. "When I had arrogantly rejected their teachings I had put them into danger as well. My mother permitted herself to be captured. Once she was in the cellblock, she was able to check the place out without fear of discovery. My mother was one of the original creations of the Psionics Project—one of the younger ones. She had escaped in the early days of the Purge and created a new identity for herself. The fire at the facility where she had been raised helped a great deal."

He placed his hand on Smokey's knee and through the link she saw red-and-orange flames enveloping a multiunit geodesic dome complex. Even as she watched, glass burst outward, transformed into a splintered glass-fall by the heat within. The image was without sound, but Smokey could easily imagine the screams of the burning man who fled out of another door, trailing flames behind him like a comet's tail.

Watching horrified, Smokey knew that these images were no creation of Bethlehem's but a memory from her grandmother, macabre family snapshots made possible by the psionic power that had passed from mother to son to granddaughter in a somewhat diluted form. The last image was of a young man, just out of gangly adolescence, reaching out his hands and pulling the viewer into safety.

"My father," Bethlehem said, "a pyrokinetic, and, I suspect, the one largely responsible for starting the fire that destroyed the complex. That fire made it impossible for the directors of the Purge to know precisely how many of the psionics had survived. It also destroyed many core records. While these two factors allowed even some of the powerful psionics to escape the Purge, they also contributed to warping the Purge into the witch-hunt that continues—in a modified form—into today."

Smokey looked down at her fingertips. Could she generate fire with her mind? What an odd thought.

"Papa? My name? Is it? Am I?"

Bethlehem smiled. "Yes, you are named, in a sense, for your grandfather, my father. As far as I know, you did not inherit his talent for starting conventional fires. Unconventional ones . . ."

He trailed off and Smokey blushed as she realized that he was alluding to her fame within her profession. Quickly, not completely certain why she was embarrassed, she changed the subject.

"So your mother let herself be caught so that she could come to your rescue," she prompted.

"That's right. My mother was a powerful telepath but, more importantly, she was also a clairvoyant and a telekinetic." Bethlehem shook his head in awe. "She was one of the Project's great triumphs, but also a person they could not hope to handle. Funneling her telepathic contact with me into a tight channel that even another telepath in contact with me at the time could not have sensed, my mother burnt into my mind a schema of the complex in which we were imprisoned."

Smokey tilted her head to one side. "Wait, Papa. If she was so powerful, why did she need to let herself be captured?"

Bethlehem chuckled, "She was powerful, but she was not a goddess. Her telepathy was most effective at short range, but she could have 'spoken' with me from outside. However, in order to clairvoyantly inspect the complex and to telekinetically affect the systems, she needed to be inside."

"I see," Smokey said. "The power certainly hasn't passed on to her descendants in the same intensity, has it?"

"No," Bethlehem said. "I suspect that she was a fluke and to have her talents maximized in the next generations, she would have had to be bred to a carefully chosen male, not be permitted to chose her own partner."

Smokey felt a flicker of sorrow for this grandmother she had never known, this rebellious girl with all the strange powers. Rebellion, at least, seemed to run in the family along with reading minds. She grinned at the notion.

"I interrupted again, Papa," she said. "Finish telling me how my grandmother rescued you."

"Working with my father, she arranged to have a fire started at the fringes of the complex," Bethlehem continued, his fingers steepled before his face. "When enough of the prison's resources had been diverted, she did something to the power system in the cellblock where we were imprisoned. That was my signal to flee and I did. Eventually, the three of us were reunited outside and went into hiding offworld, on Icedrake, if you want to know. That's where I finished growing up, got my training, and eventually met your mother. The rest is pretty much like you were told when you were growing up."

"Except that you were a telepath, using your Talent for mother's act," Smokey said. "Wasn't that dangerous?"

"It was," Bethlehem said, "but the wonderful thing about technology is that almost anything we did can be explained as microcircuitry and training."

"Still . . ." Smokey trailed off. "I'll never feel that you are safe again."

"I've felt that way about you for years," Bethlehem admitted, "but what other choice do we have? We could live in hideaways like the one I grew up in, I suppose, but that's not much of a life. Besides, now that the doppels are growing bolder—more sophisticated in their search for allies—I think hideouts have their place, but so does scattering our forces."

Smokey was in a thoughtful mood when she returned to her quarters. Bonny was absorbed by the V-net, much as she had been at home, but Smokey suspected that her attention was not always on classwork.

To keep Bonny from becoming a hermit, Smokey usually spent a part of each afternoon enjoying the amenities of the luxury liner with her. Sometimes Clarence joined them; other times, aware that he was a new member of their family group, he bowed out. In the evening, as if returning Clarence's courtesy, Bonny reimmersed herself in the V, leaving her adults to their own devices.

One afternoon, returning from playing water polo with Bonny, Smokey found Clarence seated at the round table in the front room of their suite, an assortment of cardboard rectangles spread out in front of him.

He looked up and smiled when he saw her, his gaze dropping to linger where the tight fabric of her one-piece swimsuit outlined her breasts before continuing his inspection down the mesh vee that stopped just below her navel.

"Damn, Smokey-jo, if you don't look good enough to eat," he said, rising, "and since Bonny isn't here, I may do just that."

Smokey giggled and reached behind her to flip the security lock on the door.

"You promise the nicest things," she answered. "Bonny is with her grandmother and should be so for quite a while. Let's see how seriously you mean what you say."

"Oh, I'm quite serious," he said, his accent thickening as he rolled the straps of her suit off of her shoulders. "You just set yourself on the edge of the table and mind the cards."

For a long interlude, Smokey wasn't minding much of anything, except for the touch of Clarence's mouth between her legs. Eventually, with a passion that did not quite forget tenderness, he laid her on the tabletop.

"Mind the cards," she said softly.

When they had finished making love, they slid from the table to sit on the floor. Holding Smokey in his lap, Clarence peeled a few cards from where they had stuck to her damp skin.

"Not too badly damaged," he said, holding up the jack of hearts for her inspection. "I wouldn't play poker with it, but it'd do for a practice deck."

Smokey took the card from him and ran its edge along his spine, feeling him shiver pleasantly in response.

"What were you doing with a deck of cards, anyway?" she asked. "There are good solitaire programs in the table terminal."

Clarence kissed her. "I wasn't playing solitaire. I was working through a basic guide to some poker variants."

"Poker?" Smokey said. "That's right, it was played with cards wasn't it? Do they still play it that way on Old Terra?"

"Yes, my sweet colonial barbarian, that's the only way to play. If you play a VT game, all the fun gets taken out."

"How?"

"Harder to cheat." He grinned. "Damn near impossible to cheat, actually, unless it's a full VR rig, and then you might as well be playing with real cards."

"Clarence, you can't be so bored that you want to start cheating at cards—are you?" she asked, suddenly worried.

He squeezed her. "Not at all, darling. The social coordinator has announced that any and all of the passengers can participate in programming by giving a lecture or demonstration. I've already agreed to do some history lectures, but I thought that might be a bit dry. Then I remembered some card tricks, and that seemed the way to go."

"Why not play the piano?"

"There are other musicians on board—professionals," he answered. "I suspect that I am the only card shark—at least the only one who will admit it."

Smokey kissed the tip of his nose. "You get more and more fun the longer I know you. Show me some of your tricks."

"Later," he promised. "I have something else I'd rather do with this bit of private time."

Clarence's card tricks were not the only interesting demonstration—although he was among the favorites, attracting imitators and admirers. Many of the first-class passengers were experts on something or other—wet water sailing, philately, snow skiing, and other, stranger, things. Hearing these often dull people wax eloquent on their particular hobby, the competition to provide a memorable entertainment spread beyond the lectures themselves and added a certain spice to the conversations at the first-class table.

Of course, the ship was not without its preplanned entertainment and education series. Smokey signed up for a refresher in first aid and another in ancient history. A large incentive for joining the latter class was the opportunity to see Clarence perform in his element. He proved to be an interesting and witty lecturer. Smokey felt almost embarrassedly proud of him.

And when everything else paled, she could still go and watch Joy in Motion perform—a thing that became more and more fascinating as Smokey came to appreciate the intricate byplay between her parents that made the act possible.

Joy was spinning in midair when Smokey felt the hand on her shoulder and the cool pressure of something shoved into the base of her neck. She twisted her head slightly to the left and saw a man in a dark blue uniform with a professionally indifferent expression standing behind her. The thoughts that trickled through to her were cold and focused, with the thinnest wail of a scream beneath.

"Rise. Excuse yourself. Or I will harm you."

The emotions undercurrenting the command left her with no doubt that he planned to do as he said. But. But there was a doubt—that wailing beneath the command.

Beside her, Clarence was watching Joy cavort, his hands moving to conduct an invisible orchestra. Bonny, at least, was in her room. She wouldn't have to see what would happen if Smokey guessed wrong.

So Smokey did the hardest thing that she had ever done. With the cold weapon pressing at her neck, she simply sat still. An urge to sneeze, as inappropriate as a giggle in church, rose in her nose. She fought it down and sat.

Indecision bubbled through her would-be captor's mind. As soon as she sensed that he suspected he might have walked up to the wrong woman in the dimly lit theater, she shifted her weight and snuggled closer to Clarence. Very pleased, Clarence slipped his arm around her waist. These two motions effectively moved her clear of the probable weapon.

Doubting now, and unable to touch Smokey again without alerting Clarence, the man in navy blue moved away. When Smokey risked a glance back into the crowd, she couldn't tell which of the impassively attentive staff might have been the one who had accosted her.

Turning her attention back to the stage, she realized

that Joy was in mid-somersault and that only a few minutes at most could have gone by. Aware that she could not speak with Bethlehem or Joy until after the performance, she buried her fear in a mental shelter she crafted from Clarence's pleasure, from the music, and from the odd, abstract contortions of Joy in Motion.

When she told her parents what had happened, Bethlehem expressed polite disbelief, but nothing like the outrage Smokey had expected. Only when she continued to insist did he agree to make an appointment with Captain nu-Aten—and even that had to wait until the next morning.

"That's impossible," Captain nu-Aten insisted after Smokey had repeated her tale of what had happened. "You are jumping at shadows. My Guest would know if there was another of its race inhabiting one of my crew. It assures me that it has detected no newcomers."

Smokey suppressed an indignant retort, but she saw the lines in Bethlehem's face deepen and knew that her thought had not escaped him. What if the captain's Guest was misleading her?

Instead, Smokey voiced a safer alternative. "Could the man who accosted me have been an impostor—someone wearing a purser's staff uniform?"

"That is possible," the captain admitted, "though I do normally try to meet every passenger so that my Guest can whiff 'em. Someone could have dodged me. I'll see what I can learn."

Smokey relaxed slightly as Bethlehem and the captain continued to discuss the problem. She was certain the captain would find nothing. However, at least her experience was no longer being dismissed as the hallucination of an unbalanced and excitable whore.

Waiting until there was a break in their low-voiced conference, she asked, "How long until the ship reaches Guillen?"

"Several days, yet," Bethlehem said. "Not bored, are you?"

"Not precisely," she said, though, effectively, she was.

Despite Clarence's excellent companionship, she missed the byplay of the brothel and the wheedling of secrets from her clients' minds. Returning to her suite, she found Clarence absorbed in compiling notes from his research on Arizona, and Bonny gone. The note flickering on the girl's screen said that she had gone swimming with Joy.

Restlessly, Smokey left the suite and prowled the corridors, ending up at last at an upscale passengers' lounge she hadn't been in before. Semideserted at this early hour, something about the opulent furnishings and soft music filtering in from no single source reminded her of the Gentlemen's Parlor. Grinning slightly, she sauntered in and took one of the seats near the bar.

The bartender only nodded, but not long after she entered a man with a broad, fleshy face came over, ostensibly to refill his drink. He brushed against her just enough to slosh some of the liquor from her newly filled glass.

She gave a soft cry as of dismay and he halted immediately. One hand mopped up the spill, the other patted her arm.

"My pardons, dear lady," he said, showing teeth as white and even as a strip of marble tombstones. "I have upset your glass and I fear your lovely self as well."

Smokey smiled, warmed by his spreading lust. "I'll forgive you, if you'll keep me company while I finish what's left of my drink."

"Ah, but you must permit me to buy you another." He signaled the bartender and then took a seat next to her. "I am Patrick ben Garibaldi, late of Icedrake."

Smokey muttered an introduction in return and felt Patrick's slight embarrassment that he had not quite caught her name. This did not stop him from putting a hand on her knee, then around her shoulders. By the time the drinks were finished, she had learned that he was a dealer in gemstones and jewelry, and he was suggesting that she come by and see the samples in his cabin.

She allowed him to coax her, suppressing a desire to purr as his simple, uncomplicated attention stroked her vanity. In his cabin, she eventually did see his samples and even accepted an ornate gold and ruby broach.

His gratitude—even awe—at her polished performance once they were in bed was genuine and she took the gift as her due. As she sauntered back to her own suite, she reflected how much simpler sex was than love, that maybe it was even preferable. Still, as she tucked the broach away, she decided that she wouldn't tell Clarence where it had come from. She didn't think he'd understand.

Staring at her reflection in the mirror, she wondered if she did herself. Surely her self-image wasn't so lousy that she had to lay a trick just to prove to herself that she wasn't . . . forgotten? An angry child jealous that she wasn't the center of her parents' universe?

She swallowed hard, not liking the thought. Was she that messed up? She hadn't thought so, hadn't had reason to until Joy and Bethlehem had come crashing in to ruin her peaceful life. She'd been happy—just her and Bonny and Wintering in their cozy home. A pleasant job, just the right amount of excitement, notoriety, adulation. Then her parents had to come along and mess it up, drag her back onto one of these damned starliners. Break up her home, lose her job.

Save her life.

She stopped, honestly assessing her outburst. Joy and Bethlehem had saved her and probably saved Bonny, too. If that galled, if that dependency rubbed some old memories raw and seasoned them with rock salt and lemon, well, she needed to find a solution.

Dependency and the sense that all her fragile self-respect would vanish if she just went back to being Joy in Motion's daughter were her enemies. Screwing merchants wasn't going to help with that. The only thing that would help would be if she could beat them at their own game.

Beat them?

She looked around the plush and gilt suite, all soft corners and cushioned edges. How could she fight a fight that no one else was fighting?

The thought made her uncomfortable. Pacing the length of the narrow bedroom, she focused her attention until all she was concentrating on was the doppels, most specifically on how they could be dealt with.

Gradually, her pacing slowed. Her grey eyes became a thin iron line. For a long time she stood, a statue in silver and shadow. Even when Bonny came skipping and dripping to take her to dinner Smokey's expression remained thoughtful.

"Bonita," she said after the main course had been cleared away and most of the other diners had left, "you haven't just been doing homework, have you?"

Bonny sculpted swirls in her banana split. "No."

"Want to tell me about it?"

The girl considered, ice cream dripping off her spoon into thick, sticky pools. Around their island of silence, the diners continued animated conversation. Clarence had crossed the room to discuss air current symphonies with a group of people in the floor-length kimonos of the plum-No philosophers.

Smokey tapped Bonny softly on the back of the hand that curled around her spoon handle. "Want to come for a walk?"

Bonny cut out a chunk of banana, ate it, then pushed back her chair. "Have you seen their setting room?"

"Show me," Smokey suggested, "and maybe it's a good place to talk."

The "setting room" that Bonny took her to turned out to be the liner's observation deck. At this point in the voyage, when the vista was unchanging midnight sliced by streaks of light, the room was almost deserted. Yet, to an Arizonan, for whom the setting room was the heart of the house, the vast, bare room was curiously homey.

They took two curved seats with a low table between them. Leaning back into the firm but soft sofa back,

Smokey toed off her shoes and put her feet onto the table. Bonny started to imitate her, then got up and crossed to Smokey's chair.

"Is there room for me, Mama?"

"Sure, I'll hitch over."

She tossed an arm out behind Bonny. The girl snuggled close then and pillowed her head against the offered arm.

"Can you read my mind when we sit like this, Mama?"

Smokey probed lightly and was surprised to find only curiosity, not fear, behind the question.

"I could, but if you weren't thinking about anything in particular, I would have trouble finding out about what I might want to know." She considered how much to explain. "With my clients, I would often ask questions about something that I thought would get them thinking about what I wanted to know."

"But that they wouldn't want to tell you?"

"Right."

"So you still need me to tell you stuff?"

"Yeah, I'd rather if you just told me."

"I've been trying to figure out," Bonny paused, then nestled closer. "Grandpapa doesn't know what the doppels are—I mean what they look like or anything."

"Doesn't know? Why not?"

"They aren't there if you go looking for them after the Host dies."

"What about checking in people like Captain nu-Aten? What do you find then?"

She felt Bonny searching for an answer that would explain the sparkling webwork that Bethlehem had shown her.

"They only show as activity—more thinking than a person could make all alone. Like the doppel is helping that part of the person to think harder, better."

Bonny's mind skated along the possible visualizations, selecting and discarding options rapidly, then fanning out the few remaining options. Trying to keep Bonny from feeling her shock, Smokey realized that the girl was deliberately trying to frame her thoughts in a fashion within which Smokey could share her mental images and thus add to the words Bonny could not quite find.

The options Bonny presented were represented as a series of squares of midnight blue silk sprinkled with mica dust. Each dust splatter bore fingertip tracings connecting various globular clusters of denser dust. As Smokey studied each diagram, she caught hints of eldritch music that added a fourth dimension to the pictures.

Breaking away after what felt like hours of examination, Smokey tried to put her impressions into words.

"Those are like brain energy maps—aren't they? And you've sketched out possible patterns, like fingerprints."

Bonny nodded, her round face flushed and the roses in her cheeks American Beauty rather than Blush.

"Yeah, can't know that I'm right, of course," she grinned, suddenly impish. "Can we find out?"

Again Smokey was touched by her daughter's utter trust. The girl actually expected Mama to find a way to test her theories the same way she expected her to get rid of a nightmare. Smokey tousled the girl's thick bangs.

"Maybe, but we need to know more about what they are first, Bonita. We know that a doppel can leave a Host voluntarily. So even if we suspect that someone has a Rider, let's say, and we kidnap him (which is illegal, remember), then how do we keep the Rider in its Host for us to study?"

"Yeah." Bonny frowned. "Or keep it from trying to get one of us. That's not good."

"Has Grandpapa been teaching you anything about telepathy yet?"

"Some, but he says that I'm too"—she knotted her brows—"too latent. If he teaches me too much about it, I might lose something. Does that make sense?"

"Yes," Smokey assured her, remembering how her own trial and error had helped to strengthen the Talent. "It does."

Bonny studied the star-streaked darkness. Smokey could feel the eddies of her daughter's thoughts, but made no effort to read them. Instead, she let her own thoughts drift, trying to avoid the beaten trails that she had been over before.

"Mama?"

Smokey jumped—she'd drifted farther than she'd thought.

"Mama, if I can do like you said and find a way to trap a doppel, will you help me find a Rider?"

Smokey almost choked on her own indrawn breath. "You really want to risk that, Bonny?"

"Uh-huh." Bonny grinned. "How else can I test my ideas?"

For a fleeting moment, Smokey saw Ross in that smile. Then it was just Bonny. The girl's Arizona freckles were fading under the liner's pallid light. Obscurely, sorrow for times no more clenched its fist beneath Smokey's ribs.

"I'll help you, Bonny," she promised, "but only if you can prove to me that these plans of yours will work."

"I will, Mama, I will!" Bonny leapt up, all enthusiasm and action. "I'm going to start right now!"

She was gone before Smokey could find her shoes. Listening to the observation deck door shut, Smokey looked up again into the star-smeared sky, recalling Bonny's brain maps, and wondered that the heaven's pale sparkle was less brilliant than the microverse hidden within her daughter's skull.

16

"WE ARE BORN," INTONED THE PLUM-No mystic, "before we are fully viable. Our diets are restricted by what our unformed mouths and digestive tracts can manage. Unable to move more than feebly, much less tend to our own needs, we are reduced to wailing our complaints to an unpredictable universe. As adults, many humans persist in this wailing—dignifying it with the word 'prayer'—yet no matter what it is called it is the crying of an infant for a parent.

"Others"—and here he grinned wickedly—"refuse any support. These are in continual rebellion against infant dependency. Both reactions, of course, are equally wrong. To persist as a child is weak and foolish, but to deny that we remain dependent on the charity of others—even if those others are not all humans—is equally foolish."

Listening to the lecture in the soft, pleasant light of the observation deck, Smokey started at the speaker's last words. For a moment she thought that he was alluding to the doppels, but his next words seemed to allay her suspicions.

"Our dependency is on our larger ecosystem. Even when our mouths bud teeth that can masticate food more substantial than our mother's milk we are still dependent on food grown outside of our own bodies. Even when we can move by the power of our own muscles, we still need a solid surface on which to move.

With rare exceptions"—and here he paused to bow genteelly to Joy in Motion—"we have not adapted to free fall."

He smoothed the satin of his formal kimono with self-conscious grace. "Where does this leave us? We venture out into the universe beyond our planet and continue our Terran-born pattern of dependence and rejection of dependence. When we encounter a new world that nearly suits our biological parameters, we do not shape ourselves to the world. Instead we study the world and say . . ."

Clasping one hand to the side of this face, the lecturer assumed a pose that parodied Rodin's *Thinker*. His tone shifted from that of a mature adult to that of a wheedling child. "This world is too dry and the air is a bit too thin, but if we add a bit of water and blow on it, then this world will be just right."

There were uncomfortable chuckles from the audience. The plum-No mystic waited for the room to quiet and then straightened. Clasping his hands behind his back, he studied his audience seriously.

"I am certain that all of you recognized the planet that I was describing as Arizona, our vessel's last port of call, but the same could be said about Guillen, my home-world and this ship's next port of call. On Guillen, the difficulty was not too much dryness, as with Arizona, or too much cold, as with Icedrake, but an overabundance of life and growth. Guillen has been unflatteringly described as an argument between a swamp and a tropical jungle locked in a greenhouse with the sprinkler system set permanently to 'On.'"

Smokey could feel Bonny's excited anticipation that she would actually experience such an unbelievable place. The majority of the audience didn't share Bonny's enthusiasm. Comments about fungus infestations, wormy creatures that squirmed through sodden vegetation, and perpetually grey skies fluttered about the observation deck until the lecturer gestured for silence.

"Certainly, most of you have been advised that the only humanly tolerable areas are within the geodesics or that perhaps you should avoid the entire soggy mess and stay in a lovely Terra-neutral environment in one of the space stations or perhaps never even leave the ship. If you do this, you are robbing yourself of an opportunity to experience a world that humans were not designed for and, thus far, have not been able to substantially terraform. You are also robbing yourself of a much more important opportunity, the opportunity to contemplate human interaction with the universe."

He stopped, studied his audience intensely, then spread out his hands in a gesture that was at once imploring and inviting. "Visit Guillen and consider— Should we terraform all the wonder out of the universe or should we be finding ways to adapt humans so that we can better participate in the wonder and diversity of creation?"

Beneath the polite applause that followed the speech, Clarence ducked his head down and whispered in Smokey's ear, "This announcement paid for by the Guillen Tourism Bureau."

"No." Smokey giggled. "Not really."

Clarence nodded, his expression bright with laughter. "Yep, it's true, ma'am, sort of an open secret. Mysticism doesn't pay well—at least not if you're sincere, which most of the plum-No that I've met are. Most of their lecturers only do the work part-time. Erun nu-Rakl, the fellow who was just speaking, is a microbiologist by trade. When he travels on business, he uses his free time to spread plum-No philosophy. He gets an added stipend from Guillen if he includes a pitch for visiting the planet in his plum-No talks. Erum then donates that money back into plum-No stuff—robes or reading material or VR demos for those who are interested in pursuing the philosophy."

"Nice setup," Smokey admitted, "and an interesting philosophy. You don't encounter plum-No often on Arizona, but I've chatted with some in the District."

"I can't imagine that they'd be particularly popular on Arizona," Clarence said. "It's probably the most progressive of the terraforming planets."

"And proud of it," Smokey agreed with patriotic fervor. "Progressive, open-minded, and tough."

"Also, hot and dry—lung-searingly so in places," came a new voice. Erun nu-Rakl had come over to join them. "I recognized the lady and had to come over to pay my respects. You are Smokey, are you not?"

She dipped her head graciously. "I am."

"I'm certain that you don't recall," nu-Rakl said with a blush that she would not have believed possible, "but I had a few hours of your time a few standards ago. I've never forgotten the pleasure."

"Thank you," Smokey replied. "I am always happy to hear that someone remembers his time with me fondly."

"An understatement, I assure you." He looked at Bonny, then at Clarence. "This young lady must be your daughter. I can see the resemblance. Are you on vacation, then?"

"Yes. Bonny has never been away from Arizona."

"Then, I suppose that you are not taking clients this trip." He shook his head regretfully. "Still, perhaps I can be of service to you. If you actually plan to show Bonny the planet, I would be delighted to help arrange a surface tour."

Smokey felt Bonny perk, but only smiled politely. "That might be nice. I will remember your offer."

They were walking back to their suite when Clarence said, "You enjoyed that, what Erun nu-Rakl said. It didn't embarrass you at all."

"Why should it? He was just a trick, a client. A chef wouldn't be embarrassed if someone said, 'I still remember that wonderful meal you prepared at Café le Chat two years ago.' Why should I be embarrassed that someone still remembers a good lay?"

"It's so much more . . ." He fumbled for a word, "personal, intimate. That man was in your body!"

He glanced over at Bonny, who was following the discussion with frank interest, and fell silent.

Smokey winked at Bonny. "Clarence, I'm a whore.

You knew that. You met me at my place of business. You don't think that because I love you, I'm suddenly going to deny what I've done."

Opening the suite door gave Clarence a reason to stall. Bonny scurried off to her room without waiting for Smokey to hint.

"I guess," Clarence said, refusing to meet her eyes. "I guess that something in old-fashioned Terran me did. Look, sugar, I need to think. I didn't know I was this— territorial. You won't be mad if I go walk about and try to work this out?"

Smokey refrained from touching him, not really wanting to know what he was thinking. Instead, she managed a warm—and she hoped loving—smile.

"Remember what Bethlehem said about keeping to the passenger areas," she said, "and go and do your thinking. Capi?"

"Thanks, Smokey," Clarence said. "See you in a bit."

The suite echoed with silence after the door slid shut. Smokey pondered the pattern in the carpet as if it might hold answers, jumping at a sudden, sharp sound of a door opening behind her.

"Are the good ones always so much trouble, Mama?" Bonny said from the door of her cabin.

Smokey spread her hands. "I don't know, Boniface. I've never tried to keep one around before. It sure seems that way, though. All I can do is let him cool off."

She strode over to the room bar and dialed a brandy. Sipping it, she allowed herself to admit how angry she was.

"It's not like I've ever pretended to be anything I'm not," she muttered. "How dare he get upset with me for being what I am! I have half a mind to go and lay every man on this ship!"

Bonny studied her with the same distant expression that she gave her equations. "Would that make everything all right, Mama?"

Smokey laughed bitterly and met Bonny's uncompromising gaze. "No, Bonny, it wouldn't. It would probably make it worse. I'm just angry."

"Don't be, Mama, I'm still here."

The girl looked so hopeless that Smokey set down her brandy and knelt by her, hugging her tightly.

"I know, thornbud, I know. You're awfully patient with your dumb mom."

"You're not dumb!"

Smokey smiled, honestly this time. "Think not? Let's see if you still think so after you try and explain your research to me. I bet you'll change your mind then."

Bonny's answer was an exasperated sigh, but she towed Smokey off to her room, nattering about particles, discrete matter, and quantum electrodynamics.

Later, leaving Bonny to sculpt diagrams on her VT, Smokey went hunting for Clarence. She found him in one of the larger passenger lounges, tucked in a corner with Taenia, the social coordinator, an attractive red-haired woman who managed to make a standard uniform look rather sexy.

Their heads were bent over something and they were seated so close that for a minute Smokey thought that they were holding hands.

As she came up to the table, she saw that their attention was focused on a selection of oversize cards spread out in a vaguely crosslike pattern with a bar down the side. Taenia was saying something to Clarence, but she stopped when she realized Smokey was there.

Clarence stood, somewhat unsteadily, and embraced Smokey. She smelled whiskey on his breath. The glass on the table was only half-full, hardly enough to make him shaky.

"Hey, Smokey-jo, how's it going?" he said, seating himself and patting the seat next to him. "Ol' Taenia here's been showing me a new kind of cards—tarot cards. I've read about them, but I've never known anyone who could really read them. She's good and she says that she can teach me."

"Indeed," said Smokey, giving the other woman a chilly smile. "Did she read your future?"

"Little bit," he said, "but mostly she's been showing me the basics. She says that I've got the gift for sure."

"Indeed," Smokey said, not bothering to smile this time. She knew, given her recent lecture to Clarence, that jealousy was an irrational response, but the emotion was there nonetheless.

Taenia nodded. "Clarence's background in anthropology and sociology gives him an open mind. Too many people in these technological times rule out imagination, intuition, and the like as viable sources. Of course, I view this mostly as a parlor game."

"Of course," Smokey said, not bothering to conceal her hostility from the other woman.

Clarence, however, seemed unable to sense her response. Companionably, he flung one arm around her shoulders, the other around Taenia's trim waist.

"Taenia, show Smokey how you do it, how you read the cards. Tell her about your Irish grandmother with the second sight and all the rest. Ol' Smokey, she believes stuff like that. Don't 'cha, sugar?"

Taenia delicately pulled herself free of Clarence's embrace and collected her cards. Sorting them into order, she gave Smokey a professionally friendly smile.

"It's really quite simple," she said, fanning out the cards. "The deck is larger than a standard one, containing both Major and Minor Arcana. From the royal cards, you select the signifier appropriate to the person for whom the reading is being done . . ."

Smokey sat through the explanation, through a reading that was so vague that it could be interpreted in any number of ways, through Clarence's consuming two more neat whiskeys.

At last, Taenia was commed by another passenger.

"Excuse me," she said, rising. "I must go. Clarence, why don't you keep these cards and practice what I've showed you? I would be happy to meet with you again and go into some refinements of the technique. Perhaps we could even have an occult night if enough passengers were interested."

"That would be wonderful," Clarence said, accepting the deck. "I'll memorize everything that you told me and practice a lot."

Taenia nodded. "Just remember. It's not only the rules, it's opening your mind to inspiration, to the little hints that tell you which interpretation for a card is correct."

Clarence nodded eagerly, squaring the deck and putting it in its painted box.

"I'll remember—an open mind at all times."

Smokey kept her silence, but as she took him back to their cabin, she felt disquieted. Clarence passed out nearly as soon as he was undressed and in bed. Studying him, remembering their argument, his alacrity in seeking out another woman, Smokey looked at the sober/stim patch in her bedside unit and shrugged.

Let him sleep it off. He'd deserve it if he had a hangover in the morning.

17

SMOKEY AND CLARENCE HAD NO FURTHER ARguments before the arrival of the *Ibn Battuta* at Guillen. If Clarence was somewhat more reserved, less inclined to minor affectionate gestures, Smokey excused this as part of his adjustment to the reality of her life as a whore. She let him spend his time puzzling through his work, practicing with the tarot deck, and chatting with the plum-No.

His distraction was almost welcome, for she had her own concerns. Working with Bonny, she had come to comprehend the doppels as best she could. If her own reaction to them was still largely visceral revulsion, she decided that this was perhaps safest. Bonny's comprehension was almost too intellectual. The danger the doppels presented was as abstract as death itself. Bonny was still too young, too unformed to feel a real horror at the idea of having another personality overlaid on her own.

After trying several times to caution her daughter, Smokey had given up. In a real sense, Bonny's actions were already overridden by others. Adults told her what to do, when to eat, sleep, and play, how to react in a variety of situations. Doppels might seem rather like sneaky uninvited parents to a nine-year-old. The comparison made Smokey uncomfortable.

She reflected that lots of things were making her uncomfortable lately—not the least her dread about leaving the *Ibn Battuta* and going planetside. Bethlehem and Joy would not accompany them. Their departure would be too obvious, and Joy had a contract to fulfill.

Scowling and gnawing on one thumb knuckle, Smokey eavesdropped on the "good-byes" emanating from Bonny's cabin. Joy seemed to be pressing gift after gift on her granddaughter until Bonny, who was as acquisitive as any healthy nine-year-old, was speechless. With difficulty, Smokey forbore from interrupting, pretending not to care that Bethlehem was using his casual conversation with Clarence as an excuse to study her.

Resisting an immature urge to stick out her tongue at her father, Smokey called, "Bonny, the shuttle leaves in fifteen minutes!"

Stirring in the cabin, then, "We're coming!"

Joy said with a diva's utter confidence, "They'll hold it for me."

"Ah, but it is not you who are leaving, Mama," Smokey said, balancing atop the luggage carrier a bulging duffel that apparently contained Bonny's new prizes. Even with the *Ibn Battuta*'s stores at their disposal the carrier was not overburdened; the three of them had not accumulated much luggage.

Hustling her daughter down the starliner's corridors, Smokey mentally stripped away the clever lighting and patterned paper that disguised the conduits and circuit panels hidden beneath. She breathed deeply of air that, despite the circulating pumps, was faintly tainted by the thousand, thousand lungs that had breathed it. Her steps quickened as if she could escape the bittersweet memories of a girlhood spent in such halls.

In contrast, Bonny hung back between her grandparents' hands, her eyes darting to capture every detail of the starship.

"Filing it away?" Clarence asked, his smile fond despite his serious tone.

Bonny blushed, then nodded. "I want to come back."

"You will," Smokey said, "at least to get home to Arizona."

Final farewells were a blur of embraces, promises, kisses, and advice. Then the three of them were aboard a much larger shuttle than the fighter that had smuggled them aboard. With a snap and a popping deep within the ears and a bump that was not precisely felt, they fell off through the void and toward the jungles of Guillen.

Bonny leaned against the porthole, staring at the world that they hurtled toward.

"Mama, is all that white really clouds?"

Smokey nodded. "That's right, Bonita. Clouds are water and Guillen has lots of water. You remember that from your lessons."

"I do," Bonny said, "but it's different to see it for real."

"This planet is rather pretty," Clarence said. "More green than Old Terra. There's blue there, but not like the oceans back home."

Guillen had nothing like Old Terra's vast oceans, for her water wealth was more evenly distributed. Even as they closed in on the landing site—the domed city of Custer near the north pole—only a few large lakes stood out from the tangled greenery. Once they broke through the cloud level, rain opaqued the windows, its running droplets fascinating Bonny nearly as much as had the landscape.

Upon landing, the shuttle coasted along a runway beside a covered dome. On one side was the purple-green foliage, on the other the crisp silver and shellwhite of the geodesic. From the dome extended the spider legs of a series of piers, each tented over with an accordion of translucent amber plastic. This fastened onto the shuttle's passenger door with a buzz and a click. Soon they were shuffling toward the exit while the pilot's disembodied voice assured them that their luggage would be unloaded and returned to them after being disinfected.

"Sweet lord!" Clarence exclaimed as he led the way from the shuttle into the tunnel. "It's humid here. I haven't tasted wet like this since I left Louisiana!"

Chuckling, Erun nu-Rakl, the plum-No mystic, stepped eagerly ahead. "This part is climate controlled, Terran. For real humidity you need to come outside."

Privately, Smokey thought that she could forego the experience—at least until she had rested. Even Bonny was rather wilted, although her enthusiasm for the new planet remained undiminished.

"First we head to this Shrieking Rushhour Inn that Joy and Bethlehem told us to check into. Then I dive into a cool shower," Smokey said. "Though the shower may be a redundancy. I'm dripping already."

Bonny had found a temperature gauge and was staring at it in disbelief. "Mama, this thing must be broken! It says only thirty-five degrees. It has to be hotter than that!"

"That's not broken, baby," Clarence said. "That's humidity."

"There's probably more moisture in the air here in the transport center than in all of Port City ravine," Smokey said, not completely pleased at the thought. "My hair is going to get all frizzy."

"You'll still be pretty, Mama," Bonny assured her loyally.

Smokey grunted and shepherded them to a taxi stand. Another surprise awaited them. Instead of the grav cars or tracked vehicles that served on Arizona where pedstrips and bicycles could not, what hovered at the stand was a fat, round-bottomed tub with seats around the entire rim.

The operator was a chunky brown-eyed boy with black hair parted so severely down the center that his head seemed bisected. His hairless torso was bare and golden-skinned. Otherwise, all he wore was loose nylon shorts and a pair of calf-high, form-fitting boots. He looked at them and gave a jerking bob of his head.

"Credit plus to any inn. You'll be wanting the Rushhour, though," he said.

"How did you know?" Bonny asked suspiciously.

"They got dry air," the boy answered, "and you look like 'Zonies. What say?"

"We'll go," Smokey said, making a pretense of thinking it over. "Is it a long trip?"

"Inside, yeah"—the boy stowed the luggage with neat efficiency in the belly of his buttertub—"but you wouldn't like out so we'll go by in. Trust."

"Wonder if he's taking us by the long way 'cause we're rubes?" Clarence muttered as the boy pushed a few buttons.

Smokey patted his hand. "Don't fuss. If he is, he's invoking the ancient right of guides on all worlds."

The fat vehicle slipped away from the taxi stand down a chute and splashed into a broad, placid canal. Bonny couldn't have been more astonished if the taxi had metamorphosed into a beetle and started singing.

"Mama," she said after leaning over the side to check, "they made their road out of water!"

Smokey and Clarence suppressed their laughter. Their guide wasn't so polite.

"'Zonies," he sniffled condescendingly, "every one of 'em acts like they never seen water."

"I've seen water!" Bonny retorted angrily. "I can even swim. I just never thought that you'd waste water for roads."

"Waste?" The boy steered them past a flat-bottomed barge loaded with pressed bales of greenery. "We 'taint wasting, 'Zonie. Water we can't get rid of. Dig a little hole and it's a little pool afore you put the mud down. We who live here don't call the planet Guillen."

He looked challengingly at Bonny, and Smokey realized that he probably was not much older than fourteen.

"We calls it Spongecake," he continued, "'cause it's like a wet sponge but rich, too."

"Oh," Bonny said, staring into the silty water with undiminished fascination. "Arizona's not like that. If you dig a hole, it just gets crumbly with sand."

They might have continued their conversation, but the curve of the canal took them into a section crowded with barges and buttertubs, darting canoes, and streamlined pleasure gondolas. Their young cabbie needed all of his attention to steer them through unscathed, but he managed with such consummate skill that they weren't even splashed.

The Shrieking Rushhour proved to be right on this busy stretch. It rose above the water on a thick, square pier that left plenty of clearance underneath. The building itself was solidly built, mostly out of wood, and seemed to be from a far earlier age than the overwhelmingly vast geodesic dome that loomed over and enclosed the entire city.

Bonny's brown eyes were now even wider than before. Smokey sensed her biting back questions in deference to the sophisticated wisdom of their cabbie.

"I see you build mostly from wood," Smokey said, voicing what she knew would be one of her desert-born daughter's questions.

"Yeah," the boy said, steering them under the Rushhour's pier. "Wood we got lots, but don't fuss none. It gets treated against wet and rot so you don't need to worry about the Rushhour tumbling waterward."

"Wood rots?" came Bonny's involuntary question.

"Yeah." The boy was genuinely puzzled. "Everything docs 'cept stone and glass, I guess. Maybe even stone."

"Not much rots on Arizona," Smokey explained. "It desiccates—crumbles to dust—instead."

"Ah." The boy shrugged and snugged them to a post. "Same thing then, just different ways of falling to pieces."

He steadied his vessel and helped them ashore. As Smokey was paying him, she asked, "Do you give tours?"

"Outside and in." He nodded. "Good rates. Ask anyone about Midas. They give you the splash."

"Thank you, Midas." Smokey looked at what he had handed her when he returned her credit slip. "Thank you very much."

Fifteen minutes later, Smokey was stepping from the shower. Still nude, tousling her hair dry, she grinned at Clarence, who was watching her with lusty amusement.

"If it's this hot here," she said, "can you imagine what it's like outside one of the domes?"

"Hot *and* wet," he deadpanned. "I guess you plan on letting Bonny have the tour while we wait for Bethlehem's network to contact us?"

"Half-right." She straightened, reaching for her robe, but not donning it. "We've been contacted. That boy Midas slid me an ID chit when I paid him. My guess is that we play the tourists and he sets us up with the network."

"Bonny is sound asleep," Clarence said, taking her robe from her hands, "and you are very distracting."

"Well, we can't have you distracted," she said, "not while I have a short-term cure in mind."

"As long as it doesn't involve you putting this robe back on," he replied.

"It doesn't." She reached for him. "It doesn't."

18

ON THE DAY AFTER THEIR ARRIVAL, SMOKEY paused from dabbing pastel shadows around her eyes, entranced by the jumble of boats and buttertubs outside of the Shrieking Rushhour. She no longer wondered at the significance of the inn's name. Built at the intersection of four large canals and a myriad of smaller, it seemed as if all the commerce within Custer must pass around—or under—it.

"Where's Bonny?" Clarence said, as he walked in to join her.

"Out on the deck. She's fascinated by everything, and the humidity doesn't seem to bother her at all."

"Ready for today's tour?"

"I suppose that I am," Smokey said. "I ordered this dress over the VT and I'm not certain about the fit. How do I look?"

Clarence and Bonny had both settled for shorts and shirts bought at the gift shop in the Screaming Rushhour's lobby. They had looked such universal tourists that Smokey's vanity had been unable to settle for the same outfit.

She spun slowly so Clarence could look at the fall of the mid-thigh–length, double-flounced blue-green skirt. Tucked into it was a tank top just slightly more green than the skirt and cut with a plunging neckline. A blue scarf held her long hair off her neck while still allowing it to fall loose.

"You look ravishing," Clarence said, "and if Bonny wasn't waiting for us to take her to breakfast, I think you just might end up ravished as well."

"Flatterer," she said, but she smiled.

Bonny had already been exploring and now led the way to the hotel restaurant. Once there, she examined the menu, suspicion tracing grooves between her eyebrows.

Smokey reached to smooth the lines away. "What's wrong, Boniface?"

"Do they really expect people to eat this stuff or is this just a trick menu for the tourists?" she asked.

"Stuff?" Clarence asked, his tone indicating his puzzlement. "What do you mean, Bonny?"

"Rice, fish, molluks . . ."

"Mollusks," Smokey corrected.

"What are those?" Bonny asked.

"Shellfish," Smokey answered. "Oysters, clams, mussels, scallops—I think they had some at Styler's Sea when we went on hadj. Don't you remember?"

Bonny blinked. "Sure, but people eat them? Yuck!"

"You've had rice, Bonny," Smokey said.

"Once," she said. "It wasn't bad, but for breakfast?"

Clarence laughed. "The food on this menu isn't that different from what I grew up with in New Orleans. True, some of the combinations are a bit peculiar, but these are all things that flourish where there is lots and lots of water."

Bonny still looked suspicious. Laughing softly, Smokey patted her hand.

"I thought you liked the adventure of being away from Arizona, Bon-ton," she said. "Well, this is part of the adventure. I'm certain that we could find you something more familiar—I see eggs and flapjacks listed, but don't you want to try something new?"

"Maybe," Bonny answered, frowning.

Clarence flipped off his menu with a satisfied grunt. "I'm going to have the rice-flour–breaded oysters and a side of the pan-fried noodles with cress. Good mollusks of any type are nearly impossible to get in New Orleans because of the water pollution."

"What are you going to have, Mama?" Bonny asked.

"I thought I'd have the shad roe with some noodles in bouillabaisse," she replied, "although I may get wild rice instead of the noodles."

"What's bouillabaisse and shad roe?"

"Fish soup and fish eggs," Smokey said, completely deadpan.

Bonny grimaced, but decided that she could be adventurous enough to have rice pudding along with a very safe scrambled egg—an egg she took care to make certain came from a bird rather than a fish.

"What I find odd, Bonny," Clarence said, "is that you don't have any trouble with the idea of eating lizard eggs."

"Why would I?" Bonny asked. "Doesn't everyone?"

"No, actually, where I grew up they would be considered as strange as you seem to find oysters."

"Really?"

His brown eyes not quite concealing a twinkle of amusement, Clarence proceeded to regale Bonny with accounts of the various things typically eaten in New Orleans and the surrounding regions of North America. Accustomed to the more limited cuisine available on Arizona, Bonny listened with the air of one who is not completely certain that she is not being tricked.

Smokey sat back and sipped her coffee, pleased by the rapport between her daughter and her lover. Watching Clarence sketch an alligator, complete with gaping jaws, on his napkin and listening to his explanation of how the tail meat tasted quite different from the meat from the body, she realized that she had grown quite fond of him, a fondness that was quite different from her satisfaction with him as a bedmate or her appreciation of his unquestioning adoration for her.

If this was love, then she wondered why she had avoided it for so long.

Midas arrived to take them on a tour of the city soon after they finished eating. He wore a variant on his costume from the day before, although today his shorts were a golden color a few shades darker than his skin, ornamented with a thin band of crimson piping. A headband of matching crimson kept his hair from his eyes.

Bonny, who had been arguing merrily with Clarence over the improbability of a creature like an alligator growing to any larger than maybe six feet, fell silent, suddenly shy. Midas did not seem to notice her, though he gave Smokey a grin of such unabashed appreciation that she felt indignant for her daughter's sake.

"Brought a different boat, t'day," he said, ushering them to the dock. "Buttertub is good for luggage and like, but a gondola is real pretty and goes slick as nothing in traffic."

The bow seat was immediately claimed by Bonny. Clarence sat next, with Smokey closest to where Midas stood in the stern, a long steering oar balanced deftly in his hands.

"We gonna see lots of Custer today," Midas announced, "but you let me know when the hot and wet get to you. Got?"

"Got," Smokey promised. "I don't think that heat will be nearly as much a problem as the humidity."

"Yeah, 'Zonies, they take heat pretty well," Midas agreed, pushing them clear of the dock and beginning to pole them along. "Now, when we get 'Draki here, they just curl up and melt. They think they gonna like the hot and the wet and they just go and die."

Clarence chortled. "I assume that by 'Draki you mean Icedrake natives."

Midas looked puzzled. "That's what I say, right?"

"Indeed." Clarence grinned and turned to Smokey. "What Midas said about the 'Draki reminds me of an old, old story from Earth. Back when the Christian religion was aggressively preaching its creed, the missionaries moved into regions where the winters were bitter cold—as cold as Icedrake, I'd guess. The missionaries started explaining how if you didn't follow the teachings of their god that you went to an afterlife where you were engulfed in raging fire."

Smokey felt herself smiling in return. "Let me guess. They couldn't see anything wrong with having more heat than you could use."

"That's it," Clarence said. "Of course, there were other factors contributing to the northerners thinking that the missionaries were crazy, but it's that last bit that always comes to mind for me."

"It will for me now, too," Smokey said. She reached out and held Clarence's hand, touching his mind lightly, just enough to feel his contentment flowing like syrup over the discomfort generated by the muggy Guillen morning.

Midas showed them a variety of architectural landmarks, including a museum designed to be seen in its entirety from a boat. When Clarence and Bonny were distracted by the art works, Smokey tried to question Midas about the Psionic Underground, but his only answer was the enigmatic comment "Turtles only move so fast. Hares lose, 'specially here."

Piqued, Smokey gave up wondering if Bethlehem had known that they would be assigned a guide who was clearly insane.

"Where are we going now?" Bonny asked Midas when they left the museum.

"Thought that 'Zonies like you would like to see our wet ranches," Midas said, poling steadily along. "Don't figure you got nothing like that where you come from."

"Wet ranches?" Smokey said. "Are these inside of Custer?"

"Ones I'm gonna show you are," Midas assured her. "Not the city dome, but domes linked on—little bubbles 'round the biggie. You for it?"

"Capi," Smokey said. "I don't fancy that Guillen is exactly the place to go shopping."

"Oh, you got us wrong there, lady," Midas said. "We

grow lots of stuff that makes right pretty clothes. If you not too blown when we done with the ranches, going to the shops would be just shiny, you see."

The wet ranches proved to be a series of smaller domes built over water. Unlike the city dome there was no evidence of buildings, just a few shacks up on stilts. Instead the area within was divided into ovoid sections marked by buoys strung on thick cables. Between the ovals were waterways large enough to take a fat butter-tub. Midas poled the gondola gracefully down one of these.

"Under the water," he explained, "is net that goes down to deep and catches up on the other side. Double net, really, to make safe against holes."

"So each of those ovals is like a big mesh bag?" Smokey asked.

"That's it," Midas agreed. "Little mesh, though, big enough for the water and the silt to get through and not much else."

"But why?" Bonny asked.

Midas smiled at her and she blushed. Smokey turned away to conceal a smile of her own.

"'Cause those are farm patches, 'Zonie chick," he said. "Some grow plants—rice and cranberries and muchi-mong—some grow critters—fish, tortoise, mollusks. Some grow both when the both is good for the farming."

"Oh." Bonny leaned over the edge of the gondola and inspected the plants in the nearest oval patch.

"These are kinda pretty," she said. "What are they?"

"Water lilies, different kinds," Midas said. "Some just pretty to look at. Others used to make a type of flour. Parts are good for medicine, too. They touchy plants, though. Chancy return if they get a mold or a mite."

Clarence raised his hand, for all the world looking like a student in a class.

"That had been bothering me," he admitted. "Don't you have problems with disease and infection? Do the local biologicals threaten your imported ecology?"

Midas shrugged. "Lots of questions, 'Zonie."

Bonny interrupted. "He's not really a 'Zonie. He's from Nwa'lens on Old Terra."

"New Orleans on Old Terra," Clarence chuckled, enunciating carefully.

"That's what I said, didn't I?" Bonny said, puzzled.

"I suppose you did, Bonny," Clarence said. Then he returned his attention to Midas, who had been observing the byplay with bemusement. "What I was wondering, Midas, is what are some of the problems that you people encounter farming on an alien world."

"Tha's clearer, 'Ran," Midas said. "'Sides the problems farmers always got, we got the problem that water is water but Guillen water can have stuff in it that the native plants like fine but some of ours don't. These little spit bubble domes, they get the water filtered before it comes in. Waters just get all we put in it."

"What about outgoing water?" Smokey asked. "Is that filtered, too?"

Midas shook his head. "No, we don't let it out, not really. It goes 'round and 'round 'til the plants drink it up."

"Uh, what about your city sewage?" Clarence asked. "Does that get dumped?"

Midas looked at Clarence as if the Terran was crazy. Then he shook his head.

"'Rans always ask that, always! Somebody tell me once that on Old Terra that they do just that some places, dump the sewage in the water and leave it. Maybe that's why they call the place Dirt, eh?"

Bonny giggled at his joke. Clarence looked less pleased.

"Well, it is true that in some places sewage disposal is pretty primitive—casual, even. Most areas do process their waste, now. What do you do here on Guillen?"

Midas shrugged. "Fertilizer, mostly. It's rich stuff, sewage is. Processing marshes are big business, here. You get good crops and a tithe from the government for dealing with the shit. Good job, if you can get it."

Clarence looked astonished, but Smokey, who had grown up on starships and colony worlds, understood perfectly. To save Clarence from another question that might make Midas believe him a complete barbarian, she pointed to an oval where round, flat rocks were artistically arrayed on floating logs.

"What's growing there?"

Midas smiled proudly. "Tha's sea tortoises. Good eating. Pretty shells. They going dead and drop on Old Terra with the water filth and the things eating up their eggs. Some smart one bring eggs here and set them up nice place. When breeding season comes, the ranchers open up the oval bitsy more and put in sandbars for the egg laying. Then the eggs get taken and baken and you get more tortoises."

He paused and shrugged. "It not quite that easy, but it works. Somebody say one day that Old Terra get Guillen tortoises to go in the ocean there."

"Those are animals?" Bonny asked, leaning to take a closer look at the nearest tortoise. The creature glowered at her, then plopped off the log into the water.

"Tha's right," Midas said. "These are littler ones. Some types get biggy. You can piggy-rig one. It's fun."

" 'Piggy-rig'?" Bonny asked.

"Ride back of," Midas explained patiently. "It's good time to have. I can take you if your mama lets me."

"Can I?" Bonny asked excitedly.

"I can't see why not," Smokey said. "You can swim well enough."

"Tell me, Midas," Clarence asked. "Do you people farm outside of the dome?"

"Tha' we do, 'Ran," Midas said. "Bog farmers do good when the season's right. Some Spongecake plants make good dyes, good source for medical chemicals. Not so much food, but some."

They continued through the wet ranches, Midas pausing again and again to show them some interesting crop. The boy answered questions with the patience of an experienced tour guide, keeping his sarcastic rejoinders to a minimum as the hours passed.

Eventually, they came to a small dome reserved for water sports, including the promised "piggy-rig." Swimming suits were available for purchase, but many of the people present swam in the nude. Smokey happily availed herself of the privilege. Bonny opted for a one-piece suit when Midas explained that it was necessary for tortoise riding.

Clarence dithered slightly over whether or not to swim in the buff, which puzzled Smokey. Despite the fact that he had left the first blush of youth behind, he was well-built, certainly a match for most of the men swimming around them. Eventually, he decided to opt for joining her *au naturel,* but several minutes had to pass before he relaxed.

Smokey didn't question him, privately adding the information to the pleasantly complex background history she was assembling about her lover.

At last, even Bonny had experienced enough of the heat and the wet. Midas poled them back to the Screaming Rushhour.

"If you still want to shop, ma'am," he said to Smokey, "I can come back later."

"I'm fine for now," she said. "And, honestly, too beat for a good shop. Maybe tomorrow."

"Tomorrow, maybe, I take you on tour outside of Custer," Midas said. Was that a slight wink?

"Really?" Smokey said. "Well, since I'm too beat to shop, could you buy any gear we might need and charge it to my account here? I don't think I was dressed quite right for this weather."

Midas grinned. "I take care of that, ma'am. For you and for the 'Ran and for the little girl, too. See you good and early, then."

He paddled off into the steamy heat. Clarence and Smokey between them helped Bonny off to bed. Exhausted by the heat and humidity, they tumbled off to sleep almost as quickly.

The next morning, frowning with dissatisfaction, Smokey straightened the lines of the outfit that a member of the hotel staff had dropped off the previous evening.

"Midas clearly believes that this horror is one size fits

all." She tugged at the knickers and baggy tunic in frustration before giving it up for a loss. "The 'one' this thing would look good on isn't even remotely human. I'm not sure that it's even remotely bipedal."

"You did tell Midas that you wanted something that would keep you cool," Clarence reminded her, "and that outfit certainly looks cool."

"Hrumph." She jammed on a hat that resembled a fat funnel and turned quickly away from the mirror. "Now, you look good."

Clarence wore cream-colored shorts and a pair of tan calf-hugging boots. His broad chest was bare except for wiry black hair.

"The boots remind me of swim shoes for divers," he said, and when he wriggled his toes she could see their individual motion. "They've got more traction than you would guess."

"Well, that's good," she said. "Shall we go and meet our swamp prince?"

Clarence offered her his arm and they descended. Since Midas had taken them on a tour the day before, they knew something of what to expect—a slow meander between pier and post, narrow escapes from being sloshed by the warm, silty wakes of other vessels, and then some exhilarating oddity of architecture—most viewed from angles that would have made surrealism obsolete or—more frightening—representational.

Today, Midas arrived promptly. Clad in brilliant emerald shorts with a matching short cape around his shoulders and a peaked beret over his hair, he did look something like a princeling from the swampy wilds. Bonny, clad in a mottled blue tunic and shorts closer in style to Midas's garb than to the ballooned and flowing outfit her mother wore, apparently appreciated Midas's appearance, because she slowed her restless examination of the waterfront and clambered agilely into the tub.

"So that's how it goes on!" Clarence exclaimed, digging into his shoulder bag and producing a cream-colored cape that matched his shorts. "I couldn't figure out what to do with it."

"It's a watershed," Midas said. "You got it on right now. Should be a cap folded inside. Find?"

"Yes, here it is." Clarence used a puddle on the deck as a mirror. "Do I have it right?"

Smokey scrounged up a smile. "You do, and you look so dashing that I have half a mind to go inside and put on something that will make me look less like a frump."

"No, can't," the boy hissed, motioning for them to get aboard. "It's all in the plan."

He cast off and got them moving down a swift-flowing waterway before continuing, "See, everyone notice you so pretty. You stir big comment yesterday. Today we go more quiet and with you all dressed like locals. Clarence, he look like a business uncle of mine—those even colors uncle likes. Bonny can pass as a boy like that—some boys do wear shirts and those clothes like my little brother's. You, though, you gotta look like nothing like you and nobody but nobody would believe that famous sex-sell would dress like bog farmer."

"I think I understand," Smokey said, noting that Bonny was both furious and crestfallen at Midas's description of her. So much for the girl's first crush. "You're taking us to . . ."

"Yeah." The boy narrowed his eyes. "Keep it stilly. I'm taking you out to them."

As Midas splashed them toward the nearest exit, Smokey tried to convince herself that the last couple of days on Guillen would have habituated her to the temperature and humidity outside of Custer. As they slowed outside of the dome locks and Midas handled the clearance to cycle them through, she studied the ghost images of the plants against the frost and pearl of the dome fiber with something like real anticipation.

Her anticipation wilted with her hair, which tumbled down inside her bog farmer's hat and tickled her neck. Wiping away the veil of perspiration that appeared instantly on her face, she gulped down a lungful of something that was too wet to be air. It seemed to work in the same fashion, though, and she tried a bit more.

She smiled bravely at Clarence, noting that his expression was rather blank. Bonny was leaning over the buttertub's bow so far that her shorts hitched up and her tank top was up around her armpits. Leaning forward, Smokey grabbed her by the waist and pulled her back.

"Mama!" Bonny's face was bright red, either from the heat or from hanging upside down. "I nearly had it!"

"What? Bonny, you don't just go dragging stuff out of swamps on alien worlds."

Bonny thrust out her lower lip. "Why not?"

Midas grinned. "Your mama's right, Bonny. There are things down there that would like a nip of 'Zonie's fingers right to the off and eat 'em."

Despite her current dishabille, Bonny managed to look convincingly haughty. "I'm not stupid. I know that alien things couldn't metabolize humans. I've had my basic biology and Arizona is even better at terraforming than this planet is!"

"Yes, you're right; they probably couldn't digest you," Smokey said, twitching the girl's tank top down, "but how about not giving the native life a chance to sample?"

Bonny didn't answer, but she didn't try to drag anything else from the water, so Smokey decided to call it a truce.

They were counting the varieties of the multipetaled flowers that Clarence had christened orchid-chrysanthemums when Midas raised his dripping steering oar and pointed.

"Can you see it?" he asked with an odd smile.

Bonny stood so quickly that the buttertub bobbed in the sluggish water. "What? Where? I don't see anything."

Midas only continued to point with his oar blade. Smokey studied the curtain of green and purple, of vines, leaves, and flowers. There was nothing in the verdant lushness that looked at all like human habitation. Clarence spread his hands and shrugged, sparing enough attention to wipe his sweaty brow.

"I don't see anything either," Smokey admitted when she had stared long enough to worry that she was etching lines around her eyes.

"As you shouldn't," Midas grinned. "Wouldn't be much of a hideout if even a 'Zonie could find it."

He opened a panel flush in his control board and pulled out something that looked like nothing so much as a shepherd's pipe. Puffing his cheeks, he blew across the open ends. The sound it made was haunting, lovely, and far too soft to cause the dramatic effects that followed. Smokey had a moment to suspect subsonics before the swamp waters began to stir and boil.

Coated with silt and debris, something was emerging from the water, shedding water as it came into the air.

"It's been there under the water all along." Clarence leaned forward for a better look. "Whatever it is, I bet it's made from the same material as the dome. No one would ever find something like that with all the water and mud. No one, not unless they were shown."

"Yep, that's how it is." Midas put the pipe away and began working them toward the slowly rising shape. "Moves, too, so it can't even be found by tracking people slogging out to the same place. And it looks like a monster so that anybody sees it and tells people laugh at them for a fool."

The dome that emerged from the water resembled a gigantic albino turtle, complete with leathery neck and a blunt head. The head seemed to quest about blindly for a moment before it found them. Stopping then, it reared up until a door was visible at its end.

"Uh, do we knock?" Smokey asked.

"No need," Midas answered. "They'll be opening up when the pressure is even. Place is even bigger than it looks, more under the water that never comes up."

"Bigger," Clarence said, looking at the alabaster island. "Damn!"

Smokey grabbed Bonny's shoulders, restraining the girl before she could step out of the boat.

"Wait, Bonny, the ground here can't be trusted, like around the Sea at home."

Bonny slowed and scowled, but Smokey felt no real annoyance from her. The girl was too excited.

"Mama, Midas must be right. This thing must be really huge. It would tip over otherwise, even with stabilizers. So how does it move around all these trees?"

"Not around," Midas answered. "Under. Most plants here grow ground mats, some thick enough for walking on, many not. Your mama smart not to let you get out. Can go under and gone real fast. There water under them, deep channels some places. The Mud Turtle can go under these and all around."

The door was now slowly opening, revealing a lit entryway.

"We go straight in now," Midas ordered. "Stay in the boat 'til I tell you. Got?"

"Got," Clarence promised for them all.

Smokey fought a sudden sensation that she was being trapped. Gripping her hands to the seat, she held on lest she turn and flee. Chiding herself for her foolish panic, she turned her head and rode with the waters into the Turtle's mouth.

Seen from up close, the door was clearly an airlock similar to those at Custer or on a spacecraft. Once the buttertub was through the first door, the door irised shut behind them. With a vibration that shook the very marrow of her bones, an invisible pump sucked the water from the chamber.

Lights recessed high in the curved walls glowed yellowly, revealing that the fat little boat was now resting on a silty floor in an oval-shaped room.

"My ears popped!" Bonny announced, yawning hugely. "And the walls are getting all dark."

"We're under going," Midas said, stretching his words out between yawns so broad that they showed his polished molars. "They never stay up long. When all's secure they bring us through."

"How come you're caught up in this?" Clarence asked. "Are you a psi?"

Midas shook his head. "Nope, but my auntie is and is in the network. You meet her; she called Ravenel. Hush, now they opening."

The inner door was irising open, revealing a lit room beyond and the silhouette of a male figure.

"Hold on!" the man called. "I'm rolling out a mat to keep you from slipping on the mud."

With a rumble and a slap, a roll of rough-surfaced green plastic bounced down the few steps from the inner room and snapped flat precisely beside Midas's boat. Bonny wiggled free and bounded over the side, only to stop and wait for them in one of those bursts of sudden shyness typical of her.

Midas opened a flap in the tub's side and helped first Smokey, then Clarence, down. Now that they were about to meet members of the Underground, presumably friends of her parents, Smokey was acutely aware of her sweat-streaked face and of the ugly funnel hat she still wore. Unable to do anything about the first, she compromised by tugging the hat off and tucking it under her arm. With her free hand, she tousled her hair into what she hoped would pass for artistic disarray.

Midas was already leading the way into the Turtle's shell and Clarence paused to smile fondly before following.

"Vanity, thy name is Smokey." He laughed.

"You bet," she said, taking Bonny's hand and matching the girl's now eager pace. "And you wouldn't have it any other way."

"You're right," he said. "Righter than you know."

Smokey grinned back, then composed herself. She thought she had her lessons from Bethlehem down pat. Even if everyone here was a major telepath—something she doubted—they would get little from her. Privately, she thought of herself as maintaining the enigma of womanhood. Her soft smile at her own conceit vanished as she mounted the steps into the room.

It was carpeted, clearly meant as a reception area. Furnished with several sets of comfortable chairs and low tables, it could easily seat three or four groups of a half dozen people each. Currently, it held only two occupants, both male. One, a tall Oriental with pocked skin and a kind smile, was apparently the man who had unrolled the welcome mat for them.

The second was standing by a control panel set in a pedestal near the far wall. He was Caucasian and quite pale, as if he never saw the sun. His once-golden hair was now liberally streaked with flat grey, making it seem tarnished. Altogether, he was a pale version of the person Smokey had carried in her heart and memories for over a decade. Still she knew him.

"Ross?" she said, her voice shrill with shock.

He raised his head to face her, his well-remembered sheepish grin now sculpted into the planes of his face, but no less genuine.

"Hi, Smokey. Good to see you again," Ross Styler answered. "Is this pretty girl our daughter? Is this Bonny?"

19

An hour later, a shaken Bonny had been taken off to bed. Clarence promised to stay with her until the mild sedative that the Mud Turtle's doctor had prescribed could take effect. Midas had left before he could be missed in Custer, promising that he would see them again.

Smokey wrapped her fingers around the frosted glass Ross had handed to her a moment before. Now they stared at each other, neither knowing where to start.

"Bonny's awfully pretty," Ross said haltingly. "I think she takes after you there, Smokey."

"You should see her marks in math," Smokey replied. "No doubt she got that talent from you."

She sipped from the sour, iced drink, wrinkling up her nose at its sharp bite. Ross coughed into his hand, unsuccessfully covering a chuckle at her expression. Suddenly, they were laughing somewhat awkwardly together.

"Oh, Ross," Smokey said once she had her breath. "Why? Why did you let me think that you were dead?"

"I didn't want to, Smokey," he answered, "but I had to disappear. I had warning through a man I respected and trusted that someone wanted me dead. I didn't believe him, but he had evidence enough that he convinced me to at least fake my departure on that shuttle. Our agreement was that if nothing happened, he would leave me be and I would go back to my work. That's not

177

what happened—as you know. When the craft blew up, I realized that someone did want me dead. I've been hiding out now for over ten years."

"But why didn't you get in touch later?"

He frowned, rubbing the high bridge of his thin nose. "I wanted to, Smokey, but I was convinced that knowing that I lived would endanger you . . . and me. As long as no one but the Underground knew that I lived I would be safe."

Smokey only mirrored his frown and rolled her glass between her palms so that the ice in the glass rang softly.

"You read minds," Ross pleaded with her. "Surely you can see the risk involved if more people knew than needed to. Smokey, don't look at me like that!"

"I'm trying," she replied with great deliberation, "to decide if I should forgive you. I've spent a long time mourning you, raising Bonny to respect your achievements. I've even overlooked her making you into a bit of a hero. Now I need to live with something else. How do I tell my daughter that her father is a coward?"

"Use short words," Ross said dryly. "No one ever said that physicists had to be brave."

"No," Smokey said. "I suppose not, but something you just said has me worried. Did the people here convince you not to get in touch with me?"

"Not just with you, Smoke. With anyone. They didn't want to risk a security breach."

"So you're a prisoner here!" She tried not to shout. "They don't need to put chains on you or bolt your door. They've got you so scared that you couldn't leave."

"Don't get melodramatic, Smoke," Ross growled. "I could leave. I just don't want to. I'm comfortable, safe, and I have useful work. Once we come up with a way to keep the doppels out of our minds, I'll even feel safer in public."

"Hmmph." Smokey scowled. "This Underground had better not be planning on keeping me and Bonny here. I won't stand for my daughter growing up in a 'Mud Turtle.'"

Ross only sighed. Before the silence could become awkward again, he asked, "I hope you'll let me get to know Bonny—even if I am a coward."

"Of course." Smokey relented enough to let a merry grin light her features. "I think she is going to surprise you, just as long as you don't make the mistake of talking down to her. She may be a kid, but she hates that."

"You forget. Most of the geniuses in math and physics are young." Ross pushed back the hair at one greying temple. "I'm over the hill for this area. I think I did my best work years ago on Arizona."

"So you're willing to sit in the mud at the bottom of a swamp." Smokey curled her hair around the fingers of one hand. "I've never let grey hair stop me!"

"Smokey, you haven't lost your talent for making vanity sound like a virtue. I hope that this Clarence appreciates you." Ross grinned. "He's rather cute, if you like the husky type."

"Hands off, brother." She hugged him then. "Or if you must touch, let me in on the fun."

Ross laughed at their old joke and squeezed her in return. "I've missed guy-watching with you, Smoke. I've missed you."

As she held him, Smokey could feel Ross's loneliness and his fear for his life interwoven like plaids on a tartan. She didn't relinquish their embrace, pulling back only enough to see his face.

"Ross, we've got to get out of here. You can't live this way. Or maybe you can, but I can't and I swear that Bonny won't. The answer for all of us is finding a way to stop the doppels so that they can't play puppet-master with our lives."

"Smoke"—he gave her a crooked smile—"you're hardly the first one to say that. Some of these people have been working against the doppels for years."

Smokey shook her head. "Maybe, but I'm not them. I'm going to find a way."

Ross didn't laugh at her, but she felt no confidence from him. "Maybe you will, Smokey. Maybe you will."

There was an uncomfortable pause, then Ross cleared his throat.

"Smoke?"

"Yes, Ross."

"Smoke, there's something I need to tell you." He cleared his throat again, and when Smokey looked at him she was surprised to discover that he was blushing. "Smoke, there's someone here I've . . . well, I've settled down with."

"Ross!" She beamed, concealing a slight surge of possessiveness. "That's wonderful! Why didn't you tell me right away? Where is he? What's he like?"

Ross held up a hand, gesturing for her to slow the cascade of questions.

"I couldn't tell you right away because there was too much else. Then you started acting like I was a prisoner here, and I was afraid if I told you about Pastor, then you'd think he was just a jailer—or an excuse for hiding out."

Smokey nodded. "I see what you mean. Well, tell me about him now."

Ross grinned. "His name is Pastor—Pastor Grimshaw. He's from Icedrake originally and he's a telepath and psychometrician."

"A what?"

"He reads impressions from inanimate objects," Ross clarified. "It's something psychics have claimed to do for ages, but he really can. It's a bit scary. Fortunately for him, he needs to concentrate or it would probably drive him mad."

"I'd think so," Smokey agreed. "Was he the fellow who was here when we came aboard? I know we were introduced, but I didn't catch names."

"No," Ross said. "That was Albert Cheshire. He's sort of the informal president of the Mud Turtle. You'll see more of him later."

Smokey nodded. "Well, tell me about Pastor Grimshaw. Is he cute?"

"I think so," Ross said. "And he's very kind to me. He

understands me better than anyone has—anyone since you, at least. I'm beginning to think that I may need a telepath to understand how I think."

Smokey nodded playful agreement. "I spoiled you. I know. Why hasn't Pastor come to meet me?"

Again, Ross looked uncomfortable. "He knows about you—he couldn't help it, I mean, since he reads my mind and . . . well, he's a bit jealous."

"Jealous? Of me? The two-bit whore who spreads herself around like late summer jam?"

Although she kept her words light, Smokey felt a tinge of sorrow. Clarence still had not completely come to terms with his realization of what her career as a whore meant. They still shared a bed, but he was by turns passionate and distant. She thrust her personal worries from her, for Ross was not laughing.

"Smoke, Pastor knows that what we shared was not sexual. He knows how I'm made, how you're made. He's jealous of our friendship—of what we shared. He knows that of all the people I had to abandon to go into hiding, you were the one I mourned the most."

"I see," Smokey said. "We'll just have to give him time, then. Maybe when he sees how glad I am that you finally have someone who matches you on all levels he'll give me a chance."

Ross smiled, obviously relieved. "Good. Please be patient with him, though. He's as stubborn as an Icedrake cold front."

"I promise."

They talked a bit more, then Ross escorted Smokey to the infirmary. The doctor, a round-faced, round-bodied Oriental woman, was bending over a line of bubbling flasks when they entered.

"Molly, this is Smokey," Ross said. "Smokey, this is Molly Cheshire, the Mud Turtle's resident physician."

The smile Molly gave Smokey was far warmer than Smokey had expected. The doctor bowed slightly from the waist, but did not offer her hand.

"I feel I have already met Smokey, Ross," she said. "Both Bonny and Clarence spoke of her. I had the impression that they were rather worried about her."

"I'm certain they were," Smokey said. "It's not every day that an old friend returns from the dead. I . . . I'm not certain I reacted very well."

"When we heard that you were going to join us," Molly said, "we discussed the best way to inform you that Ross was still alive. There did not seem to be any good way, but perhaps letting Ross meet you was rather sudden."

"For me and for my daughter," Smokey agreed. "How is Bonny? Is Clarence with her?"

Molly motioned toward a closed door. "Bonny is asleep, under light sedation. Clarence insisted on staying with her in case she awoke, so she wouldn't be frightened when she found she was in a strange place."

"Can I just stick my head in to check on her?" Smokey asked. "It's not like she's never spent a night with me elsewhere, but *I* need some reassurance that she's all right."

"The doors open fairly quietly," Molly agreed. "I don't see that there would be a problem."

Bonny was sound asleep, her arms wrapped tightly around a pillow, her breathing slow and regular. When the door opened, Clarence swung to his feet, holding a finger to his lips. Picking his shoes up from the floor, he walked to join them.

"She's out cold," Smokey said, letting the door slide shut. "Can we stay nearby until she wakes up? I don't want to crowd you, Dr. Cheshire, but . . ."

"I understand," Dr. Cheshire answered, "and you wouldn't be crowding me. To be honest, I think it's a good idea for you to stay near. We'll switch on the intercom so we'll be able to hear when Bonny wakes. Then we can pull a few chairs together and make tea over one of the burners. The cafeteria is closed now. Or would you like to sleep?"

Smokey shook her head. "Not me. It can't be much more than evening, can it? I feel far too keyed-up to sleep."

Clarence nodded agreement. "I just stretched out in there to tell Bonny a story while she drifted off. Might have drifted off a bit myself, but I'm not saying."

Awkwardly, Ross cleared his throat. "By the way, I didn't get to say so before, but thanks for taking care of Bonny so that I could fill Smokey in on everything."

Clarence nodded. "I feel like family with these ladies. I couldn't do otherwise, but it's kind of you to thank me anyway."

Smokey held her breath, not knowing what she would do if these two decided to dislike each other, aware that she did not dare try to read either of them in this setting. Momentary frustration flooded her. She hadn't realized how much she relied on her telepathy—limited as it was—to aid her in sculpting social situations.

Turning from where she had been filling a glass flask at a sink, Molly broke the silence.

"Ross, you know where I keep the extra chairs. Would you and Clarence pull out a couple? Smokey, if you'll look in the cabinet beneath the counter, you'll find a tea set and some tea. Could you make certain they're clean enough to use?"

The ritual of making tea filled the awkward moment, and when they settled in to sip the Guillen-grown oolong, Smokey decided to steer the conversation away from issues of family and children.

"The Mud Turtle is quite a hideout," she said. "Joy and Bethlehem didn't give us any idea of what to expect, but even from what little they said, I didn't expect this."

Molly and Ross smiled, identical expressions of pride shaping their very different features.

"The Mud Turtle is an amazing engineering feat," Ross said. "It's a mobile habitat, capable of staying submerged for up to two weeks without any difficulty, longer if one doesn't mind stale air."

"We use technology that's not much different from what you would find in a starship's life-support system,"

Molly added, "including an excellent hydroponics garden that doubles as a source of supplies. Since Ross joined us, our standard of living has really improved."

"Ross?" Smokey said. "Have you been making nixies for them?"

"Not nixies—water really isn't a need here," Ross said.

Molly chuckled. "Unless you mean the need to keep it out."

"True," Ross said, "but when I came here I started adapting my research in nanotechnology to improving conditions."

"Before Ross came," Molly interjected, "we had a tremendous problem with mold growing in valves and tubing. He's come up with something that scours it off."

"Not really scouring," Ross said, "rather converting it to components that flush away easily when the systems are cycled. I must admit, it's done quite a bit for the musty smell this place used to have."

"So you have a laboratory here?" Clarence asked.

"That's right," Ross said. "A good one. I guess we spent the better part of three years setting it up. The parts were collected in bits and pieces over that time. I still receive the major journals in my field—the subscription is pirated from the Guillen University system—and I update as quickly as I can."

"Sounds fine," Clarence said. "Is there a library that I can use? If we're going to be here a while, I'd hate to lose touch with things."

"We have a good library," Molly said. "Otherwise most of us would be at each other's throats for lack of things to do. We're not just hiding out here—we consider ourselves a rebel outpost devoted to finding a way to limit the doppels' actions."

"And?" Smokey asked. "Have you any idea how to defeat them?"

"Some," Molly said. "There are some promising lines of research. I've been working with chemicals that seem to influence psionic talents. These may give us a tool."

Ross sighed. "While tools may help, I suspect that what we are missing is a fresh point of view. When we get it, things should fall into place."

Clarence nodded agreement. "That happens more often than people realize. Sometimes all it takes is looking at existing data in a new way to realize that the answer had been there all along."

Thinking of Bonny's intent work during the weeks of travel on the *Ibn Battuta,* Smokey started to speak. Then she reconsidered. Bonny would have enough new things to deal with as they adjusted to life on the Mud Turtle. She didn't need added pressure. And Smokey was honest enough with herself to admit that she might be bringing the pressure to bear not because she believed in Bonny's insight, but out of a desperate hope that her daughter might hold the key to their freedom.

The next several days passed fairly quickly. As on a spacecraft, day was an arbitrary concept, but the community in the Mud Turtle was small enough that a regular schedule of waking and sleeping hours simplified work schedules. About twenty-five people—the mudcrawlers—lived in the Turtle full-time. All but Ross, Bonny, and Clarence were psionics. Outsiders, like Midas, came and stayed a few hours, bringing hard goods or news too sensitive to trust to even the well-shielded communications units.

Smokey quickly grasped that the three of them were there on sufferance, as a favor to Bethlehem and Joy. Clarence was able to make himself useful by turning his sociological talents to tracking probable Driver actions through media and law enforcement reports. Bonny was put back into schooling and spent much of her free time working with Ross.

Smokey found that her own skills, both as a whore and a spy, were not precisely unwelcome, but certainly were not trusted or invited. A few of the senior telepaths continued the training that Bethlehem had begun. In addition to teaching her a variety of ways to conceal her

Talent, they stressed lessons on telepathic etiquette. Her primary instructor was Bruni Hagensik, one of the best telepaths in the Mud Turtle.

Bruni Hagensik stood only five feet tall, but with her fair complexion, blue eyes, and somewhat frizzy blond hair, she resembled a petite Valkyrie. The comparison pleased her and she would often stand, hands on hips, smiling a broad, white-toothed smile, and recite tales from her Viking ancestry. Her lessons were as uncompromising in tone as the military tactics of her distant ancestors, and she had little patience with the illustrious rogue who was her newest student.

"Now, Smokey, when you're with other telepaths, common courtesy is that you refrain from reading either their minds or the minds of those around you."

Smokey had heard something similar from Bethlehem, but she couldn't resist being refractory. Bruni's smug certainty that she was the teacher, Smokey the novice, set the whore's temper on edge. Whatever else she was, she was not a novice.

"Why not?" Smokey countered. "When you look at the situation objectively, it would seem that one should be free to read minds especially around other telepaths. After all, they're the only ones who can get as good as you give, right?"

Bruni prickled, but surprisingly, she kept her calm.

"I can tell that you have never had true mind to mind contact with another telepath," she said. "If you had, you would not speak lightly of the experience."

"What's so different about it?" Smokey asked, curiosity replacing her defensiveness.

Bruni ran her fingertips through her hair, frizzing it even further. She frowned.

"There is an—an openness that can come with telepath to telepath contact. It does not always happen, but when it does, it is disturbing," she said. "Words cannot quite describe it, but if the participants are not careful, it can penetrate far deeper than mere conversation."

"I still don't get it," Smokey said. "I know that my father can 'talk' to my mother mentally. That's part of how they coordinate their act."

"Well," Bruni said, "I would not presume to speak for Joy and Bethlehem, but I would guess that they have learned how to modulate their contact so that Bethlehem only reads surface thoughts. It's either that or Joy trusts Bethlehem enough to permit him full access to her thoughts."

"Oh," Smokey said, shivering a bit at the idea of anyone having freedom of her thoughts.

"When a telepath reads a nontelepath," Bruni continued, ignoring Smokey's reaction, "the reading is one-sided, so our etiquette is to avoid such occasions without express invitation. Can you see the rationale behind this?"

Smokey nodded. "Yes, I can. If a nontelepath grows to trust the telepath's manners, then telepathy is no longer frightening."

"That's right," Bruni said. "Such little rules exist all through human societies—from little things like the formality of introductions or recognized limits of personal space to big things like prohibitions against rape and theft."

"Not all of those are merely matters of etiquette," Smokey protested. "There are laws against rape, theft, and the like."

"True," Bruni said, "but those laws would not exist without a sense that those actions are objectionable—either on lofty moral grounds or for the simple reason that most of us would prefer that they not happen to us and, therefore, we support others' right to be free from such attentions as well."

"So my use of my telepathy is criminal from the point of view of other telepaths," Smokey said, cutting to the heart of the matter.

"Yes . . ." Bruni paused, obviously reevaluating her first answer. "Perhaps 'criminal' is too strong a term. 'Gauche' might be a better word."

"Like picking my nose in public?" Smokey said, deliberately crude.

"That," Bruni said, "combined with something like innocent malice. You used your Talent to become a predator, to take from defenseless people information that they would not have given willingly."

"I also gave back for what I took," Smokey reminded her. "Not one of those men left without getting one of the best lays that he had ever had—I couldn't have given them that without touching their minds."

Bruni tilted her head and studied Smokey, pity plain on her features.

"But they paid for the lay, Smokey," she said. "You didn't get your reputation and the fees that went with it based on your mind-reading. You got it for giving a unique sexual experience."

"So I'm a predator," Smokey said, "a tiger lying in wait for the innocent and rending them with mental claws."

"You are," Bruni agreed, "and now you—without willing it—have become a different type of tiger. You now know that you have tasted forbidden flesh. If you return to those habits, you are no longer guilty of innocent malice, but malice aforethought."

"Wait a moment!" Smokey protested. "You can't impose your code of etiquette on me!"

"Within the Mud Turtle, I can," Bruni said. "If you choose to ignore our code, then the courtesy we extend to each other will not be extended to you. You are not skilled enough with your personal shield to block the stronger telepaths among us. And remember—telepathy is only one of the Talents represented here. Would you like a clairvoyant watching you go about your day? A telekinetic moving things from beneath your hands and feet? We could easily make your days and nights a nightmare, Smokey."

Smokey glowered at her. "That's blackmail."

"As you yourself said," Bruni countered, "social

codes are often enforced by laws. Our laws are no different for all that they apply to and are enforced by a small group."

A comm call came then for Bruni, and Smokey was left alone to think over what she had been told. There was a certain logic to the code that had been outlined to her, but to do without her telepathy . . . She had come to depend on the edge it gave her in interpersonal relationships.

Bruni returned, a bounce to her step that had not been there when she had left.

"There will be a supply boat here in just a few minutes," she said. "Want to come along and help unload? It's such a break when we get visitors!"

Even though she had only been in the Mud Turtle for a few days, Smokey was already tired of seeing the same faces. Compared to the variety that had been hers on Arizona, first the *Ibn Battuta* and now the Mud Turtle seemed insulated enough to be psychologically claustrophobic.

"Great!" she said, reaching almost on reflex to touch Bruni, then quickly drawing her hand back. "Sorry . . . I'm a touchy person. This is going to be a hard thing to learn not to do."

Bruni's expression was an equal mixture of sternness and guarded sympathy.

"Still, you must learn. Many of us find physical contact distasteful—a habit instilled in the days when our Talents were Awakening and we did not know how to guard against them."

They walked toward the lift, joining a general migration. Most of the Mud Turtle's inhabitants must be going to get news of the friends outside, mail, or just a break from routine.

"I know that my father's parents were there to help him through his Awakening," Smokey said, recalling Bethlehem's tale, "but do many of you Awaken without any knowledge of what's going on—like I did?"

Despite quick nodded greetings to several people, Bruni gave Smokey's question her full attention.

"Of those here, the division is about half and half, maybe even a bit heavier in favor of those who had someone around to guide them. There are wild Talents, offspring of those who fled the Project or of those who were discarded as failures by the Project, before the Project realized that the Talents were often latent, needing an appropriate catalyst or merely maturity to develop."

"I see," Smokey said. "Bethlehem said that he didn't want to tutor Bonny about her potential Talent because he could interfere with its development."

"That's right," Bruni said. "Sometimes trying too hard to make the Talent manifest is the best way to create a block against it. That's what the Project ran into in its early years. They discarded an early batch of—had they known it—fully viable psionics into the gene pool. Some of these manifested Talents later, others never did, but their children did."

"What a mess," Smokey said.

"That's true enough," Bruni agreed, "and those wild Talents became one of the excuses used for the witch-hunt of the Purges."

"So when I ran away," Smokey said, "Bethlehem knew that any Talent I had was more likely to develop, didn't he?"

"I won't second-guess Bethlehem," Bruni said, "but it is possible. He also must have known that you were smart—and I bet he made certain that you had heard plenty about what happens to careless psionics."

Remembering some of the stories and anecdotes that Bethlehem and Joy had made a part of her education, Smokey could only nod.

"They did care," she said softly. "More than I ever realized."

Bruni winked at her, a wink that replaced a hug quite effectively. "They were faced with a difficult choice. They could educate you more formally as to your potential and risk dampening it—as well as risking your rebellion against their provisions. Or they could set you free and hope. I would guess that when you ran away they chose the latter, realizing that their own public lifestyle was not a very safe place to raise an Awakening psionic."

Smokey rubbed her temples, a gesture that was only partially theatrical. Her thoughts were so busy and confused that she barely noticed when they arrived at the docking bay.

Midas was among those who had brought supplies. He stood, water streaming from him. Bonny, who had apparently forgiven him for saying that she looked like a boy, was helping him to towel off.

"Is called 'rain,' 'Zonie chick," he was saying as she clucked over him. "Happens like all the time, not much to fuss over."

Bonny sighed in mock exasperation. "I don't care what it's called, Midas, or whether it happens all the time. No matter what you say, you're still leaving puddles on the deck and those take a while to dry."

Smokey took her leave of Bruni, who was already hurrying over to talk to one of the adult arrivals, and joined Midas and Bonny. Midas saw her and smiled cheerfully.

"Going good, lady?" he said. "We get your stuff from the Rushhour. Took no trouble at all. Word is given to those who even notice—and they not too many—that you gone upside to one of the stations, nobody bother to check which one even. You free and clear."

Bonny tossed the wet towel into a heap with several others and inspected Midas critically.

"You'll do," she said. "I guess that means we'll be staying here for a while, right, Mama?"

"That's right," Smokey agreed. "Midas, are you certain that our trail was covered well enough?"

"Tha's right," he said. "Downside thinks you up, up thinks down or flown. Lots of manifests need to be checked to make certain one way or another. Anyhow things get muddled lots of times—water, fog, and mist ain't kind to computer circuits: glitches dance here."

"Good," Smokey said. "Bonny, are Clarence or Ross around?"

"Papa is checking to see if some equipment he ordered came," Bonny said. "Clarence said something about helping to move boxes from the buttertubs."

"I guess I'll see if I can do the same. Can you keep yourself out of trouble?"

"I'll keep her if you don't mind, ma'am," Midas said. "Always get a meal when I'm here for more than a minute, but hate eating alone. Auntie Ravenel is chattering like a newsie with uncle, won't have time for me for a while."

"Do you mind keeping Midas company, Bon-ton?" Smokey asked, knowing full well the answer.

"No, I can show him where everything is."

"Know that, 'Zonie," Midas said, grinning, "jus' want to study what a 'Zonie chick thinks eating is—might try to eat sand."

When they had vanished, still carping at each other, Smokey went and helped with getting the cargo aboard. Molly Cheshire handed her a dataclip as soon as the last box was in the hold.

"We need these scanned so we can start putting together an order for next time," she said. "Just record everything in that heap—I'll take this one. We can synthesize results later."

As she worked, Smokey caught a glimpse of Pastor Grimshaw helping Ross unroll the packaging around some electronic components. The stare he gave her when his eyes met hers was anything but kind.

Not part of the Underground, yet dependent on it, Smokey became increasingly frustrated as she found that very few of the senior members would take her seriously. As the weeks passed, she fumed in private, biding her time, learning everything she could about the doppels, about the Underground, and about the current state of research, all the while concealing her own impatience to leave from the others with a skill that would probably have surprised Bruni, who thought her rather frivolous.

When the murders started, all bets were off.

The first victim was Sey'zar, an elderly, dark-skinned

man with long, silvery hair that grew in a fringe that began just below ear level on his otherwise polished bald scalp. Sey'zar had been blinded by an industrial accident when he was only five, but the shock had awakened another type of vision.

His clairvoyance was so powerful that he could "see" anywhere else on the planet and often into the orbital stations above. Since his Talent worked best if someone he knew was present at the distant contact point, the psionic experts hypothesized that a form of telepathy was involved. Sey'zar claimed not to be able to read minds, however, so if he was a telepath, he was completely unaware of his gift.

Telepath or clairvoyant, he was able to do quite well with his second sight and had made a good living for himself as an entertainer before a wave of antipsionic feeling had sent him fleeing into the Underground, where he had remained since.

His death would have been dismissed as being from natural causes, for he was old and not in the best of health, but one of the mudcrawlers, an Icedrake native named Krystal, claimed to have foreseen his death. She insisted that a "dark bird" had wrenched Sey'zar's protesting spirit from his body. Again, elsewhere, her claims might have been dismissed as grief or hysteria, but the Underground took such things seriously.

Krystal's precognition was an erratic but recognized Talent and so a detailed autopsy was ordered on Sey'zar's body.

Molly had barely begun work when Piet, Krystal's lover, found her dead body in their cabin. The cause of Krystal's death could not be dismissed as accidental. The sharp, curving fang of an Icedrake sabertooth had been thrust repeatedly through her chest and then left in the pooling blood beside her corpse.

The Underground's ruling body, five seniors popularly called the Coven, assembled with Smokey hastily elected to fill the place of the deceased Sey'zar. Smokey was not permitted to let the honor go to her head. Brushing against Albert Cheshire, the Coven's chair, she learned that she had been included because she was viewed as the least indispensable of the Mud Turtle's inhabitants.

She kept her chagrin at this cutting, if accurate, estimation to herself and resolved to use her new rank as a means of learning what she could to get her and Bonny out of an asylum that was rapidly becoming a death-filled prison.

Coolly, Smokey assessed each of her cohorts. Albert Cheshire was the man who had been with Ross the day they had arrived at the Mud Turtle. He was also Molly's younger brother. An Oriental of middle years, he wore his jetty hair blunt cut across his forehead and below the level of his ears. Normally, his dark, almond-shaped eyes danced with an appropriate mischief. His Talent involved poltergeist activity—including a variety of embarrassing audio illusions he used with less than good taste to discomfort those he deemed too self-important. As this category included almost everyone, he made a relaxed and popular chair for a singularly sensitive and often socially inept group.

Midas's aunt, Ravenel, was also a member of the Coven. A plum-No mystic and native of Guillen, Ravenel was the only name the woman claimed, perhaps because it suited her so well. She wore her long, thick brown hair drawn back from her brow, usually with a silver bar clip, though at times she held it in place with wooden combs carved with Guillen vines. Copper-skinned, of average height, and given somewhat to plumpness, she exuded an aura of calm that reminded Smokey of her fellow mystic, Erun nu-Rakl. Unfortunately, Ravenel's Talent was telekinesis accompanied by a gift for common sense, neither of which was likely to recommend her over Grimshaw as the chief investigator.

Bruni Hagensik was a member of the Coven as well—not surprisingly, as she was the probably the most skilled telepath. Smokey suspected that Bruni had wanted to correct her when she had "bumped" Albert, but the Arizona whore had greater worries than the ire of a miniature Valkyrie.

The most immediate of these worries was Pastor Grimshaw. Ross Styler's lover was an attractive but stern man with a grizzled beard and glossy chestnut hair. Despite the fact that Smokey had done nothing to threaten his relationship with Ross, it was quite apparent that he still viewed Smokey's appearance as a dreadful catastrophe, one that was certain to lead to Ross's destruction.

As the Coven convened to discuss how to deal with the murders, Pastor's flat blue stare fell on Smokey in a fashion that made it clear he would be delighted to pin the crimes on her. Knowing that his Talent combined telepathy with the ability to sense impressions from inanimate objects did not comfort Smokey at all. Grimshaw was clearly the logical person to be put in charge of any criminal investigation.

Nervous energy was running high enough throughout the Mud Turtle that several of the telepaths and empaths had been issued mild sedatives. With an expression of relief, as the Coven convened, Albert Cheshire ordered the conference chamber sealed and rapped them to order—without touching his gavel, Smokey noted.

"I move for skipping the usual routine and addressing the emergency," Bruni Hagensik said.

Her motion was seconded and passed by unanimous vote.

"I have the medical report," Ravenel stated. "Sey'zar's death was caused by a triple dose of the medication that he had been taking to control heart irregularities. Perhaps someone who wasn't part of the Underground could believe that Sey'zar accidentally overdosed, but we all know that his blindness made him methodical in the extreme. A double dose I might believe, but never a triple."

"Did the report note how much medication would be needed to assure his death?" Smokey asked, ignoring Grimshaw's glare.

Ravenel flipped screens. "Yes, it does. Two doses might have been enough, but three was a guaranteed overdose."

"That seems rather much of a coincidence," Albert said. "I know from experience that the Turtle's medical records are officially considered sealed, but in practice nearly anyone could get access to them. Molly has her virtues, but she is not very security conscious."

"And why should she be?" Pastor Grimshaw replied, his tone rough and level. "Until now, we have always been safe within our own community."

Smokey acutely felt her exclusion, but she bit back the sharp retort that came readily to her lips. Perhaps Ravenel was sensitive to the tension, for she hit a tab that brought her into her next file.

"I have the medical report on Krystal's death." She hesitated. "It's very technical."

"Molly always gets technical when she's upset"— Albert's affection for his sister was clear—"but I don't think we really need the gory details. Most of us 'heard' them after Krystal's body was found."

"Poor Piet," Bruni said with uncharacteristic gentleness. "I don't think he would have projected that way under any other circumstances. His control had become flawless, but he and Krystal had just started sharing a suite a few days earlier. He was still on a lift from romantic euphoria, then this . . ."

Grimshaw nodded sharply, his fingers worrying the left edge of his beard. Smokey wondered if he was reflecting on how he might have reacted to finding Ross murdered. When he spoke, his voice was even, if a shade more gravelly.

"If we've finished with the medical reports, let me proceed to my reading of Krystal's room and of the tooth."

The assembled Coven members leaned forward as one, but Pastor's gaze was turned inward.

"I found little that will be useful. Krystal and Piet's traces were both in the room, but that is to be expected. The tooth itself has such a violent history that one more bloody killing did not mark it." His face contorted as if the memory of what he had sensed was physically painful. "Krystal had it from one of the sabertooths that has been gen-engineered and released on Icedrake. I had always believed that it was a facsimile, but it was the genuine article. I am curious as to how she acquired it; I thought those creatures were protected."

"They are," Ravenel commented. "Krystal told me that this one had to be killed when it contracted a disease—something like rabies. She had a relative who made her a gift of the fang as a memento when Krystal was forced to flee Icedrake."

Albert Cheshire glanced at Ravenel and then Pastor. "Anything else, Pastor?"

"No, whoever it was took precautions. I doubt that the killer was in Krystal's suite for more than the time it took to stab her."

Albert sighed heavily and began drumming the table-top with his fingers. Continuing the short tattoo, he studied each of them thoughtfully.

"Thus far, no one has raised any reason we should believe that these deaths were accidental. Does anyone wish to do so?" Silence met his question and after a moment Albert continued. "Does anyone have any provable suspicion as to who might have committed one or both of the killings?"

"Except to comment that evidence strongly suggests that the same party or parties did both killings—Krystal's because she might have come up with evidence to convict Sey'zar's murderer," Pastor said, "no, nothing certain. Yet."

"Anyone else?" Albert asked.

"I agree with Pastor," Ravenel said, "but no."

Short negative gestures met the chair's inquiring gaze. Another moment passed during which Albert's almond eyes narrowed as if contemplating an unpleasant task.

"Then our next duty must be to appoint an official inspector. Although this person does not need to be of the Coven, I advise that we choose from our own numbers to reduce debate."

"I nominate Pastor Grimshaw," Smokey said quickly,

having decided that the best way to deal with the unpleasant was to embrace it. It had worked with certain men.

Grimshaw looked sincerely surprised, not so much at the suggestion as at who had made it. The others were nodding agreement, but Ravenel raised one graceful hand.

"I think we are overlooking another logical choice," Ravenel said. "Smokey may be a less powerful telepath, but as a newcomer she may see us all with less bias. Also, she has done investigative work before this and may have resources we lack."

Bruni nodded. "Yes, she can always ask Pastor to touch read for her."

"Why not have them both do the job?" Albert offered. "Not only could they rely on each other, but if, as we suspect, the killer may seek to eliminate an investigator, this would broaden the field and protect both."

By common consent, Smokey and Pastor had remained silent while the others debated.

"I'd be happy to work with Pastor," Smokey said seriously, inwardly cringing, "if he'll have me."

Her words clearly made him the one who would govern the choice and Smokey felt certain he would not wish to seem petty before the Coven. She was right.

His smile looked as if it hurt his face, but Grimshaw extended a hand to her. "I accept the Coven's suggestion and will work with Smokey."

Smokey grinned and pecked him on one prickly cheek. "Thanks—partner."

Grimshaw was too skillful a telepath to let anything go, but Smokey was certain that she had caught him off guard. Good. She was actually beginning to feel like her old Arizona self.

They started working as soon as the Coven adjourned by reviewing the locations given in the official report for the Mud Turtle's population at the time of Krystal's death. All of the mudcrawlers had filed reports (Smokey noted that Bonny had been with Ross; Clarence had been in the library), but not all of them had someone who could confirm their word. In fact, the members of the Psionic Underground were largely loners, something that might be expected from a group whose abnormal abilities had set them apart from their peers and had finally driven them into hiding.

Only three of the Turtle's residents—Ross, Bonny, and Clarence—were not psionic. They were dually isolated, for not only were they in hiding, but Smokey knew the Underground was unlikely to let them leave. Bethlehem and Joy could be permitted, even encouraged, to wander the spacelanes, because to reveal the Underground would be to betray themselves. A nonpsionic might be tempted by the rewards some governments still offered, might even seek out and join the doppels.

Smokey shivered and then hid her reaction from Pastor Grimshaw by reaching for the loose jacket she had flung over a chairback. She had been so busy bitching about being useless and caught in others' plans that she hadn't seen the obvious. She wasn't trapped. The one who was trapped was Clarence. His love for her had led him into a prison and the only key to his escape was her standing bond for him. For that, she would need to win the Underground's gratitude and trust.

Buttoning on her jacket, she scrolled through the screens of accumulated data, urgently aware that she—not Pastor—must be the one to find the killer, equally aware of how slim her chances of success truly were.

20

"SHE'S REALLY SOMETHING, SMOKE," ROSS SAID, pouring her an iced glass of bitter green tea. "There are days when I forget for hours at a time that she's only a kid."

"She is though," Smokey said, "and her birthday is at hand. She'll be awfully disappointed if you forget."

"I won't," he promised. "I've been working on a surprise. Pastor's a great pastry chef. I'm sure we can requisition the makings for something sweet."

"Ah, you've found the way to her heart. Can you get ice cream? She's practically addicted to it, and it's fairly hard to get on Arizona." Smokey smiled. "When I took her up to the Wheel to see Joy perform, it was all Bonny could do to choose for all the flavors. I remember thinking that Daniel Chinue wouldn't have been so impressed with her if he could have seen her then."

"Chinue? What does that fossil have to do with Bonny?"

"Fossil? He didn't look that old to me," Smokey teased. "He was a plant of some sort in some of her classes on the V. Got the shock of his life when he found out that his hottest classmate was a girl of nine. I think he wants to recruit her for some fancy university."

"I'm sure! Don't let him have her. She's too original to fill up with other people's methods. He'd be real surprised if he could see what she's doing here." Ross emptied his glass. "Bonny has a way of coming fresh to what we've been doing that keeps unraveling minor tangles. If she keeps up this way, she'll be undoing knots."

Smokey glanced at her timepiece. Still ample time before she had to meet Pastor and Molly to review medical reports on Sey'zar's overdose and Krystal's wounds. She sipped her drink and nodded.

"Good. Ross, are you making certain that Bonny is getting her rest?"

Ross chuckled self-consciously. "Yeah, I'm learning. I hadn't realized that she would work herself to collapse if I didn't make her quit. Now the computer locks her out for an hour for every two and six for every twenty.

"Oh, don't worry," he went on hurriedly, misreading Smokey's expression of concern. "She has an override she can use once every eight hours so that she won't need to stop working if she's on a roll."

"Ross, you idiot," Smokey swatted him, "she needs more rest than that. You'll burn her out and then she'll be no good to either of you. I'll give you the schedule we worked out on Arizona and you two can adapt it. Fair?"

"Fair." Ross paused, then stared uncomfortably at the tabletop. "How are things going with the investigation? With Pastor?"

Smokey considered lying and discarded the impulse immediately. "So-so. He seems to accept that I have some abilities that don't involve spreading my legs, but he's hostile. I think he'd still like to pin the deaths on me or, failing with me, on Clarence."

"Yeah." Ross stood and took one of her hands in his. "Smoke, give him a chance. Even more than a chance. He's worth it. It's just that not only are you an outsider—and on some level we all want to deny that the killer has to be one of us—he's also trying to adjust to Bonny. A kid is the one thing we can't give each other, and as long as we're locked away in here we can't even adopt. Pastor's taking your arrival with my daughter rather hard because it's reminding him of things that we've tried to forget."

Smokey rose and embraced him. "I'll give Pastor a chance—and more—Ross. You make certain that Bonny gets a rest from math and physics."

"Capi," Ross agreed. He paused halfway out of the door. "Oh, and find the killer, too, while you're about things. Would you, Smoke? I'm tired of having Pastor out at all hours doing cop work."

"Right." She checked the time. "In fact, I have just time to stop and give Clarence a hug before my next meeting. See you!"

She didn't tell Ross that she was worried about Clarence. His moods had been erratic lately—friendly one time, grumpy the next. Sometimes he spent hours shuffling his increasingly worn deck of tarot cards, examining the painted pasteboard rectangles as if they really held the answers to future dilemmas. Only to herself did she admit that she was rather glad to have the investigation as an excuse to get away.

"Molly will be joining us in a few minutes," Pastor said when Smokey entered his office. He glanced at the chronometer built into his desk. "Actually, I expected her several minutes ago."

Smokey paused in the doorway. "Her labs and office are one level down, aren't they? Let me run down."

Pastor actually smiled. "I would be grateful if you would, Smokey. Molly can be touchy and, if I call her, she's likely to get prickly and stall just so she can prove that I can't order her around."

"I'll be faster than a chulo through a cactus pear," Smokey promised. "I won't even tell Molly that you were asking for her."

Grimshaw's muttered "Thanks" followed her out into the corridor. In the days since coming to dwell in the Mud Turtle, Smokey had memorized the concentric rings of the corridors. Only one long curve separated her from a service ladder. She shinnied down it, pleased with her tactics. This way if Molly was heading toward the lift, they wouldn't have a potentially awkward meeting. If Molly was in the lab, she could claim that she had been passing by on her way to meet with Pastor and had looked in to see if Molly wanted to walk up with her.

The door to the lab was closed when she arrived, so Smokey tapped the intercom. When there was no answer, she started to turn away, convinced that Molly had already headed up. Some impulse she didn't consciously understand made her turn back and rekey the intercom.

"Pastor," she said, her thumb still bearing down on the lab's door buzzer, "is Molly with you? No? I'm outside the door and she's not answering. Yes, it's locked. No, I can't unlock it! I'm an honest whore, not a lockpick. If she doesn't show up in a few minutes, you'd better get someone down here."

Someone came in the form of Piet, followed by Pastor himself. Piet put his hand on the electronic doorplate, bent his head and scrunched up his eyes. He exhaled so gustily that the sound nearly covered that of the door opening.

Pastor was through the door as it was opening, but Smokey ducked under his arm and was in before him.

"What's that?" she coughed. "Smell. Smoke."

The lab was filled with acrid, grey-green vapors and sulfurous fumes burning the eyes, scouring the throat and nose raw. Smokey started to take a deep breath, immediately decided that this was a mistake, and bulled ahead to where a figure bulked against the floor.

"Pastor! Piet!" she choked, touching it. "It's Molly and she still has a heartbeat. Hurry!"

There was some confusion as to where to take Molly, since Molly's lab was also auxiliary to the Turtle's infirmary and she the doctor. Somehow they ended up in Ross's lab and, with Bonny tucked under her arm, Smokey shoved through the dithering group.

"Do any of you have the least idea of what you're doing?" she said. "Get oxygen. Pull up her records on the computer. We can't stabilize her fully until we know what's normal."

She probed Molly's supine form, noticing the pallor beneath her normally golden skin.

"Why are doctors always chunky?" she asked no one in particular. "In Molly's case, it was probably a good thing that she was carrying some extra weight. We're going to need to get liquids into her, but if her throat feels as raw as mine does, she's not going to want to drink."

Albert Cheshire had come panting to the door and now shouldered his way through the crowded room to his sister's side.

"What are you doing, whore?" he snarled. "Don't you specialize in a different kind of playing doctor?"

Smokey leveled a steely gaze at him. "I grew up on starliners. I ran away when I was fifteen. I learned a lot of odd things, both growing up and to survive. Doctoring is one of those. I'm not in Molly's league, but I'm better than any of these hysterical psychotics. I'll back off, Cheshire, if you've got someone better."

She coughed violently, the speech too much for her raw throat. No one spoke. For a long moment, no one breathed. Nor did anyone meet Smokey's glare. Finally, Bonny put a timid hand on Albert's arm.

"Really, Mama does know what she's doing. She even taught a class at my school. Can't you tell she just wants to help?"

Albert shifted embarrassedly. "The Turtle is short of anything more than first aid techs; we have never needed more. Molly's a psychic surgeon, you know, as well as the usual kind. Can you help her?"

Smokey took the IV equipment Piet extended to her and checked the style. "Yes. I think so. I'd rather set up in a cleaner room than this."

"Molly's own room is just a level away," Albert offered. "We can go there."

Nodding, Smokey checked Molly's vital signs.

"Good, she should be coming around soon. Let's get her moved before she'll feel it. Once she's resting, I want someone with her at all times, but not a great mob like this."

"I'll stay with her," Albert said. "Do you think she's in great danger?"

The arrival of the gurney and the work of shifting Molly gave Smokey a moment to think. She considered hiding her thoughts, but decided that with telepaths around this might be more dangerous than speaking bluntly.

"Not from these injuries, Albert," she said, "but you don't think that her 'accident' was just chance, do you?"

"No?" Albert had clearly been too worried to think about implications. "You mean . . ."

Pastor Grimshaw nodded. "Yes, Smokey is right. This is clearly a third murder attempt; probably the only thing that kept it from being a third murder was that Molly was late for her meeting. It probably saved her life."

"That has to be the first good thing I've heard about a meeting," Albert muttered.

The lift stopped. After helping guide the gurney out, Pastor turned to Albert and Smokey.

"Excuse me, but I've got to start finding out where everyone has been. I'll also need to check the lab—though that can wait since it's sealed now." He gave Smokey an awkward bow. "If you could join me as soon as you are sure that Molly is safe and stable, I would be grateful. I could use your help."

Smokey returned the bow. "I'll be there."

Stabilizing Molly took the better part of an hour, partly because Albert was so anxious that Smokey had to explain every procedure.

"She's always been there," he explained, stroking back his sister's shiny black hair and tucking a coiled braid into place. "The big sister, the wise one. Our parents died in one of the Psionic Purges, but they got us away. I'm lucky, I guess, that my Talent can be dismissed as mere chance. Molly's can't be, though. Do you know what a psychic surgeon does?"

Smokey considered strapping Molly's arm loosely to the bed so that she wouldn't jostle the IV free. The woman was beginning to stir now, her flat, Oriental features contorting as she tried to swallow.

"Hand me that bottle, Albert," Smokey said. Then, to distract him as she began the messy task of getting her semiconscious patient to swallow some liquid, she asked, "Wasn't there a man on Old Terra who was supposed to be able to do surgery while possessed by the ghost of a German doctor? I saw a play about him back on Arizona."

Albert nodded. "Arigo, the Brazilian. Molly could do things like that—surgery without tools and without scars afterward—even when we were little. She didn't think she was anybody else either, but she had this—aura—for lack of a better word. Really confident, really calm.

"Almost any other set of parents," Albert continued, wiping the liquid that had spilled onto Molly's neck, "would have ignored what she was doing as an elaborate 'pretend,' but our mother was a clairvoyant telepath. She saw the truth right away, just like she knew I had a real poltergeist problem, not just a bad temper. Dad pulled strings and Molly started medical school young. Miracles were done in private, but now she had justification for her knowledge."

He sat for so long, silently stroking his sister's hand, that Smokey thought that the story was over. When the carved jade figurines set around the room began to vibrate in their niches and shelves, she suspected that Albert had only been finding the courage to go on.

"Mother must have known that the vigilantes were coming for her and Dad," he said, his exuberance gone, his voice husky, "but she didn't try running. I think she knew that Dad wouldn't—couldn't. He had been paralyzed a few years earlier in an 'accident.' She sent Molly and me to visit some friends—for a birthday party of all the stupid idiocies. We never went back home."

Smokey nodded. "You didn't come here right away, though, did you?"

"No." Albert twinkled, his normal good temper surfacing for a moment. "First both of us went to Oxford; then I took a job in Singapore. Molly became a surgeon in London. Do you know what surgeons see every day?

The misery? The pain? Molly broke down under the stress and started hauling out tumors, cleaning gooped valves—all without the benefit of UMA approved tactics. She found that she could do a—I'm not sure what to call it—a remote, field hypnosis?"

He shrugged. "Something like that, so observers wouldn't notice anything odd about what she was doing. Usually she remembered to forbid cameras, but she forgot one day when a brain tumor ruptured and she had to go after the parts, pronto."

"And that was the end," Smokey said, "or close."

"Yeah, we . . ." Albert jumped, his almond eyes bright with hope. "Smokey! She's opened her eyes! Look!"

Smokey did and met the grateful gaze of a miracle healer, who, having cured hundreds with no real desire for recognition or remuneration, now in her hour of need found herself being treated by a 'Zonie whore with jumped-up first aid. Smokey felt acutely humble, but covered her emotion by reaching for the water cup.

"Prop her up gently, Albert," she said more brusquely than she intended. "Let's see if she can handle more than a few sips of this."

Molly did, choking only slightly. Then she signaled that she needed to rest—but not before squeezing Smokey's hand and letting her gratitude and affection flood through the contact. The sensation was a balm for Smokey's lacerated, isolated soul, and she broke the contact reluctantly.

"I'll stay here all night," Albert promised, "and call someone if I get sleepy. Probably Ravenel."

"Sounds good." Smokey squeezed his shoulders. "Now, I need to go and help Pastor. Call if you need me."

She hurried through the curving corridors, her mind racing ahead, wondering what Grimshaw would have learned. His office door flashed open as she raised her hand to buzz for admittance. Momentarily, she wondered if he had detected her. Then Clarence's bulk filled the doorframe.

"Smokey-jo!" His smile was warm, wide, and bright. "How's the patient?"

His embrace was quick, but not perfunctory. She savored the flavor of love and friendly lust.

"Fine and resting. Whatever Molly inhaled was caustic only as a secondary effect. Its first effect had to be to put her down and out." She squeezed her lover's hand. "How does my diagnosis sound?"

"Don't discuss such sensitive matters in a public corridor," Pastor chid. "Clarence was just leaving. He was here to turn in location reports for his section of the Turtle."

Smokey ignored the hint that Clarence should leave and kept his hand in hers as she entered Grimshaw's office. Technically, she and Pastor were partners in the investigation, just as technically they were equals in the Coven. She didn't need to take his hints, and she had been seeing too little of Clarence. Clarence, for his part, seemed content to let her tow him along.

"What did the position reports show?" Smokey asked.

Grimshaw sighed, obviously deciding against making an issue of Clarence's presence, and ordered his desk unit to project a schematic diagram on the wall.

"There's everyone's reported position for an hour before you found Molly. Note that some of the ID codes shift. In this mock-up a second equals one minute. The codes in green reflect those for whom there is a human confirmation." He grinned without any real humor. "An alibi."

He continued, "The gold are those for which we have some other cross-check—a computer memory, a food request, etc. The red are for those times there is no confirmation. One ID up there may shift colors over the hour mock-up according to location."

Clarence watched the somewhat jerky progression of the codes around the Turtle's layers with absorption. "Hey! My code is mostly red—but I told you that I was at my computer reading files and doing data entry."

Grimshaw nodded apologetically. "Yes, but mostly

you were passive. The computer was running but not being interacted with. You, theoretically, could have left at any time."

Clarence still looked displeased and Pastor hastened to add, "Look at my code. It's all red. I was in here alone preparing for my meeting with Smokey and Molly. I've not given myself any greater leeway than anyone else."

Clarence grunted, his brown eyes still tracking the unchoreographed ballet of the Turtle's populace.

"I don't suppose we found anything easy and obvious," Smokey said, "like someone claiming to be two places at once or an alibi that didn't pan out?"

"No," Grimshaw said, tugging at the fringe of his beard with frustration. "And we have no idea when whatever got Molly was set up. It could have been hours or even days earlier. I have a database for most of today. Reliability becomes more fragmented as we move back through the day and people's memories get less certain. Human memories are fallible."

"No!" Clarence breathed mockingly.

Smokey elbowed him. "Pastor, you can't have had time to check the lab yet, but the air should have cleared by now. Shall we head there?"

This time Clarence didn't ignore Pastor's pointed stare. Giving Smokey another hug, he rose.

"I need to get back to work," he said, "though given what I've heard, I don't think that I'd better keep to my scholarly peace and quiet. There should be space for me to work in Ross's lab, and I'll just let the elevated discussions he and Bonny have wash over my aged brain bumps. Might do some good."

Smokey walked him to the corridor. "I'll be by when we're done here, Clarence."

The brief walk to Molly's lab was undertaken in brisk silence. Grimshaw silently handed Smokey a compact respirator with goggles and slipped on one himself before overriding the door lock.

Smokey hated looking foolish, but complied, well aware that less obvious and more noxious poisons than those that had roughened her throat might still linger. The lab was apparently unchanged from its usual appearance. Except for what debris had been created getting Molly out into clean air, the room might have been awaiting some yet-to-be-performed bit of research.

"See if you can learn what she was working on from her notes," Pastor ordered. "I'll check . . ."

He let his words trail off and Smokey did not protest that she could learn Molly's activities easily from the woman herself. Ross had told her that Pastor found using his Talent for reading inanimate objects unnerving. That Pastor was permitting her to be present at all was an acknowledgment of their growing accord—and of his awareness that someone was stalking their numbers with singular attention for those who could best unravel the killer's identity.

Obeying his request as quietly as she could, Smokey watched as Pastor drifted about the lab. His graceful motion reminded her a bit of both a bird dog and a ballet dancer. Finally, he came to stand precisely where Molly had been when Smokey had found her. His hands hovered, fingers spread, at his sides.

Gradually, his eyelids drooped so that only a thin white slash was visible. When he spoke, his voice was level and emotionless, unmarked by pauses for breath. With a start, Smokey realized that the raspy whisper was purely telepathic, its softness a measure of the demand the object-reading made on Pastor.

"Molly, Molly everywhere. Bottles, vials, knobs, tongs, and handles all radiate her." As he named each item his floating, boneless-seeming hands brushed against the indicated object. "She has saturated this room with her presence. Will the scent be so strong as to mask . . . Ah!"

The last exclamation burst from his drawn lips. His eyelids flew open to examine a canister that rolled among the debris on the lab's floor. His hands wrapped around the container as if jealously guarding it. Then he extended it so that Smokey could inspect his find.

She took a step forward, bending to look closely but

not touching it. There seemed to be little to excite
interest. Seven centimeters high and about half that
wide, the cylinder was made of dull, yellow plastic. A
square series of characters marched around the rounded
side.

"E-O-M-Trin," she spelled. "What does that mean?"

Pastor set the canister on the countertop, a speculative
expression lighting his features. When he stopped scowling, Smokey could easily see why Ross found him
attractive. Absorbed by the puzzle, his features stopped
being merely handsome and became compelling.

"What is it?" she prompted. "Was Molly using it for
her experiment. Was this just an accident after all?"

"We'll see," Pastor said. "Did you find her notes?"

Smokey indicated the computer terminal set into the
countertop. "This says that the last file she was working
on was something to do with psionic boosters."

"That fits." Grimshaw nodded. "She has been working on ways to enhance psi powers on and off for years.
Lately, she thought that she was onto something—a
derivative of one of the plants here on Guillen."

"Psi-boosters?" Smokey said. "To make Talents
stronger?"

"Or to last longer," Pastor answered, his tone not
quite condescending. "Your own Talent is comparatively
slight and you have usually used it erratically."

"Or erotically," she added flippantly.

He ignored her. "Prolonged use, especially of a greater
Talent, can exhaust the user. So can particularly intense
use, like telepathic contact with someone who is half a
planet away. Molly was particularly interested in this
problem because she feared that her own Talent would
phase out during a critical operation."

Smokey recalled Molly briefly discussing her search
for tools for psionics. "This E-O-M-Trin is related to her
research?"

"Precisely. However, it reduces psi powers, rather
than enhancing them. Molly has also done work with
psi-dampers. There are Talents that can flare up as if
they have a will of their own."

"Like Albert's poltergeist activity," Smokey said.

"Right. There are also times when it might be convenient to effectively not be psionic."

"Like when a Purge is on," Smokey said, "or if you want to hide from one of the doppels."

"Right." Pastor grinned. "This canister contained an organic sedative derived from the venom of an animal native to Icedrake. It is fairly unique in that it paralyzes mental rather than physical processes. However, concentrated like this and released as a gas it is physically dangerous as well. As you experienced, it is quite caustic, and there are nasty side effects from prolonged exposure—including electrical impulse suppression, I believe. What this means is that we will somehow need to check Molly's nervous system to make certain that she hasn't taken permanent damage."

"Aye-aye, Cap'n. I believe I can handle that." Smokey saluted. "Where did you find that canister?"

"In the general mess on the floor, but I have a suspicion." He gently touched the mesh covering a ventilation shaft and it swung loose at the bottom. "Look, Smokey, the grime shows that something the size of this canister was set in here. I would hazard that there was a timer set to open it at a time that Molly should be in the lab. Either the mesh wasn't set tightly enough or the timer jolted it free. Even if she wasn't alone, the gas would be blown into the lab in sufficient quantities to affect several victims. The electrical impulse suppression would not only guarantee confusion and ineffective response, but also that even a powerful telepath would have difficulty getting help."

Smokey stared respectfully at the canister. "That means that the canister or ventilation area may have some trace of whoever put it there. Do you sense anything?"

Pastor rubbed his bearded chin—nervously, she thought.

"I haven't tried yet, but I guess I should. We can check for physical traces later."

He wrapped the fingers of both big hands around the canister, effectively concealing it in their embrace. Closing his eyes, he began to breathe steadily from deep in his abdomen. The breaths increased in depth and decreased in frequency so at last he appeared hardly to breathe at all.

Smokey watched in silent appreciation of his effort. Even though she was not in physical contact with him, she could feel the astonishing strain he was under. Then, with a dreadful, shuddering gasp like a swimmer surfacing after a too-deep dive, Pastor straightened. His eyes opened, but Smokey was certain that he did not see her. When he released the canister, she saw that it was crumpled from the pressure of his grip.

Without speaking, he grabbed the ventilation mesh and again his gaze turned inward and his breathing slowed. When he broke his trance, he let the mesh fall beside the canister.

His clearing gaze rested on her and he whispered, "Nothing. My Talent is working. I could have followed that thing back to its making. Yet the only hands it recalls are Molly's own. Either our enemies can fully mask their presence from me, or somehow Molly herself set the trap that nearly killed her."

21

"OF COURSE IT'S IMPOSSIBLE," SMOKEY CON-
cluded as she sat with Bonny and Clarence at
a meal that she thought of as dinner, though
she had lost track of the Mud Turtle's cycle. "Molly
wouldn't have done that to herself. There are more
certain, less painful ways of committing suicide. Even if
she wanted to divert suspicion from herself, we aren't
suspicious of her—at least not any more than of anyone
else. So we're faced with someone who is invisible to
Pastor's Talent, which is not a comforting feeling."

Bonny let her finish, then hesitantly spoke. "Maybe I
shouldn't say, I mean, we don't know—not yet anyhow,
but it could be important."

Clarence chuckled at Smokey's confused expression.

"Bonny and Ross may have learned something about
the nature of the doppels," he clarified. "What this is,
I'm not sure, but they were pretty excited about it today
in the lab."

He winked at Bonny. "I eavesdrop, honey. Go ahead,
tell Smokey. That way I can find out, too. I've been half-
eaten with curiosity."

Bonny nodded. "Mama, I told Papa—Ross—about
what I had been thinking—that all the studying has gone
on the idea that it doesn't matter what the doppels are,
only what they can do and how we can stop them from
doing it."

"Right." Smokey poured out a cup of tea made from

the same plant as the astringent green drink Ross had served her at their reunion. This preparation, oddly, was sweet.

"Papa thought about what I said and said that I was right—that in worrying about 'why' and 'how,' he had forgotten all about 'what.' So I asked if I could work on what and he said yes and"—Bonny paused for effect—"he even opened up his files for me—gave me the password."

Smokey smiled and gestured. "Go on."

"I worked on it, like I'd been working on the ship. There were lots of false starts, but they're useful too, like getting to a dead end in a maze, so you know at least that you shouldn't go that way. And then I got to something—it was so obvious that Papa said he felt really dumb for not seeing it sooner—because it was like what he did to make the Sea."

"Slow, Bonita, you're losing me. I don't know how Ross made the Sea except that it was terraforming of some sort."

Bonny slowed with a visible effort. "To make the water for the Sea, Papa made tiny machines—his nixies—you know that."

"Yes, but I don't know how the nixies work, Bonny. Having a name for something isn't the same as understanding it."

"Oh." Bonny stopped, then started rearranging the utensils on the table until she had made a letter "E" from the pieces.

"See that?"

"That's an 'E,'" Clarence answered for them both.

"Right. Now, if I take out the bottom piece, what do I have?"

"An 'F,'" Clarence said.

"And if I put the bottom back, but take out the middle, what do I have?"

"A 'C,'" Smokey guessed, "though it's rather square cornered."

"Right, one more." Bonny pushed the bars of the C until they met. "What's that?"

"A 'D,'" Clarence said. "Or a triangle."

"A 'D,'" Bonny said firmly. "That's how Papa's machines work, except that what they move around are the atoms that make up molecules. The nixies are programmed to take apart other molecules and recombine them until they make H_2O. It's more complicated than pushing around silverware, but not really if you know how to do it, and the nixies do. Papa built them to know."

Smokey could tell from Clarence's tightening grip on her hand that he was anticipating the drift of Bonny's argument and, like her, he wasn't happy with where it was leading. He smiled a trifle too bravely to be sincere and gestured to the girl.

"Go on, Bonny, we're caught up now. What do Ross's nixies have to do with the doppels?"

Bonny stared strangely at him for a moment, but her eagerness was more powerful than any curiosity she might have felt that grown-ups could be scared of the implications of an idea.

"The doppels must somehow be like the nixies," she said. "Only they're not made to change dirt into water— they're made to change people's minds."

Smokey couldn't even muster a grin at the pun. Taking a long swallow from her tea, she tried to shape words for the bevy of uncomfortable thoughts Bonny's theory had awakened.

"Even if," she managed at last, "we ignore why anyone—or should that be 'anything'—would do this, how does it help us deal with the doppels? The nixies are tiny, I remember that. If the doppels are on a similar scale, then we can never hope to deal with them. Does this mean that we have to give up?"

"No, Mama!" For the first time, Bonny seemed exasperated. "No, not at all. My guess—mine and Papa's— is that the doppels are part of something that's gone wrong, lost its original programming. We've got three basic types, each with its own way of 'terraforming' a mind, right?"

"Drivers, Riders, and Guests," Clarence said.

"Yeah, only one of these is really bad, at least for us—the Drivers." Bonny waited until she had nods of at least provisional agreement from them. "So, what we need to do is find a Guest who will let us study it, reproduce its program, and then make our own machines to carry in the replacement—maybe a virus—and then reformat the Drivers into Guests or Riders. That's it!"

Smokey blinked at her daughter, a sense of unreality curving her lips into a smile.

"That's it, Boniface?"

"Yeah, neat, huh?"

Now Smokey started laughing, a warm, bubbly thing that was so infectious that Clarence and then Bonny joined her. When she was finally able to stop, she wiped the tears from her streaming eyes and explained.

"I'm sorry, Bonny. I don't know whether to praise you for a genius or hail you as a dreamer. Either way, you certainly have made me see our entire problem differently. Up 'til now I've felt like we were dealing with devils and angels, spirits of some sort. Now I keep envisioning tiny little windup toys marching around in people's heads and oiling mental gears. It helps, but it's all a bit much."

Bonny grinned. "You're doing really well. You should have seen Papa when we started working this out. He nearly went crazy. But I think we're right—I really do. We need time to do tests and proofs, that's all."

"And time," Clarence interjected soberly, "is what we suddenly don't have much of, not if someone is trying to kill off all of the big players."

"Yeah."

Smokey fell silent, glad that the others couldn't read her mind, gladder still that she had learned how to shield her thoughts. Something ugly had occurred to her and she didn't like the implications. Leaving her worries to brood, she studied her lover and her daughter.

"Folks, we need to keep this idea to ourselves. Oh, I'll ask Ross to tell Pastor, but otherwise we stay quiet. I don't like the idea of this getting out before it's proved."

Clarence patted her. "Be blunt, Smokey-jo. If this killer realizes that Ross and Bonny have something, they'll be the next targets. Otherwise, no one would ever think of physicists and mathematicians as dangerous."

Bonny's eyes widened. "I hadn't thought of that! It's just a neat idea and I thought you should . . . Oh!"

"Good," Smokey said. "You two might as well know now, Pastor and I are going to announce it first cycle anyhow. As soon as we have the gear together, everyone is going to wear a passive tracer, locked under the skin. It will feed data at all hours to a computer base. It won't just give location, either. It's going to mark body temperature, heart rate, and a few other vital signs. It should become impossible for anyone to even be injured without the computer giving an alert."

Clarence bared his teeth and she caught a flash of his merry, wicked thought. Bonny, innocently, was nodding serious agreement.

"Will the tracer hurt?" she asked.

"Maybe some when it's put in," Smokey admitted, "but it should hurt a lot less than getting murdered."

Not everyone in the Mud Turtle was as accepting as Bonny and Clarence at the announcement that they would be tagged. Oddly, one of the most voluble protesters was the usually equitable Ravenel. She stormed loudly about this being the type of harassment she had entered the Underground to escape. When Grimshaw tried to reason with her, she pushed past him and out of his office.

Bruni supplied the answer that even Pastor was at a loss to find.

"Didn't you know?" She grinned. "Ravenel's a great counselor, all of that plum-No insight. She's not a great believer in hands-off therapy, though. I would guess that she doesn't want anyone to know exactly how many people she is intimate with, especially—pardon me, Smokey—after some of the catty comments about whores that were circulating after a certain arrival."

"This is what I get for having a steady relationship," Pastor complained. "I miss out on all of the gossip."

"Oh, Ravenel is discreet enough," Bruni said. "I'm simply nosy."

"Well," Smokey said, "she's either going to have to discontinue her 'therapy' or be a bit more honest about it. These tracers aren't just to keep track of people; they're to let us know if anyone else is attacked."

"Let me speak with her," Bruni offered. "I think I know how to get through to her. The other holdouts will fall into line when she does; most of them are simply reacting out of fear and a desire to feel they have some control."

After Bruni had left, Pastor pushed a series of computer graphs across to Smokey.

"These are what I've come up with for our three 'incidents.' The problem is that Sey'zar's murder could have been arranged well in advance. Krystal's is easier to check for time and opportunity, but we still have lots of possibilities. Too many of us prefer solitude. Molly's accident is just like Sey'zar's. Again, too many of us would have had both opportunity and the skill. Fewer have the knowledge of what that gas would do, but Molly wasn't really quiet about her research. Her computer files could have been accessed easily."

Smokey studied the interweave of colored lines and blocks and concluded silently that all they demonstrated was a lot of work to tell them what they already intuitively knew.

"I don't suppose that we could have an intruder?" she asked hopefully.

"No," Pastor said, "I'm afraid not. One of the joys of the Turtle is that since we have controlled life support and limited resources, a stowaway would be almost impossible. I coordinated a level by level sweep and we didn't find any evidence of a stowaway or the gear to support one. The senior telepaths haven't detected any trace of another mind either."

The computer graph's swirl of lights and colors tempted her with rationality, but she decided to share her odd insight anyhow.

"Have you talked with Ross about the research that he has been doing?"

"With Bonny?" Grimshaw shook his head. "No, I haven't had time. We do have a more serious problem than theoretical physics to deal with."

Smokey drew in a slow breath, remembering that Pastor resented Bonny, realizing that she could be damaging her hard-won accord with her partner, remembering, too, Sey'zar, Krystal, and Molly.

"I think you should," she said, finally. "Soon. I've got a feeling that it's important to solving this somehow."

Maybe Grimshaw felt a trace of the intensity she was trying so hard to smother, maybe he just decided that he would humor her, that it would not be that much of a difficulty. Whatever the reason, he nodded.

"I will ask him about it when he comes home. Or maybe I can stop by the lab and get them both to show me."

"Thanks," she said. "Soon. I'm going to check on Molly now. Do you have any message for her or Albert?"

"No, but why don't you bring the tracers along? That will finish everyone except for Ravenel and her holdouts. If Bruni is good as her word, we should have those done soon."

Smokey took the two tracers from the desk and slipped them into her pocket. "I'll let you know if I learn anything new. Otherwise, I think you should get some rest."

"I will, but the more I think about it, the more curious I am about what Ross has been doing. I'm going to stop in the lab first."

"Great."

Then Smokey went right and Pastor went left. As she tapped the call buzzer to Molly's room several minutes later, Smokey wondered if Pastor would see what she had seen and if their tentative accord would survive the revelation.

22

DESPITE THE TRACERS, THEY NEARLY DIDN'T GET to Ross in time. Smokey was jolted from deep sleep by Pastor's frantic shout.

"Smoke! Do you have Ross with you?"

She sat up in bed, peripherally aware of Clarence rolling sleepily beside her, scrubbing sleep from his eyes with the back of one black hand. Her gaze darted wildly around the room, but Pastor was nowhere visible, though his words were ringing in her head.

"Smoke!" came Pastor's shout again, and this time she was awake enough to realize that the communication was telepathic. "Ross isn't with me and I can't find his tracer on the screen!"

Not bothering with a robe, she tabbed the VT for Pastor's room and office.

"Pastor!" she said as calmly as she could. "No, Ross isn't with me. Why would he be?"

"I—" The word echoed oddly in her ears and in the listening paths of her brain. "I don't know."

He stared blankly at her image. "What I'm really worried about is that the computer map doesn't show him anywhere—nothing. Like he's vanished."

"Or dead," Smokey thought aloud with new/old pain. Seeing Pastor jerk as if slapped, she realized that in some way he was still in touch with her thoughts. Pushing off the blankets, she started dressing.

"Let's start a quiet search, Pastor," she suggested.

"Clarence and I are awake and can be looking as soon as we're dressed. Have the computer track back to the last reading it has for him and we'll start there. Capi?"

Pastor was recovering enough to spare Clarence's nude form the unconsciously appreciative glance Smokey hadn't aroused from him. He nodded.

"Thanks, Smoke. Better haul Bonny out of bed. We can't have her left alone."

"Now."

Smokey heard the final word in her mind and knew that Pastor was worried for Bonny, not just as an inhabitant of the Mud Turtle, but as Ross's daughter. Telling the girl as little as possible, Smokey awakened Bonny. Clarence hoisted her up into his arms, having less trouble with her weight than with her tangled limbs. She'd grown even since their hadj on Arizona.

"The computer's last record of Ross shows him heading down to the Neck Room," Pastor greeted them as they entered his office. "He only left here within the last fifteen minutes."

"I'm gone," Smokey said. Clarence put Bonny down in a chair and followed her. "No, Pastor, don't argue. You can follow us mentally; Clarence and I can't do the same and, as you said, someone needs to watch Bonny."

The office door had slid shut behind them, and they were running for the lift even before she was finished. Nevertheless, Pastor's reply reverberated in both of their minds.

"*Hurry!*" he said. "*And good luck. I'll continue a computer search and make calls to people who are awake.*"

When they reached the room from which the "neck" that was the Mud Turtle's most usual connection to the outer world was extended, it was deserted.

"Can you figure out if that thing has been used?" Smokey asked Clarence. "Maybe Ross went outside."

Clarence moved toward the control bank. "I think that I can work it; it didn't look much more complicated than some of the levee setups back home. I should . . ."

His speech dissolved into a flow of curses in what

Smokey vaguely thought was French. She was running before he found his English again. Ross lay crumpled behind the console, blood running freely from a gash in his head. His left arm was twisted awkwardly beneath his torso.

"He can't be dead," she said, half to assure Clarence, "not if he's bleeding like that."

She tore her shirt off over her head and started stanching Ross's head wound. A pulse came faintly to her fingers.

"Yes, I've got a pulse, but it's wild. He's nearly bled out. Call Molly. No, she can't get up."

Clarence was already on the intercom. "Easy, Smokey-jo. Do what you can. I've got Pastor."

As Smokey mopped up blood, she reached for Ross's mind. It was there but weak and too confused even to be afraid. She lulled him, keeping up a steady flow of mental butterflies to distract and amuse him. When Pastor bolted into the room, Bruni and Bonny at his heels, she was able to accept the medkit with a confident smile.

"He'll make it," Smokey promised. "Come and hold his hand, Pastor—the right one—and feed him the most calming thoughts that you can. This is going to really hurt, and I don't dare give him even a mild painkiller."

She paused to look at her daughter. "Bonny, you had better step out of the room."

The girl shook her head stubbornly. "No. He's my father. I want to help."

Pastor dragged his attention from Ross. The expression on his face told her that his Talent had traced the nature of Ross's injury and he knew how serious the situation was.

"Smoke," he said, "don't let Bonny go out alone. Don't."

Smokey frowned. "I can't spare any of the adults to watch her. Fine. Bonny, this won't be pretty."

Bonny paled but held steady.

Smokey arrayed a selection of items from the medkit. "Now, Clarence, anchor Ross's feet. Bruni, get by his head. Pastor, you keep his right hand." She picked up a pressure bandage. "Pastor, you already know the situation, so I want you to pull his left arm free."

"Smoke, it's . . ."

"Do it!" She knelt in the pooled blood. "Only the angle that he has fallen at has saved him from bleeding to death so far."

Pastor gingerly eased Ross's left arm out. It was horribly mangled and from the elbow on down it was hanging by a bit of bone and tendon. Shivering at the violence of Ross's scream, Smokey wrapped the pressure bandage to hold the ruin together.

"I can't save it," she quietly explained. "I don't have the skill. But the bleeding is stopped. The head wound is superficial. I would guess that he hit his head when he fell."

While she explained, she inserted an IV and started neutral blood substitute flowing into Ross's veins. She might have been fooling herself, but his breathing and pulse seemed to strengthen.

"Bruni, you brought a gurney?"

"I did," the petite Valkyrie replied, "and I've been in contact with Molly. She says that we should bring Ross to sick bay. She's already there."

Smokey couldn't find the energy to protest Molly's being out of bed. Ross's blood was stiffening on her skin and Pastor was frantic.

"Good," she said. "Pastor, Clarence, take him to Molly. Bruni and I will look for anything here."

When the others had left, Smokey mutely accepted the water and hand towel Bonny had drawn from the refreshment center, the same refreshment center from which Ross had drawn their drinks on her arrival.

"I couldn't go up to sick bay," she said, not hiding her exhaustion. "If I've messed up, made a wrong decision, Ross will still lose his arm and maybe he'll die. I couldn't bear that."

Bruni patted her awkwardly, then offered Smokey the green print vest she wore over her shirt.

"You can't go topless out into the halls. The rest of us would never survive the comparison." Bruni managed a shaky smile. "Well, something good will come of this."

"What?" Bonny said, narrowing her eyes in disbelief.

Bruni winked at her. "I don't think we'll have any holdouts for the tracers. Even Ravenel will listen now—continued refusal would be a mite suspicious."

Smokey pulled on the vest. Bruni was broader across the back though smaller in the breast. With a bit of pulling, Smokey could get the vest somewhat modestly fastened. She glanced at her reflection in a polished tabletop.

"It's lots better than nothing," she said. "Thanks, Bruni. I'm afraid that I'm not very clean. I may ruin this."

"Minor sacrifice, isn't it?" Bruni said softly. "Given what is happening here. I don't know if you and Pastor have thought about this, but we can't stay submerged indefinitely. We synthesize most of our food, but we'll need supplies eventually."

Smokey stared at her hands, seeing fingernails rimmed with darkening blood. Exhaustion welled up, thick enough to choke her.

"I have to go and change and wash if Molly can spare me. I'll do a better job clean. Right?"

Bruni stood on tiptoe and pressed her palm to Smokey's head. Instantly, the headache she hadn't known was pressing behind her eyes vanished.

"Better?"

"Thanks." Smokey put her hand out to Bonny. "Come on, Bonita. We'll walk Bruni to—where are you headed, Bruni?"

"The main cafeteria. I'm not sleeping yet—maybe not at all. Several people are certain to have gathered there. I can at least dispel rumors."

"Thanks."

As Smokey was scrubbing Ross's blood off—some had even soaked through her trousers to stain the skin on her legs—Bonny climbed up on the sink counter.

"Mama, is Papa going to die?"

She looked somberly at her—their—daughter. This was certainly not the time to start lying.

"I don't know, but I don't think so. Whoever went after him wanted the tracer deactivated first and got overenthusiastic. That's what happened to Ross's arm. When Ross smashed his head into the console, the killer must have thought that the job was done. He looked gory enough."

Bonny frowned. "Mama, I don't see how anyone here could do that to Ross. And I know we didn't do it, not us or Clarence. I'm scared."

Smokey hugged her. "Me, too, and that's good. If we weren't scared, then we would be crazy—wouldn't we? Anyone in her right mind would be scared with what we've been through, both here and on Arizona."

She stopped and pushed Bonny back lest the girl read her thoughts. Parts and pieces of ideas, fragments of suspicions fell into place at that moment. Anyone in her right mind . . .

"Mama!" Bonny reached out. "What did I do?"

"Nothing, thornbud." Smokey masked her thoughts, carefully locked them in an old-fashioned safe and twirled the dial until the buzz filled her mind with white noise. Then she pulled her daughter close.

Careful not to lie, she answered, "I just got scared for a minute. I didn't want you to feel it from me. Bethlehem told me that telepaths have to be responsible that way."

The VT saved her from further explanation.

"Would you get that while I find some clean clothes?"

Bonny giggled. "Yeah, like Bruni said, we don't want the other women getting jealous."

The caller was Albert. His face looked tired and a little grey; his hair poked up at odd angles as if he had been tugging at it.

"Good news and bad news, Smokey," he said without preamble. "Ross is stable. Thanks to Miracle Molly, he may even regain full use of his arm. Pastor is sitting with him now. He says that Ross's thoughts are pretty clear. His brain didn't lose enough blood to cause permanent damage."

"The bad news?"

"Molly has collapsed again. I think—hope—all she needs is rest, but I would feel better if you checked her out. Then, Bruni has called. The holdouts are clamoring for their tracers. Pastor is in no shape to insert them. Can you take over?"

"I'll be there." Smokey flipped off the switch and put a hand out to Bonny. "I know you're tired, sand cat, but I can't leave you alone. Clarence is probably still in sick bay. If you want, he can bring you back right away."

Bonny bounced a few times to prove her energy and grabbed a computer link from the desk.

"I'm coming. Mama?" she asked as they hurried down the corridor. "They need you, don't they? That's why you're so busy, right?"

Smokey considered. "They need me now because some of their most central people are dead or hurt. If that hadn't happened, I'd still just be another 'Zonie whore. I'm not sure that I'd mind."

She winked at Bonny. "It's easier making a living flat on your back. You get your sleep, too."

23

MOLLY TURNED OUT TO BE SUFFERING FROM nothing worse than acute exhaustion. To be safe, Smokey ordered her to bed. Instead of sending Molly back to her room, Smokey opened up the infirmary. With Ross in one bed and Molly in the other, only a single mudcrawler would need to be spared to serve as nurse. And, no matter how devoted Pastor was, he couldn't be permitted the luxury of sitting by his lover's side.

The tracer emplacement also went well. Bruni and Albert supported and enforced her suggestion that in addition to the electronic tracers people assign themselves buddies. Bruni went as far as to inform the Mud Turtle's inhabitants that the Coven would consider refusal to remain in company highly suspicious.

"They'll prefer partners to guards," she said. "No one who has made it into the Underground is stupid. That is one good thing the doppels have done for us. Stupid psionics never survive unless, like Bonny, they have family to guide and educate them."

Albert smiled sleepily from where he had resumed his vigil at Molly's side.

"And Bonny's not stupid, but having a family is a survival factor all in itself," he said. "Why not send Bonny in here? She can roll up in a blanket or something. Then Clarence will be free to help you."

Smokey agreed. Collecting Clarence and Pastor, she

bustled them off to Pastor's office. When they had confirmed both that every tracer was working and that everyone was obeying the buddy order, Smokey poured them each a cup of iced green liquor.

"Gents," she said, "I need to work through a train of thought. I think I know who our killer is."

Pastor was on his feet, reaching for a sidearm that Smokey hadn't realized was in his desk.

"Who?" he growled.

"Sit, Grimshaw," she snapped. "I need to run through the records we've compiled. I'm not going to start accusing people until I make certain that my theory has support. We've pulled the killer's fangs for now. So sit!"

Pastor looked as if the emotional force of her outburst had physically struck him. Clarence merely seemed impressed. They sat, though, and Clarence fiddled with the keypad.

"What do you want to see first, Smokey-jo?"

Smokey spared Pastor an apologetic smile. "Start with the notations for the day of Sey'zar's death. I want a floor plan scheme with people's locations done in—oh, make it orange. Then follow it with the Krystal data in blue. Then the Molly data in purple. We had tracers in almost everyone tonight, so tell the computer to reconstruct locations for occupants a half hour before Pastor found Ross was missing. Put those in bright yellow and let those . . ."

Clarence's hands were flying. "Whoa! Whoa, Smokey-jo! Give me a mo'—I've only just learned this system."

Pastor crossed and helped him. When the wall screen was aglitter with orange, blue, purple, and yellow icons pulsing in their various zones, Pastor nodded curtly.

"What next, Commandante?"

"I want the icons to move through the pattern we have for them for the critical half hour before each 'accident' was discovered. Let it run at the rate of a second per minute."

Pastor complied, his hands sketching out the commands automatically, his eyes on the wall. When the thirty second cycle ran, he hit the tab so that it would rerun. After a third go through, Smokey was frowning. Then she began chortling dryly. Pastor and Clarence stared blankly at the wall.

"Smokey, I don't see anything to laugh about," Pastor said. He did something so that the blue and yellow icons glowed brighter. "Even with comparing these two occurrences, where the killer couldn't have gotten too far away before there was an alert, there isn't any overlap that can't be explained by random habit. If you add the other patterns in, it's all shot to pieces. And you're laughing?"

"No, well, not from finding any humor in this," she said. "I'm upset because I think that my guess is right, and I'm afraid that you won't believe me, and even if you do, then you'll hate us."

"Damn you, Smokey," Pastor said. "Who?"

"The doppels. I believe that they have evolved a new form"—she bit her lip—"and I think that we brought it in with us."

The silence was so pure that the faint hum of the computer became cacophony to which the icons on the wall swept through their halting ballet. At last, Pastor expelled his breath explosively and, clenching his fist, brought up a level stare to meet Smokey's steel grey eyes.

"I would be lying if I didn't admit that a few days ago I would have welcomed that theory and have done everything in my power to prove it." He spread his fingers, wincing as if he had bruised the joints. "Now. Now I'm not happy at all. Give me your theory, Smokey."

She looked to Clarence for support, but his dark face was impassive, the faintest trace of hurt deepening the lines of his mouth. Hiding her own hurt behind brisk professionalism, she leaned to banish the wall display.

"First," she said, "did you ever find time to have Ross explain to you what he and Bonny have been working on?"

Pastor quirked a swift grin. "Yes, though I needed a brushup on atomic structure and nanotechnology before I could follow it. I gather that he and Bonny believe that the doppels are biological nanomachines that have had their programming go haywire."

His agreeable tone couldn't conceal his doubt. Smokey nodded seriously.

"Yes, it sounds crazy, but on Arizona we make hadj to a Sea filled with water that Ross's nixies made from dust. That Sea keeps me from doubting too quickly."

"Why would anyone—anything?—want to reshape thoughts?" Pastor shook himself. "That's a stupid question. Who wouldn't? That's why so many normals are scared of psionics. Telepaths can influence thoughts and underneath the fear of having it done is a guilty awareness of times that they would like to have the Talent."

"The implications that the doppels are created to shape minds are so wide-reaching," Clarence said, "that I hurt just thinking about them. From the lectures Bethlehem gave us on the *Ibn Battuta,* I gathered that the doppels have a long history of coexistence with the human race. I was startled by the thought that many unexplained leaps in culture or technological development could be explained by the assistance of a Guest or the prodding of a Driver. But what if human intelligence itself is a by-product of the manipulations of these proposed nanomachines? It would explain why the vague but undeniable quality that we term sentience is so rare."

"You have a paper or two there, Professor Beauduc," Smokey said, "if we ever dare publicize this. I fear that if we do, we will end up with a witch-hunt that will make the Psionic Purges seem mild."

"That decision belongs to a future we may not get to," Pastor reminded. "Let's get back to our basic problem."

Smokey sighed. "Yes. It goes back to terraforming, really. The human reaction to an inhospitable universe has been to adapt the environment to our needs—to make Arizona wetter, Icedrake warmer, Guillen dryer and cooler. The plum-No mystics have a point. We never give a thought to adapting us to the world, only to adapting the world to us.

"I think that whatever developed the doppels took a different approach to the same problem. Instead of shaping the world, they chose to shape the minds of the inhabitants to accept them as co-residents. If this was done, the aliens would be perfectly adapted to whatever world they chose. The doppels may be little more than 'landscapers' evolved into something with its own volition."

Pastor pulled his lips back from his teeth in a feral grimace. "I don't know that I buy this. What good does just riding along in a Host do for a doppel? Don't they risk losing their own identity?"

"Maybe," Smokey countered, "but first you tell me what identity is."

Pastor blinked at her, clearly uncertain if she was serious. "Identity is what you are—how you perceive yourself—maybe even what theologians and philosophers have termed the soul."

"If Molly can't save Ross's arm, is his identity still there?" Smokey asked.

"Sure. He might need to rework a few things, but he would essentially be the same man."

"Then you would still love him?"

Pastor's anger was as solid as a blow. "Of course. What kind of man do you think I am? I'm not going to stop loving him over a physical accident."

Clarence put a hand on his arm. "Easy, old man, Smokey wasn't insulting you. It's her way to refuse to get to the point quickly. Instead she puts out all the pieces of the puzzle for you to see. Sort of the reverse of normal thesis and proof."

Pastor actually blushed beneath his beard. "I apologize, Smokey. I must be more tired than I had realized."

"Me, too." She smiled ruefully. "I'm losing my touch. I used to be able to convince people day was night if I tried. All I'm trying to show you here is the truth."

"Maybe that's harder," Pastor said softly. "I do get your point. Whatever designed the doppels must have had a concept of identity distinct from a specific physical form. So, as long as the doppels continued to reproduce and spread, the race that made them had effectively infinite choices of habitat."

Smokey nodded. "Right, but over the millennia, the programs have shifted. I tend to see the Guests as closest to the original design, though that could be wishful thinking on my part. The Riders may be dormant Guests or incomplete in some way. They certainly lack initiative."

"The Drivers have too much initiative," Clarence added, "which could indicate another deviation."

"And now you suspect that there is a fourth type," Pastor said, "a fourth type that is here in the Mud Turtle."

"Call them 'Infiltrators,'" Smokey said, "because that's what they do. They can hide their presence both from psionics and from those of their own kind. Undetected, then, they can move among us."

"And cause havoc," Pastor said. "I can see how this makes sense. It seems a logical evolutionary step."

"They sound like a form of Driver," Clarence added.

Smokey keyed the wall screen back to life. "Yes, I think that they are. I also suspect that they have a more developed form of whatever program permits a doppel to shift Hosts. And you realize what that means?"

"What?" Pastor growled.

"It means that any one of us could be the killer—any one of us or, in an odd way, all of us." She pointed to the flow of icons against the floor plan. "Let me show you."

Pastor shook his head. "No, I follow you. Even if psionics are difficult hosts for the doppels, it can be done, especially short term. All the Infiltrator would need to do is occupy a Host who is likely to have contact with the intended victim. Then with a mental nudge or so, the situation . . ."

He let the words trail off. "I understand what you're saying. Sey'zar was simply prompted to overdose. Molly herself probably rigged the situation that would expose her to the gas. Krystal's death and the assault on Ross both had to be done more directly."

Smokey interrupted him. "Do we really want to know who wielded the sabertooth, especially if that person is

essentially innocent? We can narrow down the attack on
Ross to one of those who wasn't wearing a tracer, but—
again—is that person really guilty?"

Pastor considered, then slowly shook his head. "No,
but we should keep the information that will let us track
more conventional subjects, just in case your brainstorm
is incorrect. Right now, we need to put our energy into
finding this Infiltrator if it exists and doing something to
immobilize it before someone else is hurt."

Smokey could almost hear her own pulse pounding as
she waited, hoping that someone else would raise the
obvious next question. Wanted to hug Clarence when he
did—wanted to, but didn't.

"How do we find it?" Clarence said. "Isn't it pretty
much insubstantial? And if we do find it, what do we do
with it? The solution to the doppel problem that Bonny
outlined for us earlier involved a Guest willing to be
examined, a virus of some sort, and lots of other things
that will take time to develop."

Smokey toyed with her glass before answering. "I have
a thought about what we can do once we find the
Infiltrator, and I even have an idea of how to go about
finding it."

She let the silence fall, again weary, but there was no
Bruni near to politely remove her headache, and what
she had to say must still be said. Pastor moved restlessly
in his chair, apparently impatient of another long explanation, but something in her expression made him hold
back whatever he had been about to say. Smokey coiled a
rope of her silver-grey hair about her hand and staring at
the hair she finally spoke.

"Psionics are intolerant of the doppels. Apparently,
they simply don't make good Hosts. Maybe we're too
familiar with the workings of our own minds to miss the
external prodding. I would guess that telepaths and
empaths are the worst Hosts of all. Now, almost everyone in the Mud Turtle has some trace of telepathy or
empathy. Right, Pastor?"

He steepled his fingers, lips moving beneath his beard
as he counted. "Yes, that's right. Ravenel, Culwych, and

Giaccomo all have either a null or a low rating. Albert and Molly are not very skilled telepaths, but empathy is strong in both of them."

"Culwych and Giaccomo," Clarence mused. "Weren't they two of the holdouts?"

"That's right," Smokey said, "but we're overlooking three candidates who are neither telepath nor empath."

Pastor spoke for her. "Ross, Bonny, and—Clarence."

Clarence neither jumped nor looked ashamed. He turned a dark, unsettling gaze on Smokey. The words locked in her throat behind a wave of pity and fear.

"Ross could hardly have ripped his own arm off," she said softly, "and, in any case, he has been a resident of the Mud Turtle for many years. He has had barely any contact with the outer world. He may have been a stopover Host for the Infiltrator, but I don't think that he was the means by which it got in."

Pastor added, "I am a telepath and a strong one. A doppel would be risking my detecting it in Ross's mind. Even if it could conceal itself, I know his way of thinking. I believe that I would notice some change."

Silence, then Smokey said, "Bonny is at least a latent telepath—"

Clarence interrupted, his voice harsh. "Just say it, damn you! Just say it! You think that the Infiltrator rode in on me—burrowed in my brain and then leapt out to slay its enemies!"

"It would make sense," Pastor said, "except that Smokey is also a telepath. Not as strong as I am, but she has finely tuned her awareness when she is in physical contact. She surely would sense any change in her lover."

"Except," Smokey said, not bothering to hide her anguish, "except that since we left Arizona there have been many times that Clarence has either avoided me or been less leisurely than he might. I had been excusing him—blaming myself, believing that he was angry at me because he had been ripped from a stable situation, because I wasn't sure that I wanted to give up my work, because . . ."

She stopped, tears running down her face and raining into her lap. "Because maybe he didn't really love me after all . . ."

"So it could have used Clarence as a Host," Pastor said uncomfortably. "How long ago did he start acting differently?"

Smokey glanced up from her tear-dappled lap, but Clarence wouldn't meet her gaze. He wasn't going to make this any bit easier for her.

"Since soon after we joined the *Ibn Battuta*," she said.

"I wonder if an Infiltrator had been set on the ship to observe—spy on—Bethlehem, Joy, or Ha'riel nu-Aten?" Pastor said. "If it somehow gathered where you were being taken, it might have chosen to piggyback along then."

Smokey managed a politely interested sound, but his question awoke an internal turmoil that nearly drowned out Pastor's theorizing. What if Clarence had been infiltrated even earlier—perhaps as early as when they met on Arizona? Bethlehem had indicated that she had probably given ample evidence of her telepathic abilities to Lee when he had first visited the Victorian Mansion. Might Clarence's strange and sudden love for her have been the effect of an Infiltrator? Could she, all this time, have been sleeping beside a man whose thoughts and emotions were not under his own control but instead were subject to the pulls and tugs of a near-invisible puppet-master?

Disgust and revulsion filled her. She struggled against an urge to gag, uncertain if she could face Clarence.

"Smokey? Smokey? Are you all right?" Pastor's tone was urgent. Peripherally she realized that he must have been trying to get her attention for some time.

"I . . . I think that tonight has caught up to me," she said, managing a smile she knew was unconvincing, unwilling to admit that with murder and betrayal threatening the inhabitants of the Mud Turtle that among her darkest terrors was the loss of a love she hadn't realized how much she treasured until that moment.

Clarence sat wooden and still, not reaching for her.

Part of her wanted him to hold her, to let her sob into his shoulder until this all became a dream. Part of her suspected that she would scream if he opened his arms to her.

"Smokey," Pastor was saying, "you deserve a rest, but I can't give you one. We've got to find this Infiltrator before it can do any more harm. You said you thought you knew how we could do it. Tell me!"

Smokey tried to detach herself from the moment, as she had when laying an especially unpleasant client. It worked somewhat.

She raised one hand and pointed. "It's there, in Clarence again. It fled there after it attacked Ross."

To her everything in Pastor's office froze, became deathly still. Even the motion on the wall screen seemed to stop its electronic progress. Then Pastor reached for the override to make certain that his door was sealed. He found that it was already locked.

Staring at Smokey with unguarded horror, Pastor said, "Smokey, you've known all this time!"

She nodded, her surface detachment holding for now. Clarence had not yet stirred; his eyelids had fluttered closed and he slumped slightly in his chair. Except for the rise and fall of his breathing, he might have been dead for all the reaction he showed.

"Yes," she said, "I knew—suspected—from the time I first figured out that the Infiltrators might exist that Clarence was the most likely Host. Sometime after Ross's accident, I noticed that Clarence was acting distant again. He had been quite—affectionate—when we had gone to bed. At first, I thought that his change was shock, then I noticed that he was avoiding my touch. I brought you both in here to discuss what we would do next because I knew you were a powerful telepath and would be safe from infiltration. I didn't think it could touch me because I am acutely aware of it."

Pastor rose and gently prodded Clarence. The man didn't move. Carefully, Pastor rolled back one of Clarence's eyelids. The eye beneath did not react to the light. Knee reflex also showed no reaction.

"It has frozen his nervous system," he said with something like awe, "all but the most basic life support. Clarence is still alive. How could you take so long to tell me where it was?"

Smokey rubbed her face with her hands. "How could I tell you quickly? First, I had to make you believe that they existed. Then I had to show how only a few residents were possible Hosts. If I had just started accusing Clarence, you would have rightly wanted proof, and he would have been able to defend himself, probably quite eloquently given his own ability and the doppel's assistance."

"Hmm, I see. Yes, I might have ended up locking you away and no doubt been sorry when the next 'accident' was to you"—he stroked his beard—"or to me. What do we do now? Clarence may be in danger. This isn't exactly a normal way to live."

Smokey stared at the passive form. "I think—hope— he is not in danger. The doppels need Hosts and Clarence is the only available candidate. If it kills him, it is dooming itself."

She didn't speak of suicide or hostages, remembering what Bethlehem had said about the doppels being as different from each other as humans were. This particular doppel might not have acquired those concepts. Clarence would have, but it had taken his mind out of the loop. In any case, she felt certain that the imperative to live must be very strong in its programming. For now, they had a stalemate.

Carefully, she extracted the sedative patch she had dosed earlier. Palming it, she made as if to check Clarence's throat pulse. Then she pressed the patch into place. She sensed a flicker of awareness as the doppel felt Clarence's system come under a control that was not its own, but it couldn't activate Clarence's dormant reflexes swiftly enough.

Before Clarence fell into a deep sleep, she felt the doppel's anger and beneath that, so faintly that she might have imagined it, she thought that she sensed a faint gratitude that could have been Clarence's own.

Pastor helped her heave Clarence onto the sofa in his office. Without asking her, he extracted two sets of restraints from his desk. They looked newly synthesized; he must have had them made in anticipation of a more normal arrest. One set was fastened around Clarence's wrists and the other about his ankles.

Clarence did not stir during all of this and try as she might, Smokey could not touch even his dreaming mind. She could not find the doppel either, which raised interesting questions about its dependence on its Host.

"Or—" Pastor said, looking up from where he had been rummaging through his desk. "Or it has escaped despite your care."

Smokey gulped. "Are you . . ."

He shook his head, expression serious. "No, I'm me. So I say. And I wasn't trying to snoop, but you were projecting. There's only one way we can be certain, Smokey. We need to let each other in."

"That—" Smokey realized that the idea frightened her, more than she would have imagined. "I can see your point, but . . ."

"Ironic, isn't it?" he said, walking around his desk with measured steps. "That you're afraid after everything."

"You mean, being a whore and all?" she replied a bit defensively. "That was my body; my mind was mine alone."

He had come to face her. "I know, but still you used your Talent to do something like this and your partner—victim—wasn't even willing."

"They all benefited," she said. "Not one of them ever had a better lay. I gave back for what I took."

Pastor's eyes bored into her own, blue against steel. "So you did. This isn't that different. I'm giving you the same thing I'm asking for. And if it helps you to know, I'm scared, too. Telepath to telepath contact goes way beyond surface thoughts. I've never entered into it except in a crisis."

She could smell his scent now, just slightly masked by the soap he had scrubbed with after tending to Ross.

This close, she could see the minute beads of perspiration along his brow. The pale blue eyes were very near to hers and framed with more lines than she had realized. His breath hissed between his teeth, coming faster than it should and not from suppressed passion. He opened his arms to her as in an embrace.

"Touch me," he said. "I know it will help you to make contact."

She could have settled for his hand, but she stepped forward into the circle of his arms and pillowed her head so that her cheek rested against the exposed skin of his throat. She slipped her arms around his waist, wondering if he needed a hug as badly as she did.

—*Yes*—came the thought as his arms tightened around her—*I do. This has been too much to bear alone.*—

She was not even aware of her own reply, for it did not come in words but in a final pulling aside of whatever last veils had separated their selves from each other.

Together they were Smokey pacing the too-regular corridors of the *Venture Rose,* the first ship on which she remembered feeling trapped between the metal and ceramic walls and the conduit-clogged ceilings. They were Pastor roaming the frost-rimed hills of an Icedrake summer, going farther and farther away from the settlements because recently human minds had begun to clamor their thoughts into his own.

They were Smokey sneaking away from the theater in which Joy in Motion was performing, selling her body for the first time for passage on a tramp trader to a man with no taste for fine art, and finally escaping the limits of a ship for a world. They were Pastor camping with the shaman who had taught him not only how to shield his thoughts from the outer world but how to love.

They were Smokey weeping as a fireball claimed the shuttle on which her best friend had been immolated and weeping again as a medical technician confirmed that Ross would have his small bit of immortality in the daughter she would bear. They were Pastor looking with guarded dislike as Ross proudly introduced him to the round-cheeked, fair-haired girl who looked too much like Ross to be denied, whom Ross would never wish to deny.

They were these and a host of memories more, too fast, too bright ever to be remembered except as depth and foundation to a friendship and a trust that was sealed to endure until their deaths. When they were themselves again, Smokey realized that she was weeping.

"I've got," she sniffled, "to stop doing this. You're going to lose all respect for me."

"Silly Smoke," Pastor said, kissing the top of her head before releasing her from his embrace. "Weep if you want, but first come with me. I don't want to plan the logistics of how we will proceed where this doppel might hear."

Smokey saw the reasoning behind this. Mopping her eyes on her shirttail, she reflected that mutual telepathy had its advantages. Pastor now not only knew the entire plan she had evolved for extracting the doppel from its unwilling Host, but he had also weighed it against his greater knowledge of psionic abilities and still found it sound.

She glanced at her timepiece. Their communion had taken about twenty minutes. She had dosed Clarence so that he would be asleep for several hours. Pastor, of course, knew this, too.

"Molly may not be able to work yet," she reminded him, as they hurried through the corridors. "Whatever she did to help Ross wiped her out."

Intellectually, she knew what Molly had done, for Pastor's memories had shown her. Molly had submerged herself into Ross's damaged arm, reattaching muscle, tendon, vein, artery, skating though blood vessels and nerves, mending and aligning so that the shredded arm would have a chance at rebuilding.

Her ability combined clairvoyance, telekinesis, empathy, and probably even telepathy, for she monitored her patient on levels that no scanner yet built could. Yet, such use drained her. She might not be able to do surgery again so soon. If she could not, Clarence might need to be kept in isolation and sedated.

If the doppel which was hiding in him regained autonomy during that time, there was no telling what it would do. As Krystal's murder and Ross's mutilation showed, while it could be subtle and canny, when thwarted or panicked its response could be brutally destructive. Again, how like a human it seemed.

Smokey tried, but could find no pity for the creature. Fleetingly, she wondered if the doppels were themselves creatures or merely, as she had proposed, landscaping for some other type of entity. She suspected that she would never know.

The only person awake in sick bay when they arrived was Bruni. Bonny slept at Ross's feet, and Albert had retired to the sofa in the infirmary's antechamber. Bruni set down her reader screen when they came in.

"How's Molly?" Pastor asked.

Bruni's expression showed what she thought of Pastor not asking after Ross first, but she responded to his inquiry.

"Weak. I've dipped in and she's gotten past immersion nightmares, but probably won't come around for hours yet, maybe even a day. We have her on supplements."

Pastor cursed, but Smokey managed to ask, "Immersion nightmares?"

"Yeah, whenever Molly does an intensive surgery, her mind won't let go even after she has done. It keeps replaying the details until she's able to relax. Drugs don't help. They actually can make it worse by locking her in at one level of brain activity. We've been experimenting with gentle telepathic suggestion until she relaxes into deep sleep. I think it worked tonight, but she was weak to start with. I don't think she should be bothered until she awakens naturally."

Pastor cursed again from where he was now sitting by Ross. Bruni looked puzzled.

"Why do you want to wake Molly? Ross is resting easily." Her voice rose in sudden panic. "Where's Clarence? There hasn't been another attack, has there?"

"No," Smokey reassured her. "Not exactly. Come out into the anteroom and I'll explain. Pastor can take over the vigil."

"Albert's out there napping," Bruni said with a doubtful glance toward Pastor. "Can't we just talk in here?"

"Albert will need to know this, too," Pastor said. "Smokey can fill you in while I watch. I know her mind as my own."

Bruni looked as shocked as if someone had announced that the Mud Turtle would dissolve into the swamp within the hour. She rose, however, and while Smokey assembled a snack from the supplies in the infirmary's cabinets, she woke Albert.

Munching on protein jerky, crackers, and sipping tea, Smokey filled in Bruni and Albert on the events since Ross had been found. Once they saw the drift of her report, they insisted she stop until Ravenel could be summoned and the Coven assembled.

After Smokey's report was completed, there was some debate but little argument. Pastor's judgment was valued, and when they learned that he and Smokey had permitted each other a deep mind probe, they trusted her so implicitly that she was vaguely uncomfortable.

"The only thing that I don't understand," Ravenel said, "is why Molly's accident was so elaborately set up."

"I can guess," Smokey offered. "Sey'zar's death could have been dismissed as accidental, but there was no way that Krystal's could have been. We would have been suspicious of any accident, whatever the circumstances, so the doppel engineered a situation that would leave us doubting each other. Only an intimate of the Underground would have known of the E-O-M-Trin gas's effects. Therefore, we were diverted from looking for a stowaway—which the doppel Infiltrator is in an odd way—and toward doubting each other."

"Sensible," Ravenel said, "and frightening. I had always assumed that the doppels were more or less adjuncts to the minds that they inhabited. Now their real abilities are coming through. I wonder if we will ever know why they were created?"

Albert had been quietly listening while Smokey talked, offering little to the general discussion. Now he stopped chewing on his right thumbnail.

Staring at the ragged edge, he offered, "We will probably never know for certain, but I wonder if they weren't created for the very reason that Smokey has proposed. We usually think of improvement in terms of affecting the body—curing illness, experiments with mechanical enhancements—or of things that will make our environment more suitable—like terraforming. But I imagine that the doppels are the product of a culture that felt that the mind was what needed improvement, not the outer self. They may have created the doppels for themselves and eventually their machines adapted to us as well."

"The idea makes sense," Bruni agreed. "Except for psionics and sporadic attempts to breed for some artistic talent, we still tend to view the workings of the mind as a mystery."

"People may even be happier that way," Ravenel added. "With science rapidly expanding the known, the last land of wonder most people can hope to explore is no longer an unmarked portion of a map bearing the legend 'Here there be Dragons.' It's the grey matter between their own ears. How many times have you heard someone say, 'They still don't know what most of the brain does—you don't expect me to believe that it does nothing.'"

Smokey tried unsuccessfully to smother a yawn.

"Poor Smokey," Bruni said. "You haven't had any sleep since Pastor woke you. I suppose you could safely go back to your room. We'll wake you when Molly does."

"I don't want to wake Bonny to go back," Smokey said, "and I know this sounds stupid, but I don't really want to be alone."

Albert looked quizzically at her. "I'll sleep with you Smokey, if that's what you want."

She managed a smile. "No, Albert, I'm too tired for that. I just need to rest."

Albert didn't look angry or even disappointed, and she was obscurely touched to realize that he had offered not only because he found her sexy, but because he genuinely wanted to offer her some comfort.

"You could have the sofa, then," he said. "I'm awake now, and I can take over and let Pastor sleep."

"Good idea," Bruni interjected authoritatively. "We'll all need to be rested. Ravenel and I will brief everyone else. I don't think we need to give the full story, but enough so we defuse some of the tension."

"Albert, you'll be the best judge of when Molly is strong enough to do surgery," Ravenel said. "Don't let her try to tell you that she can work sooner. Clarence may be at risk, but this is the most delicate surgery she'll ever attempt. We may not have another chance. The Infiltrator will surely realize that she is a danger to it. That may even be why she was attacked."

The two women left and Albert went in to join the patients. Smokey heard Pastor agreeing to rest only if he could sleep on the floor by Ross's bed. Albert agreed with minimal protest. Smokey finally drifted off to sleep, haunted by a memory of Clarence asleep on another sofa, just a level away, his hands and feet bound.

When Albert came out later to check on her, he saw that her sleeping face was streaked with tears. Her palms were spread outward in a gesture of mute apology so powerful that all he could do was turn away and hope that sleep at least would bring her some peace.

24

"BUT, ROSS, WHAT WERE YOU DOING UP AND roaming about?" Smokey heard as she walked into the infirmary.

Night, or what had remained of it, had passed uneventfully. Clarence, when they had checked, still slept. So, unfortunately for her and Pastor's plans, did Molly.

She had taken Bonny to their rooms to wash and change clothes, but Bonny had balked at eating in the cafeteria, asking if instead they could take a picnic into the infirmary. Wheeling a cart loaded with enough food for not only the two of them, but also Ross, Pastor, Piet (who had taken nursing detail from Albert), Molly (should she awaken), and probably for the legendary Mongol Hordes as well, they had marched in on a playfully heated argument between Pastor and a now-alert Ross.

"Papa!" Bonny crowed, covering her mouth when Piet waved toward sleeping Molly. "How do you feel?"

"Not well enough to swing you around," he said, patting her with his good hand, "but much better."

Smokey judged from Pastor's pleased expression that Ross was indeed out of danger. She shared a fleeting smile with him.

"Bonita," she said, "leave Ross alone for a moment and help me with the food. Piet, you must be hungry."

The dark-skinned, button-nosed, redhead shook his head stiffly. "No, but I would accept a cup of green tea."

Smokey poured for him, wishing that she believed that she could do anything to mitigate the pain he still so obviously felt over Krystal's murder. Not long ago, she would have routinely offered her body, but with what she had learned from the telepaths about the workings of the human mind, that easy answer no longer seemed reasonable.

Instead, she made no effort to pretend that he was not hurting and patted his knee as she passed him his cup. He gave her a curt nod, but his smile seemed less forced.

Bonny carried a tray over to Ross, struggling a bit with the weight. He looked at the enormous meal that she had proudly placed before him.

"I hope you'll let Pastor help me with this, Bonny," he said with evident consternation. "I haven't been getting much exercise in the last day or so."

After Bonny nodded, Pastor leaned over Ross to grab a round bread topped with a thick, sugary preserve made from one of Guillen's native fruit.

"By the way, Ross," he said, "I'm not going to let you keep dodging my question. What were you doing up and roaming about last night?"

Curiously, Ross's reply involved reaching out and grasping Pastor's wrist, tilting it so that he could see the face of his timepiece.

"Ross," Pastor said, "are you feeling light-headed? How much blood did you lose?"

Even Piet was curious by now, but Ross only sat up straighter in bed, favoring his injured arm. He looked straight at Bonny, an odd smile playing about the corners of his mouth.

"Happy birthday, Bonny," he said. "I'm very happy finally to be able to tell you that in person. However, I am afraid that your present will be delayed. Midas was delivering something for me last night. I suspect that the poor boy was quite puzzled when I didn't make the rendezvous."

"Very little surprises Midas," Pastor observed dryly. "I'll make certain he is contacted."

Bonny's brown eyes had widened. Clearly, in all the

excitement she had forgotten her own birthday. When she started to leap up into Ross's lap Pastor interposed a polite but firm arm.

"Gentle, girl. Have you forgotten? He's still recovering." He relented enough to lift her up alongside Ross. "Happy birthday, Bonny. How old are you?"

"Ten," she said proudly. "Ten standards. Arizona years are shorter. What are years where you were born?"

"On Icedrake? Longer. The world is about the same size as Old Terra, but the world is farther out from the sun so the years are longer. The world is at a different stage in its development. It's cooler and the flora and fauna are less sophisticated than on Old Terra."

Smokey interrupted long enough to offer her own birthday congratulations, then drifted back and watched Pastor gradually let Bonny charm him with a constant stream of questions. She sipped her tea, nibbled a biscuit, and tried hard not to be impatient for Molly to recover.

Ross suggested that they hold a birthday party for Bonny. Since Smokey did not trust her medical skills enough to permit him away from the medical gear, they set up in the antechamber that connected the infirmary with the lab/surgery.

Albert blew up surgical gloves into makeshift balloons. From her wardrobe, Ravenel produced an abundance of silk scarves that made admirable streamers. The hydroponics lab supplied flowers.

Once under way, the party provided a welcome diversion. Smokey would have been more distracted if someone had not programmed a selection of Dixieland jazz. The brassy buoyancy reminded her with forceful clarity of Clarence's piano playing.

She was leaning against a viewport, watching the grey-green water eddy by, when an excited shout from Albert brought her out of her brooding.

"Molly's awake!" he announced, grinning broadly. "She asked for a bite of my cake and she wants a look at Ross's arm."

Smokey nearly ran to Molly's bedside. "How are you?"

"Better, rested even." Molly's voice was still hoarse, but her eyes were clear. "How is Ross?"

"Sore," he said from the doorway. "What did you use to put my arm back on? A staple gun?"

"Such gratitude," she scolded happily. "Pastor, push that wheelchair over here so I can look at his arm. What's this?"

Bonny had popped up next to her and was extending a plate bearing a luridly blue slice of frosted cake.

"Bonny, what's this? One of those chulos you're always telling me about?"

"No," Bonny said, not certain that she was being teased. "A chulo is an animal. This is a birthday cake."

"Birthday cake." Molly smiled. "Yes, I remember now, just as I was waking up, my little brother was gobbling down the last of a slice. Happy birthday, Bonny! Can you hold that cake for a moment longer while I take a look at your father's arm? Last time I took a look at it, he had apparently decided to give up cuddling Pastor in favor of bear traps."

Ross shook his head. "No bear traps down here, Molly. Just snapping turtles."

Pastor intently watched Molly inspect Ross's arm, the worry lines around his eyes smoothing as Molly chirped her satisfaction. Smokey resisted the urge to pat him.

"We'll need to talk with you about that snapping turtle, Molly," Pastor said. "Are you up to a long lecture or should we come back?"

Molly studied his expression and then Smokey's. Her bright eyes lost some of their sparkle as she scanned the people who had crowded into the infirmary and noticed that Clarence was missing.

"If Bonny will give me my cake," she said, "and baby brother find me some green tea and remember that I don't take sugar, I will be ready to listen. Has anyone else been attacked?"

"Well," Pastor said, motioning for the infirmary to be

cleared, "in a manner of speaking, yes. Clarence is in trouble but to explain how we need to go through a rather detailed report. Smoke, you take it from here."

Smokey barely noticed Molly's surprise at Pastor's giving her the floor. She launched into the details of nanotechnology, doppels, Infiltrators, and the theories that she and Pastor had evolved about the varied attacks. Ross and Bonny had been permitted to stay and they nodded approvingly, even when she was discussing technical aspects. Pastor confirmed the role that the tracers had played, but mostly Smokey talked uninterrupted.

As she concluded, Molly sat thoughtfully still for several moments. Then she looked at Smokey.

"You want me to go after that Infiltrator, right? You think that I should be able to pull it out without hurting Clarence."

Smokey whispered softly, "Yes."

"Can you?" Pastor asked. "I've spoken with Ross and he thinks that he may be able to rig some sort of containment field so that we would be able to study it afterward."

Molly frowned. "How long would the rigging take, Ross?"

He shrugged, his injured arm still and awkward. "A couple of hours, maybe less with my nimble-fingered sorcerer's apprentice here to help. We're not looking for an elegant solution, just something that will work for now."

Bonny beamed. "I'll help, Papa. I've learned where everything is in your lab."

"Good." Molly managed to strike a commanding attitude even though she hadn't stirred from the bed. "Do that. Pastor, I am going to want to speak with you and Bruni before we do this. I am going to want a shield of some sort. Ravenel and Albert can match for it, but I'll want one of them to gather the other mudcrawlers and keep them together; the other is going to sit on Smokey."

Smokey jumped. "Me? Why? What have I done?"

"Nothing, but you're ragged on the edges, woman."
Molly allowed a bit of her own worry to show. "If this
doesn't work, you're going to need to be ready to cope
with the crisis. I want you rested and relaxed."

Smokey blinked and straightened. "Yes, ma'am."

Closer to six or seven hours passed rather than the
hoped-for "couple" before Ross and Bonny could rig a
field that they thought would hold the Infiltrator. During
that time, Molly rehearsed the planned surgery with
Bruni and Pastor. Despite ample small details to keep
her busy, Smokey grew more and more tense. No matter
how she tried, she couldn't let go of the image of
Clarence as she had last seen him, bound body and
mind. An increasing conviction grew in her that somehow she was responsible.

When the time for the surgery finally came, Clarence
was moved to the sick bay; Pastor's office was simply too
small. The surgery team—Molly, Pastor, and Bruni,
backed up by Ross and Bonny—gathered. Molly shooed
everyone else out.

Politely but firmly declining company, Smokey went
to her suite. The bed was still rumpled from when
Pastor's frantic call had awakened her. Kicking off her
slippers, she climbed into the bed and wrapped her arms
around Clarence's pillow. It still held some of his scent.
Breathing slowly and steadily, she squeezed the pillow to
her as if it could fill the aching hollow inside.

The call from the sick bay startled her sufficiently that
she knew that she had actually drifted off to sleep, but
the shift from waking into nightmare had been so
smooth that jolting awake was welcome. She rolled and
hit the VT on.

"Mama?" Bonny said. "We're done now. Molly said
that you can come down."

"How did it go?" she asked, even as she stuffed her
feet into her slippers.

"Molly says to tell you that it's too soon to know.
Clarence is still sleeping. She wants you here when he
wakes up."

Smokey compromised with her reluctance to go out looking like an unmade bed by combing her hair but not changing her slept-in clothing. Then she ran to sick bay, suddenly panicked that Clarence would have awakened during her delay. The others were talking softly when she arrived and Clarence, of course, was still unconscious.

Bonny ran over and hugged her. Smokey could feel that the girl was troubled—no wonder given that her first venture into adult responsibility involved psychic brain surgery and molecular physics. Pastor followed her over some moments later.

He found a smile for her. "I think it is promising, Smokey. Molly forced something out. Ross and Bonny trapped it, though I suspect that they didn't trap it all. According to the monitors Molly had us set up before she collapsed, Clarence's nervous system shows more normal levels of activity. We don't—"

"Molly," Smokey interrupted, feeling terribly guilty that she had forgotten the risk that Molly had taken. "How is she?"

"Resting. So is Ross," Pastor said. "Albert is with them. Oddly, this ordeal may have been good for him. I haven't tested him, but I suspect that he had a stronger Talent for empathy that hadn't been tapped until now. That is often the case with poltergeist manifestations. The wild activity is a cover for something that the person doesn't want to deal with. Empathy is particularly rough since it involves feelings without concrete thoughts to explain them."

Bonny had been listening intently, her expression growing increasingly worried. When Pastor paused, she tugged at Smokey's arm.

"Mama, Clarence is going to get better, isn't he?"

"I don't know, Bonita, but we'll find out soon. Want to come and sit by him with me?"

Clarence's dark face was serene as he slept. Smokey resisted the impulse to see if she could touch his dreams. At best, the experience was unsettling, as she knew from occasions when his limbs had tangled with hers in sleep and her mind wandered across that tactile bridge to enter a silent film of his own subconscious world.

She had seen New Orleans in his dreams, not only the place, but the people as well. One strong-featured woman with skin as dark as Clarence's but hair like fine-spun steel wool featured frequently in his dreams. By chance, she had learned that this was Clarence's mother, dead a dozen or more years now and still missed.

No, she would not touch his mind and see what roads he walked. She might find that serenity was a mask for a mind emptied of any thought.

"Is he still one of the good ones, Mama?" Bonny asked.

"I think so, Bonny," Smokey said. "I hope so."

"Me, too. I'm glad that we found Papa and he's nice, but he has Pastor. I want you to have someone, and I've known Clarence even longer than I've known Papa."

Smokey hesitated, then decided that she couldn't start lying to Bonny now.

"He might not care about me the same way now, Bonny. The doppel could have been affecting how he thought; maybe it made him like me more than he did. Now that the doppel is gone, he might change his mind."

Bonny smiled at her, shaking her head in obvious amazement that a grown-up could be so dumb.

"Don't worry, Mama, he won't change his mind. You're the best."

". . . whore on Arizona?" Smokey added when Bonny didn't finish the phrase.

"No, Mama, just the best. Clarence will remember that. You just wait and see."

Clarence wasn't remembering much when he first awoke. He blinked several times, as if his eyes had never before been exposed to light. Like an infant, at first he studied Smokey's face as nothing more than an obstruction of the light. Gradually, his focus sharpened and he studied her features as if he would draw them.

Through all this scrutiny, he never spoke. Smokey could feel Bonny growing agitated and pushed her away from the bedside with a reassuring pat.

"Go sit with Ross, Bonita," she murmured. "Please."

Then she put her hand on Clarence's, searching for his thoughts. At first she found nothing more than simple, remarkably sharp, sensory impressions. His mind was like a receiver drawing in data that it lacked the means to interpret.

She felt a flicker of interest as the sound of Ross's voice saying something comforting to Bonny drifted over. On an impulse, she started to sing softly, choosing one of the jazz ballads he had played for Ami back in the Gentlemen's Parlor.

Peripherally she was aware of Pastor and Bruni easing the others out of the sick bay and raised her voice to fill the silence. She was no artist, but she could carry a tune and slowly she felt the sounds unlocking memories in Clarence's mind. When tears welled up in his eyes to flow unchecked down his cheeks, she knew that she had gotten through to something.

"Hey, lover," she said. "How are you feeling?"

He shook his head slightly, then more vigorously. The flood of information into his once-blank mind had reached overwhelming levels. She slid her hand from his bare skin to rest on the blanket over his chest.

"I . . ." he croaked, licking his lips with a tongue she saw was thick and dry. Hurriedly, she nursed the nearest liquid—a sweet punch that had been brought in for the birthday party—into his mouth. He swallowed a few times and grimaced.

"Water?" he suggested, his voice husky but improved.

She quickly brought some, and he propped himself up on one elbow to take the glass. He drained it thirstily, only spilling a few drops, and mutely held the glass out. She refilled it, allowing her hand to touch his.

Jumbled information was still being sorted; that he had found a word to express his need was hopeful.

"How are you doing?" she asked again.

His expression went from tranquil to frustrated. He let the cup fall to clatter on the floor. The noise was clearly unanticipated and he froze.

"Clarence," she comforted, "look at me—remember me? Smokey? Your Smokey-jo?"

Part of her chid the rest for asking such a selfish question, but she couldn't bear that blank, terrified expression. Whatever else, Clarence had been steady, even in his irrational devotion to her. Seeing him reduced to infantile panic frightened her.

At first she thought that her question had meant nothing to him. Then his lips moved, slowly, as if testing the word before speaking.

"Smokey?" His gaze sharpened and she realized with a thrill that he was actually seeing her as a person, not just as a jumble of images. "Smokey!"

He wrenched himself into a sitting position and grabbed her. "Smokey! Oh, god! I thought I'd lost you, honey. I thought . . ."

He didn't finish the phrase, nor did he need to. Rocking back and forth, they held each other, taking comfort in the other's nearness. She didn't try to sort out the images and emotions that flowed from him into her. It was enough to be clasped to that barrel chest and feel the woolly softness of his hair under her hands as he bent his head and held her in the shelter of his body.

They might have stayed that way much longer, but there was a polite clearing of throats behind them. Albert stood in the doorway to the infirmary, Molly leaning a bit heavily on his arm.

"Pastor didn't clear us out with the rest," Albert explained, "since Molly was asleep. We heard the noise though and . . ."

"And I wanted a look at my patient," Molly said. "Right away. I've never done anything like that before. I hope I never need to again, but I suspect that I will. So, I had better make certain that I haven't scrambled too many neurons."

Clarence had viewed the Cheshires initially with puzzlement, but Smokey felt his memories falling into place. He smiled, some of that childlike wonder at discovering that his mind did hold the answers still shining forth.

"What have you been doing to me, Molly?" he said.

"Mucking around your grey cells," she replied, "and you had better decide if you would rather have Pastor or Bruni rooting around in there later. I'm not going to feel sure that you're rid of that thing until someone else takes a peep."

Clarence looked startled. "This is more serious than gulping drugged gas, isn't it? What's happened?"

"What do you last remember?" Smokey parried.

He didn't remember much after Ross had been found in the entry foyer. The memories that remained were cloudy. Learning that nothing remained of the meeting in Pastor's office, Smokey was somewhat relieved. While Molly continued her inspection, Smokey filled Clarence in, offering only minor editing. He was too dark to blanch, but his hands worked nervously as she told him what the Infiltrator had done to him.

"And you folks ask me to have Pastor or Bruni snoop around?" he asked as she finished. "Hell, yes! I don't want even a trace of that thing left, not a cog nor a gear."

Entering the room with Ross, Bonny heard enough to giggle.

"You are okay!" she chirped, her relief so evident that Clarence beamed. "You do know that it didn't have any cogs or gears, don't you?"

Clarence frowned. "Actually, I don't know what it was—except tiny. Most of what Smokey told me had to do with what it did, not how it did it."

"If I told you that it was a combination of biological and electronic nanoengineering, probably of nonhuman origin," Ross said, "would that help?"

Clarence grinned. "Not much. How's the arm?"

Ross shrugged. "Feels stiff and a bit sore, but I think I could even do without this sling if Molly would trust her own work more."

"I trust my work," Molly retorted. "I don't trust you not to bang it up."

Smokey couldn't resist a sigh of relief as if with their banter she could finally set down a tremendous burden. She knew that somewhere in the Mud Turtle, Piet still wept for Krystal. Sey'zar, too, was missed. At least, he had died peacefully and among people who would mourn him. The time had not been his choice, but was anyone's?

She knew her sensation of an ending was an illusion. In many ways they were just beginning what would be years of struggle to detect and neutralize those Drivers and Infiltrators who would do them harm. Now, however, things were on somewhat more level ground.

As she listened to Bonny and Ross babbling to Clarence about self-assembling nanotubes of carbon and zeolite, DNA software, and solar propulsion systems with chemical backup, she realized that her role in the battle would be support, rather than the front lines.

"But those also serve who stand and wait, eh?" Pastor said, coming up beside her.

"Do you read my mind freely now?" she said.

"No," he replied, "but you looked about the way I feel. So I took a lucky guess. The future has become overwhelmingly complex all at once."

"Yes"—she winked at him—"but it beats dealing with demonic possession, which is what seemed like the only explanation at first. The Mud Turtle is too isolated for the type of work Ross and Bonny will need to be doing. I wonder where we should go?"

"I think Bethlehem may have some suggestions," Pastor replied. "I nearly forgot to tell you what I was coming to speak to you about. Bruni and I just had contact from Bethlehem. He and Joy are back on Guillen. They will be coming here as soon as it's safe, probably with Midas and supplies."

"Do they know?" she asked.

"About all of this?" He shook his head. "No, long-range telepathy can be rather exhausting. I'm afraid that you've just been elected to explain the whole mess one more time."

"Lucky me!" she groaned, but inwardly she was terribly pleased—and oddly nervous.

Thoughtfully, she returned to Clarence, who reached out to take her hand.

"Yes, lucky me," she repeated so softly that no one else could hear.

25

"THAT'S THE WAY IT IS," SMOKEY CONCLUDED. "Ross and Bonny have been examining the—thing—that was taken from Clarence's head. They're fairly certain it is inert—dead. They haven't reached any decisive conclusions. You see, they have one major problem."

Bethlehem studied her. "No comparison. Lack of a control sample."

"Right. It's very hard to draw conclusions from a sample group of one. Aside from the unlikely event that a horde of doppels turns up for us to capture, we have only a few options." She raised a hand and ticked them off. "One, we can do with what we have. Two, we can pursue those Wickerwork executives—Lee, Morrel, etcetera—who are carrying Drivers. Three, we can find a doppel willing to cooperate with us."

Bethlehem traded a glance with Joy and then nodded for Smokey to continue.

"Option one," Smokey said with a sip from her tea, "is a poor choice for the reasons we've just mentioned. Option two is superficially quite attractive. We know where several Drivers are—or at least where they were several months ago. I suspect that Morrel, at least, is ill adjusted to his. We might be doing him a favor. Lee, well . . . I didn't like Lee."

"Your tone says that you don't think this is a good option," Joy prompted.

Smokey nodded. "Yes, I've talked with the residents of the Mud Turtle at length. This Underground simply lacks the resources to carry out a kidnapping or two. Most of its energy and resources have gone into building hideaways like this one or in helping Purge victims obtain new IDs and such. We could recruit or hire outside help, but that is a risk. We would always be vulnerable to blackmail.

"Moreover"—Smokey refilled her teacup and Joy's— "even if we did succeed, we would need to have Molly or someone with similar talents try and haul the Driver out. That's chancy—dangerous both to her and to the subject."

"So, you would prefer to let Wickerwork be?" Bethlehem asked.

"Not to ignore them," Smokey assured her parents, "but not mess with the Drivers directly. Not yet. Let Ross and Bonny do their research and then maybe we can 'reprogram' the Drivers into Guests who would accept our way of thought."

"Your third option seems to be the best, for now," Bethlehem said, "and I can take a hint when I hear one. I'm not certain if Captain nu-Aten will be able to volunteer, but I will ask. I can be very persuasive."

"I knew I got the talent from someone." Smokey smiled.

They continued to refine their tactics, but at last Smokey realized that she had been smothering yawns for some time.

"I apologize, Mama, Papa, but I'm so tired that I'm thinking in loops and spins. How soon can you talk to the captain?"

"The *Ibn Battuta* is orbiting Guillen now," Bethlehem answered. "However, I prefer to wait until I can do a very tight beam communication. Compromising the Mud Turtle after all this time seems foolish."

"Wake me if there is a crisis," Smokey said. "Otherwise, I'm going to try and make my daughter get some rest and get some sleep myself. Last I saw, Bonny went tearing off with Midas and her birthday presents. I think they're the only things that would have gotten her out of Ross's lab."

"You're a good mother, Smokey," Joy said unexpectedly. "Better, I think, than I was."

"I try," Smokey replied, "to be a good parent. It's not easy trying to be right for someone else."

"No," Joy said, "it's not. Sleep well."

Bonny was bundled away from her birthday presents with little protest, especially when she learned that Midas was staying overnight.

Clarence had been dismissed from sick bay and proved to Smokey that he was feeling better—much. Several hours later, as they lay cuddling in the dimly lit room, Smokey's thought returned to her conversation with Bethlehem and Joy.

"When do you have to go back to your position on Old Terra?" she asked. "I hadn't thought much about it, but you've had a very odd sabbatical."

"Falling in love with a 'Zonie whore, getting possessed by a minute, mechanical monster, then rocketing along the spacelanes to hide in a swamp with a bunch of renegade psionics?" He chuckled. "Yeah, guess I have. To answer your question, I should report back for this coming term. Why do you ask?"

She could feel that he was teasing her, just a little. It warmed her spirit just as his body warmed hers.

"Bethlehem and Joy were talking about what needs to be done next. I ran the options that we had come up with by them and they agreed that perhaps studying a Guest or two is our next logical option."

"Good, good," he said, stroking her hair, playing with the intricacies of a long curl. "Tell me what they have suggested."

"They're going to speak with Captain nu-Aten"—she poked him in the side—"as you have already guessed. And if nu-Aten says 'yes'—as I think she will—the next logical move is to suggest that we relocate to the *Ibn Battuta* for a time."

"You aren't crazy about that idea, are you?"

"Well, I didn't enjoy growing up on a variety of space liners. Bonny is different. She might thrive. She practically lives on the V unless you pull her out." Smokey sighed. "I suppose that even hoping to move back to Arizona is unrealistic, isn't it?"

Clarence paused. "Probably, Smokey-jo. Kyu isn't going to have forgotten Ami's murder and, with you under suspicion for murdering both Fox and Gary, she is probably not going to welcome you at the Victorian Mansion. The places that would want you on staff in order to capitalize on your notoriety would not be places that you would care to work."

"No, you may be right."

She fell silent, feeling Clarence slip into a drowse. He was still far weaker physically than he cared to admit, but she saw no reason to hound him. He was stronger than she had believed in many more important ways.

With a pang, she realized that she would miss him when he went back to Old Terra, but she couldn't follow him there. Leaving Bonny was out of the question, even if Ross and Pastor would watch her. They didn't have her experience. A growing girl needed a mother more than the mother needed a man.

They could visit Clarence when the *Battuta* ported at Old Terra, see the sights, take Bonny to the ocean. They could . . .

She shook Clarence awake. "Hey, Clarence. Wake up! I have a question for you."

"Yes," he muttered, sitting up halfway and looking down at her sleepily. "Ask away, Smokey-jo."

Suddenly, she was scared and almost found something innocuous to say. Her tongue, however, had a will of its own and she heard herself asking him, "Would you marry me, Clarence? Come and live with me and Bonny full-time, wherever this takes us? I just realized that I don't want to see you go."

His smile was so joyous that it was answer enough, but

he replied solemnly, "Yes, I will. I had been hoping to find a way to ask you, but you had too much else to fuss over. You *are* serious, aren't you?"

"As serious as I've ever been," Smokey promised. "I'm not even scared anymore. And I really was—I think because I thought that you would say no."

"That would be crazy, Smokey-jo. Life would get awfully flat without you in it. Of course this means that I'll have to quit my job. There is no way that you and Bonny could settle on Old Terra now." Clarence grew somber. "Are you willing to quit your job, Smokey? I'll admit that I'm a jealous man."

She nodded without hesitation. "I don't doubt that you are, Clarence. If knowing makes you more comfortable, I should tell you that I'd not be doing it just for you. I'm ready to leave whoring behind. I don't need that kind of admiration—hell—that kind of power game. Not anymore. I'm learning new things. I'd like sex to be just you and me."

"Thanks, honey." He held her close. "Tell Bonny in the morning?"

"Yeah, let her sleep now. Don't think I'll let you sleep yet"—she ran her hand down his midsection—"now that you're up again."

When they woke the next morning, a message short and neat waited for them. "Nu-Aten says yes. Awaiting your decision. B."

"What does that mean?" Bonny asked.

"It means that if Ross and Pastor agree, the five of us are going to live on the *Ibn Battuta* for a while with Joy and Bethlehem. That way you and Ross can continue your work. You'll have access to equipment and such without compromising the Mud Turtle."

Bonny's face brightened hopefully. "I hope they say yes. Do you think they will, Mama?"

"I do. You're doing important work and Pastor knows just like I do that we should be relatively safe on a star liner. We may be safer than on a planet, since Captain nu-Aten scans her passengers, and we know to be careful of Infiltrators now."

Bonny danced in place, then stopped. "Five, Mama? You and me and Papa and Pastor are just four. Is . . ."

Smokey nodded. "Clarence and I are getting married. He's going to quit his job and stay with us."

"Papa was right!" Bonny crowed. "He told me that Clarence would be staying."

"That's the problem with friends," Smokey said ruefully. "Sometimes they know you better than you know yourself."

Bonny hurled herself into Clarence's arms. "I'm so glad! This is going to be the best! Can I tell Midas and everyone?"

"Go ahead," he said, setting her down. "I'm glad that you're so glad. I know that I am."

Moments after Bonny had gone barreling out, the VT beeped. Smokey switched it onto 'Hold,' turning so that she could ignore the blinking light.

"There's still lots to work out, you know. We'll need jobs of some sort on the *Ibn Battuta* if we're there long enough. We'll need new identities, no matter.

"Pastor has been working on a plan using posthypnotic suggestion to create mental shields for you and Ross and probably for Bonny. I'll need to find a way to sell my house; you'll have to resign from your university or get a leave of absence."

Clarence put a finger gently across her lips. "Slow, Smokey-jo. Of everything we've been through since we met, this is going to be the easiest. Trust me."

Looking up, she met his warm brown eyes.

"Trust me?" he repeated.

She hugged him. "Said the Chinese nightingale."

Enter the Realms of
Romantic Fantasy with

Sharon Green

"An acknowledged master
of the fantasy adventure"

Rave Reviews

Discover the Magic that Awaits . . .

DARK MIRROR, DARK DREAMS
77306-6/$4.99US/$5.99Can

GAME'S END
77725-8/$5.50US/$7.50Can

DAWN SONG
75453-3/$4.99US/$5.99Can

SILVER PRINCESS, GOLDEN KNIGHT
76625-6/$4.99US/$5.99Can

WIND WHISPERS, SHADOW SHOUTS
77724-X/$4.99US/$6.99Can